MURDERING MADELEINE

THE CLAIRE BASKERVILLE MYSTERIES
BOOK 11

SUSAN KIERNAN-LEWIS

SAN MARCO PRESS

Murdering Madeleine. Book 11 of the Claire Baskerville Mysteries.

Copyright © 2023 by Susan Kiernan-Lewis

All rights reserved.

Books by Susan Kiernan-Lewis

The Maggie Newberry Mysteries
Murder in the South of France
Murder à la Carte
Murder in Provence
Murder in Paris
Murder in Aix
Murder in Nice
Murder in the Latin Quarter
Murder in the Abbey
Murder in the Bistro
Murder in Cannes
Murder in Grenoble
Murder in the Vineyard
Murder in Arles
Murder in Marseille
Murder in St-Rémy
Murder à la Mode
Murder in Avignon
Murder in the Lavender
Murder in Mont St-Michel
Murder in the Village
Murder in St-Tropez
Murder in Grasse
Murder in Monaco
A Provençal Christmas: A Short Story
A Thanksgiving in Provence
Laurent's Kitchen

The Claire Baskerville Mysteries
Déjà Dead
Death by Cliché

Dying to be French
Ménage à Murder
Killing it in Paris
Murder Flambé
Deadly Faux Pas
Toujours Dead
Murder in the Christmas Market
Deadly Adieu
Murdering Madeleine
Murder Carte Blanche
Death à la Drumstick

The Savannah Time Travel Mysteries
Killing Time in Georgia

The Stranded in Provence Mysteries
Parlez-Vous Murder?
Crime and Croissants
Accent on Murder
A Bad Éclair Day
Croak, Monsieur!
Death du Jour
Murder Très Gauche
Wined and Died
A French Country Christmas

The Irish End Games
Free Falling
Going Gone
Heading Home
Blind Sided
Rising Tides
Cold Comfort
Never Never

Wit's End
Dead On
White Out
Black Out
End Game

The Mia Kazmaroff Mysteries
Reckless
Shameless
Breathless
Heartless
Clueless
Ruthless

Ella Out of Time
Swept Away
Carried Away
Stolen Away

The French Women's Diet

1

I often think that Parc Monceau would be a good place to hide a body. I'm not often given to such ghoulish contemplations—in spite of the fact that I'm a private investigator and a lot of my stock in trade leans in that direction.

The park in question—where I was currently sitting—is a popular park in the eighth arrondissement of Paris. Triangular in shape, with its vertices coming together at the Place de l'Étoile and the avenue de Friedland, it has a direct view of the Arc de Triomphe.

Aside from being a good place to hide a body, it was also a pretty nice playground for a kid to grow up with.

That was the other thought I had as I watched my foster grandson, Robbie, running after my partner Jean-Marc who held the string of a kite that bobbed and soared above the manicured lawns and flower beds of the park.

I sat on one of the park's many green wooden benches—all benches are green in Paris as it happens—and enjoyed the heady scent of the park's gardens, the sounds of the fountain gurgling and the children laughing all around me. My little

French bulldog, Izzy, sat at my feet, her ears tweaking and twisting at every child's squeal.

I was getting over a summer cold and was still feeling a little lethargic. As much as I enjoyed watching Jean-Marc and Robbie clearly having such a good time, I was looking forward to a hot tisane at a small and fairly new tea place I'd recently discovered that was on the walk back to our apartment.

A bright blue sky was capped by a thin layer of white clouds, the sun overhead nearly blinding me, yet the temperature was moderate. Families strolled by, a man and woman were holding hands, and a few business people were eating their lunches in the park while checking their smartphones. Still, they were out in the sunshine and the fresh air.

My partner Jean-Marc and I had been spending too much time lately working our most recent case. A wealthy American family living in Paris had asked for help finding their au pair who'd gone missing—along with the wife's credit cards. They didn't want to involve the police and were certain she'd run off on her own accord. After meeting the family, both Jean-Marc and I were inclined to agree.

I watched him jog down the grassy slope near the Egyptian obelisk with Robbie right behind him. Watching the two of them gave me a shiver of pleasure. I couldn't help but see, as I watched Robbie, laughing and running after Jean-Marc, how much he took after his father—my late husband. I couldn't imagine Bob running with the child or playing with him. That wasn't his style. Neither was fidelity, it seemed, which was why Robbie was my *adopted* son, and not my biological child.

Well, that and the fact that I'd been sixty-one years old when he was born.

From where I sat, I could detect a mixture of fresh-cut grass mingling with the aroma of French fries and hot dogs from the various park vendors.

I turned and waved to Jean-Marc and Robbie who both

turned and began to make their way back to me. As I watched them, I felt a tug of wistfulness. Six months ago, I was here in this park with my granddaughter Maddie who had now gone back to the States to live with her mother, my daughter Catherine. That was all well and good and as things should be. I was delighted that Catherine had gotten to the place in her life where she could take the baby. But it still hurt to lose her.

Somewhere off in the distance a cello was being played from one of the apartments that ringed the park.

Only in Paris, I thought with a smile. It was such a beautiful day. Perfect actually, and only one thing, really, to spoil it.

And then only if I let it.

2

The delectable fragrance of sautéing garlic and onions wafted through the small apartment. I'd hesitated to cook both—a cardinal sin to even consider not to in France—but I was going to a formal event tonight and I didn't want to smell like I'd just taken a bath in garlic. On the other hand, I was going with a Frenchman as my date so that might not be such a bad thing.

Robbie sat at the kitchen table drawing in a coloring book waiting for the moment when I'd allow him to go into the living room and watch TV.

Raising Catherine, a hundred years ago, I'd been very careful to restrict her screen time, but I was much more lenient with Robbie. Mostly that had to do with my age. At sixty-six, drawing too many lines in the sand was just exhausting. I had to hope that genetics would fill in the gaps for Robbie. That, and a ton of love from me, his pseudo-grandma.

I continued to stir the cooking onions and garlic, feeling a rare moment of peace and contentment as I glanced at Robbie bent over his project. The apartment where we live in Paris is a two-bedroom on the third floor in an old building on rue de

Laborde, a very well-to-do area of Paris in the eighth *arrondissement*.

"Look, Grammy," Robbie said, holding up his coloring book for me to appreciate.

"Very nice, darling," I said.

Small digs or not, I thought, watching him go back to work, I wouldn't change anything for the world.

Just then there was a tap at the door which set off both Izzy and Robbie who bolted from his chair.

"Ask who it is first!" I called to him. The security mechanism in our building was such that nobody was supposed to be able to get past the two security doors downstairs, so I wasn't too worried that it was someone from the outside but still, it was good to have rules.

"*Qui est là?*" Robbie called as he simultaneously opened the door.

"*Bonsoir, mon petit!*" a happy voice called out. "What is Grammy making tonight, eh?"

"*Bonsoir, Mamie*," Robbie said. "I think omelets."

Geneviève Rousseau was my eighty-four-year-old downstairs neighbor. Wise and accepting—especially considering all the tumult I bring to the apartment building—she has become one of my dearest friends in Paris if not the world. And she is definitely a beloved grandmother figure to Robbie.

She came into the kitchen, a small bowl of niçoise olives in her hands and looked at what I was cooking on the stove.

"Bonsoir, Claire," she said, eyeing critically the skillet I was working on the stove. "I thought you could use a hand tonight."

"You're a godsend," I said as I took the bowl from her.

Immediately, she pulled down an apron from a hook in the kitchen and robed up.

"Let me do this," she said. "Are you ready for tonight?"

"I've got time," I assured her.

"Well, set the table then," she said as she moved to the hot skillet on the stove.

Robbie stood in the kitchen doorway. At seven hundred square feet, my kitchen is really only a sort of alcove. After living in the US my whole life—and recently coming from a thirty-two hundred square foot two-story in Atlanta—that took some getting used to.

"Grammy?" he said hopefully.

I smiled indulgently at him. Robbie, with thick brown hair and blue eyes, was the spitting image of my husband Bob which, depending on what day it was, either pleased me or irritated the heck out of me.

"Yes, all right," I said. "Go ahead."

He was gone before I finished speaking, little Izzy at his heels. I heard the sounds of the TV turning on.

"You spoil him," Geneviève said. "He should be the one to set the table."

"I like spoiling him."

"Of course you do," she said pointedly. "It's not about what you like. It's about what's best for him."

"When he knocks over his first gas station, I'm sure your words will come back to haunt me."

"*Très amusant, chérie*," she said as she reached for the salt and began liberally seasoning the egg batter in the pan. "How was your day at the park with Jean-Marc?"

I smiled because Geneviève's question had underlying implications. She adored Jean-Marc and had been very unhappy last summer when I'd torpedoed the relationship. I'd heard her views on that quite a bit all autumn and through the holiday season until Jean-Marc reached out to me after the new year, and I'd gotten a second chance with him.

"It was good," I said. "For someone who never had kids, he's so good with Robbie."

"When you marry, that will come in handy," Geneviève said. "Especially if Robbie is having children of his own by then."

"Anyone ever tell you you're not subtle?" I said as I went to the cabinets to pull down three plates.

"And what about the other thing?" she asked without looking at me.

I didn't answer her right away. The Other Thing as she so subtly put it, was something I thought about pretty much every day, if not every hour of the day. I know she didn't approve—she'd told me that in many different ways. But like anything that's become a minor obsession, not thinking about The Other Thing was something that was currently out of my ability to do.

"Have you talked to Catherine recently?" she asked as she grated cheese into the nearly cooked eggs in the pan.

I sighed. I wasn't currently my daughter's favorite person. After what had happened at Christmas, I was lucky she was still taking my calls.

On the days that she *was* taking them.

"Not recently," I said.

Two years ago, Catherine was having fertility problems with her late husband and had frozen seventeen of her eggs where they were then stolen from a facility in Florida. At the time—Tod had just been brutally killed—and Catherine had bigger emotional fish to fry and had let the theft go. She believed, as any sane person might, that there was nothing in fact to be done about it.

But nobody had ever accused me of being sane.

I spent nearly a year tracking down those stolen eggs—obsessed with the thought that someone was going to fertilize them and implant them in a surrogate where they would then be born out of reach from me forever. I eventually discovered that all the stolen eggs except two had been deemed unviable and had been destroyed.

The remaining two eggs were fertilized and implanted in

surrogates. One of the babies born—my granddaughter Maddie—had been returned to me by the monster whose sperm was used to create her since he was only interested in a male heir.

Catherine had Maddie now and was raising her back in the States. The other baby, born earlier this year, had been a boy.

This one was not going to be handed over to me. This one, I would need to find on my own.

To that end, I have scoured the Internet and used every resource at my disposal to find him. I make my living as a private investigator and have many resources for finding people. In fact, finding missing people is the bulk of what I do. I found Maddie when everyone told me it was impossible. I'll find the boy baby, too. No matter how long it takes or how insane it eventually makes me.

I think that's what Geneviève is afraid of.

"Robbie needs your full attention," she said to me.

"I'm pretty sure he has it," I said as I opened the drawer for silverware knowing what was coming.

"Jean-Marc said you still spend too much time trying to find the baby."

I felt a flash of irritation at Jean-Marc's betrayal. I knew what he thought but unlike Geneviève, he wasn't quite as free as she was with his comments about it.

"When did you talk to him?" I asked.

"When you were getting ready today," she said. "He and Robbie were in the courtyard with a soccer ball. You know it is hopeless, *chérie*. You are only driving yourself mad."

"If you say so," I said, hoping she would drop the topic, knowing she wouldn't.

"What is that saying about the very definition of insanity?" she asked.

I felt a headache coming on.

"Geneviève," I said, "if I'd given up on finding Maddie, we'd never have gotten her."

"No. Abd-El-Kader let you have Maddie. He will never let the boy go."

My stomach clenched at the sound of that monster's name.

"Just because finding Maddie was easier," I said, "doesn't mean finding the boy is impossible."

Geneviève turned from the stove to face me.

"It *is* impossible," she said sadly. "Everyone sees that but you. Even Catherine has accepted it."

She was right about that. But Catherine had also accepted that none of her stolen eggs would be recovered.

"Look, Geneviève," I said. "I'm just doing some basic research. I'm not screwing up anyone's life and Robbie is still getting plenty of my attention."

"It's not research," Geneviève said firmly. "It's obsession. The search is hopeless, and you need to give it up before it interferes with your life and the ones you love."

"Thanks for your input," I said, turning away to bring the plates and silverware into the dining room—and to move away from the voice of loving but aggravating reason in the kitchen.

3

The night was a warm one with a gentle breeze rustling through the trees along the rue de Chevreuse, providing a pleasant respite from the day's thick summer heat. The streetlights cast a soft, golden glow, illuminating the facade of the US Club of Paris where the taxi stopped.

Because of my multiple folds of crinoline and satin Jean-Marc had to help me out of the cab. I was born and raised in the American South and have had plenty of experience wearing ballgowns as a result, but I must say it had been a while.

Tonight, I wore a volumous black velvet dress with strappy rhinestone heels. The only thing missing was a tiara and I'd actually seen one in my favorite consignment store a few weeks ago and had seriously considered it.

Once safely out of the taxi without catching my train in the door, I stood on the sidewalk in front of the US Club and smiled at the other similarly dressed guests as they made their way to the club entrance. The street in front was lined with cars, and gleaming black limousines.

I'd always thought that the outer appearance of the US Club of Paris, which was made of thick, white slabs of weathered marble and brick, seemed more like an austere place of business than the center for expat parties, secret deals and clandestine dinners. Menacing gargoyles perched atop the stone lintels and leered down at Jean-Marc and I as we walked up the marble steps to the entrance.

"Are you ready for this?" I said to Jean-Marc under my breath as the club doorman, a chubby man in his late fifties smiled and opened the door to allow us entrance.

The foyer alone nearly took my breath away. The walls were marble and the ceiling was painted in vivid colors and images.

The US Club of Paris Summer Gala was held every year in the club's main ballroom and included every senior member of the US Embassy along with any celebrity or prominent—meaning wealthy—expatriate American currently visiting or living in Paris. I'd never attended any of its events before now—the membership being very strict. The fact of my being an American in Paris was not enough to gain entrance.

As I surveyed the ballroom which was anchored by a small stage where a small orchestra played jazzy background music, I tried to take it all in: the ornate interior balconies, the soaring columns, the crystal chandeliers, the uniformed wait staff, standing at attention by lavishly set tables, and of course the guests themselves in their tuxedoes and ball gowns.

"*Incredible,*" Jean-Marc murmured in appreciation. "Are we working tonight?"

I frowned as he led me to the perimeter of the room where we were a little less visible and so that the next person coming into the room would have the spotlight.

"No, we're not working," I said and then frowned. "Why? Do you see someone?"

"I see lots of someones," he said.

That was ominous since for a former homicide police

detective to recognize someone, it was usually not in a positive way. But then, there would be a whole lot of politicians here tonight, so perhaps that was as it would be.

A young woman dressed in a formal waiter's attire appeared before us balancing a tray of nearly a half dozen filled champagne flutes. Jean-Marc relieved her of two of them and we made our way to the tables of food.

The buffet table was groaning with crystal platters of smoked salmon canapés, *foie gras* on toast spears, oysters on the half shell and escargots.

I was too excited to chow down at the moment, but it was lovely to see it all. I did pick up a small plate with two raw oysters and a spoonful of caviar. Jean-Marc took a little longer to make his selection. Food was important to him and while that usually translated into wonderful restaurant meals as well as his own creations, it also allowed for a certain amount of obsessive analysis that I quickly become impatient with.

Once he settled on a small plate of escargots and foie gras, we turned to watch the people in the room. Amid all the swishing ballgowns and glittering gems sparkling from the throat and wrist of nearly every woman waltzing under the ballroom lights, was a man in what looked like a military uniform and a striking woman on his arm wearing a low-cut gown. Unused to seeing Joelle so dressed up, it took me a moment before I recognized who it was.

"Oh my gosh," I said to Jean-Marc. "Don't look now. It's Joelle."

"Where?"

"Don't look."

Too late. Joelle, with the unerring radar of a heat-seeking missile turned to look straight at me. I smiled woodenly and toasted her with my champagne glass. Her face appeared frozen. Right then the lights dimmed, and a gentle swarm of people glided between me and my stepmother.

"What is she doing here?" I asked Jean-Marc. "She hates Americans."

Well, it was probably only me that she hated but it was still a shock to see her here. The sounds of clinking crystal champagne flutes, the collective noise of a hundred voices laughing and talking, rumbled lightly over the soft music.

"Who was she with?" I asked. Jean-Marc. "Did you see?"

"She's not slumming," he said wryly, but when I turned questioningly toward him, he merely shrugged.

Determined not to let Joelle's presence ruin my night, I signaled to a passing waiter for another glass of champagne and turned my attention to the rest of the gala guests.

4

I had just about decided to make another run on the raw bar when something truly extraordinary happened.

I saw someone I knew.

This fact alone is highly unusual for me since I suffer from face blindness which makes me unable to tell most faces apart. Now if the face is scarred or hideous in some way or has a Cyrano-sized nose, I'll likely recall them. But otherwise, no.

The disability is a definite handicap, especially in my line of work as a private investigator, but I have developed several workarounds over the years. But tonight, I didn't need any of them. That is because as I was passing an elderly man with a kind face and his very young date, I overheard the man he was speaking to, exclaim: "Senator Andrews! What brings you all the way from Georgia?"

I knew Ethan Andrews, His Excellency, the right honorable Senator from Georgia from my days back in Atlanta. More specifically, my late husband Bob knew Ethan much better as he had had been involved in several of Ethan's campaign fund raisers over the years.

I turned to the Senator and waited for a pause in his

conversation.

"Ethan?" I said.

I was all set to remind him of who I was but one look at his face told me that would not be necessary.

A handsome man with close cropped silver hair and dancing blue eyes, Ethan smiled warmly at me.

"Dearest, Claire," he said in a deep voice as he pulled me into a long embrace. "My dear girl, it has been so long."

Jean-Marc was still by my side, and I wondered what he must be thinking. The Senator was tall, like Jean-Marc, his body was still muscular and trim—denoting a powerful presence. In his day Ethan had been known across the Senate for his tenacity in pitched political wars and for his fierce honor when it came to military combat.

He was a senator who had achieved his position through hard work, and he commanded the respect of every man and woman who stood before him in the Senate chamber or in one of the committees he chaired.

When we separated, I could see his eyes glittered with emotion and I knew he was thinking of Bob. They'd been friends until their separate careers had made get togethers harder and harder to manage.

Ethan came from a South Georgia town where his family had been farmers for generations. He put himself through college and law school, and as I recall, he campaigned on the fact that he'd seen the disparities between urban and rural life and wanted to improve the economic disparities between the rich and the poor. He and his wife Dilly lived comfortably, but not lavishly.

I turned to present Jean-Marc.

"This is my partner, Jean-Marc LaRue," I said. "Jean-Marc, this is Senator Ethan Andrews. We knew each other a very long time ago."

Ethan shook hands with Jean-Marc and then turned to

introduce the young woman by his side. Before he even spoke, I realized it must be little Madeleine who of course was no longer little.

"You remember my daughter Madeleine?" he said to me.

Madeleine turned to smile, her delicate features even more refined by the soft light of the ballroom. Her dress was befitting the most elegant cotillion, a shimmering column of seafoam silk with an intricate beaded embroidery that dripped with pearls and shimmered in the lighting.

"Your gown is lovely," I said, as we shook hands.

A slight movement behind her made me look and I noticed a young beefy man in an ill-fitting tuxedo standing behind Madeleine.

My first guess since no one made an effort to introduce him was that he must be some kind of security since he looked a little rough around the edges to be her date.

"I was so sorry to hear about Bob," Ethan said, glancing briefly at Jean-Marc.

"Thank you."

"How are you holding up these days?"

I was fairly sure he didn't mean anything by that, it was just cocktail party chatter. But for some reason I found myself blushing as if by being out with Jean-Marc tonight I was somehow cheating on Bob.

"I'm working as a private investigator in Paris," I said. "Mostly for expats in trouble."

"That sounds fascinating," Madeleine said, but her eyes were scanning the room as if looking for someone.

"Well," I said, taking Jean-Marc's arm. "It was lovely seeing you again, Ethan."

But by then, Ethan the consummate politician had already moved on too. When I followed his gaze to see what had so captured his attention, the only person I saw in his sightline was Joelle.

5
―――

After we walked away from Ethan and his daughter, Jean-Marc wasted no time in asking how I knew the handsome and powerful statesman.

I laughed with pleasure at Jean-Marc's jealousy, if that's what it was.

"I knew him through Bob," I said. "Most of our social interactions were at fundraisers and of course we lost touch once he was gone to Washington."

"He was watching you very closely," Jean-Marc said. "He looked to me like a man who would say more to you."

"Well, that's because you are a romantic Frenchman," I said, leaning over and kissing him on the mouth which went a long way to assuaging him. "And he is American, so he doesn't look at any woman over thirty in a romantic way."

"That is difficult to believe."

"That's because you are an amazing, intuitive and evolved man, Jean-Marc," I said and then saw a flash of lavender out of the corner of my eye. "Uh oh."

Jean-Marc frowned and looked around. The sea of guests had parted as it had ebbed and flowed all night and now Joelle and her mystery man once more stood fully revealed. This time, instead of glaring at me and waiting for the crowd to cover her once more, her date tucked her arm firmly in his and advanced on us.

Joelle dazzled in a low-cut gown as she glided across the floor. Her hair was swept up in an elegant twist, her red lipstick the only touch of color on her face.

I was always astonished whenever I ran into her—and because she hated me, our infrequent run-ins were never planned—as to how beautiful she was.

I felt Jean-Marc stiffen by my side which unnerved me. I had an issue with Joelle, but Jean-Marc did not.

Which meant he must have an issue with Joelle's date.

The man stopped in front of me and clicked his heels and gave a small half bow. I was shocked because I'd only seen that done in Nazi movies but with the brilliant tricolor sash he wore against his tuxedo, he was most certainly French. He was also slight, balding, and with a face that I think even I might remember. His eyes were dark blue and as cold as the arctic.

"*Bonsoir*, Madame Baskerville," he said to me, as his eyes raked Jean-Marc from head to toe. "Allow me to introduce myself. I am Députée Michel Leblanc."

As I shook his hand, I could easily see that Michel Leblanc was charming. His handshake was firm, and his smile engaging. If he hadn't been on the arm of my archnemesis, I might even have believed that he was happy to meet me.

"Joelle has told me so little about you," I said.

He laughed and Joelle scowled, her eyes flickering to Jean-Marc in resentment and animosity. He'd arrested her once. And saved her life once. So, all in all, I could see why she hated him.

I was just about to formally introduce Jean-Marc—however unnecessary that was beginning to seem—when Ethan walked up.

"Madame Lapin!" he said enthusiastically to Joelle. "How good to see you tonight."

Ethan's gaze then darted to take in Leblanc, and I swear the temperature in the room dropped ten degrees. There was no way his look didn't broadcast that they knew each other. And not in a good way.

"I am sure you are mistaken, Monsieur," Joelle said abruptly before turning and making her excuses and walking away.

The look on Ethan's face was not one of confusion. Although rebuffed, he didn't seem surprised. I wondered what that was all about. Mostly, I wondered how it was that Joelle knew Ethan Andrews.

"Députée Leblanc," Ethan said to Leblanc with a curt nod before turning and walking away.

Before I could think of what to say, Leblanc himself nodded and left, leaving me and Jean-Marc staring after the back of him.

"What do you make of that?" I said.

"Your stepmother seems to know the Senator," Jean-Marc said. "But lied about it."

"Yeah, she did, didn't she?" I said.

"What did you think of Leblanc?"

"Your typical charming politician," I said.

"Perhaps not so charming," Jean-Marc said.

I looked at him.

"What do you know about him?"

"Only rumors."

"That doesn't sound good."

"Trust me, *chérie*, it isn't."

Curious but not enough to pump him for more, I began to head back to the oyster table when my earlier assessment of who the man standing behind Madeleine was, proved correct when I turned in the direction of the entrance in time to hear raised voices.

"I'll thrash you myself, son!" Ethan's voice boomed out.

There were nearly thirty people between me and Ethan and whomever he was shouting at, but I had no doubt that the target of his ire was the so-called bodyguard I'd seen earlier. I turned to make my way through the crowd with Jean-Marc close on my heels.

The crowd quickly parted as we pushed through until I saw Ethan, his tie pulled loose and his face flushed with fury, standing over the burly young man we'd seen earlier who was now on his back on the floor.

Something in the expression on the young man's face along with the tense coil of his muscles told me he wasn't going to let his employer humiliate him any further.

6

The bodyguard jumped to his feet, his fists clenched by his side as he confronted the older man, fury emanating from him from every pore. Ethan stood his ground, squaring off against the younger man, but I could see doubt and even fear on his face. People began to gather around, unsure of what to do as they watched the escalating tension between the two men.

I could feel Jean-Marc tense beside me, but I also knew that unless someone produced a weapon, he wouldn't intervene. I was seconds away from stepping between the two men myself when a commanding voice called, "All right, let's bring it down a notch, shall we?"

Stanley Cole, the US embassy's diplomatic coordinator, stepped out of the crowd and slipped between the young man and Ethan. His face was tense, but his voice stayed calm and reasonable as he addressed them.

"Let's just both step back and take a few deep breaths before things get out of hand," Stanley said.

The young bodyguard continued to glower at Ethan. I

wondered what had started it. What had Ethan said? What had prompted him to hit the younger, more powerfully built man?

Stanley put a hand out as if he would touch the young man's chest but stopped short of that.

"What do you say?" Stanley said to him, smiling hopefully.

The young man snorted in disgust and reached up as if to push Stanley's hand of restraint away. But instead, stepped away from the scuffle.

Ethan wasn't backing down though; his eyes still blazing with rage but as Stanley turned to him, I saw Ethan slowly uncurl his fists. Stanley sighed with relief and put an arm around the older man's shoulders.

"Okay, Ethan?" I heard him say.

"Bastard," Ethan muttered and allowed himself to be led away.

I saw Ethan's daughter on the perimeter of the gathered crowd, a horrified hand to her mouth as she watched her father leave. I felt a moment's impulse to go to her, but I didn't really know her that well. I didn't want to make her more embarrassed than she already clear was.

I have to admit that was the moment I saw that Ethan wasn't really the totally civilized man that I thought I'd known.

Even when I'd seen him gladhanding and schmoozing with people at the gala there was something about the way he held himself that made me think he was on edge and uncomfortable. Granted, I really didn't know him all that well, but he was a politician which everyone knows is a different animal from your average person. I'd imagined he should be fairly skilled in the art of dissembling, so it was disconcerting to see him so rattled.

"What do you make of that?" Jean-Marc said as the crowd finally seemed to lose interest in the altercation.

"It's hard to know what to think," I said as I saw Stanley reappear, smiling and shaking hands with people as he made his way back into the thick of the party. He turned and caught my eye and grinned sheepishly as he walked over to me.

"Sorry about that," he said.

Stanley was short and balding, but his eyes crinkled with delight. I'd known him for the full time I've lived in Paris—over five years now—and he never failed to impart his sheer joy at landing this dream gig in Paris was one he would never fully believe was his.

I was dying to know what the argument had been about, but I could see Stanley would appreciate moving on from it.

"The party is wonderful," I assured him, knowing how much he'd had to do with organizing it. "And a little excitement here and there doesn't make it any less perfect."

"I like your attitude. Now I just hope my boss shares it."

Just as he turned to look at Jean-Marc and I prepared to introduce them, Stanley's wife, Jenny, a petite brunette from Texas, hurried over to us. She was wearing a gown made from yards of pale ivory silk, lined with intricate lace detailing. It was absolutely stunning but the billowing material was very nearly swamping her. Jenny seemed to peer up from within a literal barricade of silk ruffles.

"My hero," she said, lifting up on tiptoe to kiss Stanley on the cheek.

I watched him blush happily at her praise.

"Jean-Marc," I said, "allow me to introduce Stanley Cole, US diplomatic coordinator and his wife Jenny. Two reasons why I'm still making a living in Paris."

Stanley smiled broadly.

"You earn your keep, Claire," he said. "Every case I've sent your way you have literally saved my bacon."

"*Enchantez*, Jean-Marc," Jenny said, dimpling as she and Stanley shook Jean-Marc's hand. "Stan and I have heard a lot about you over the years."

"All good," I hastened to add since that would not be at all presumed, given my history with Jean-Marc.

"Yes, of course, all good," Jenny said hurriedly, reaching over and giving my hand a squeeze.

Whenever I see Jenny, I always wonder why I don't make a point to get together with her more often. She's one of the warmest and most generous people I know. As the wife of a midlevel statesman in the most popular posting in the universe, she was on nearly every charity and fundraising committee there was. If we didn't see much of each other, it was because she was always so busy.

"We're here tonight because of Stanley and Jenny," I told Jean-Marc.

I'd already briefed him before we came that I got at least fifty percent of my business through Stanley and the expat community the embassy served.

I knew Stanley took his job very seriously. I think he might have mentioned one time that a dull but safe project management position awaited him back in Indianapolis when his time in Paris was done. He did not sound as if he was looking forward to that and I couldn't blame him.

How can any place else compare after you've lived in Paris?

"It really is a wonderful event," I said to him. "You should be proud."

"I am," he said, glancing and smiling at Jenny who smiled her agreement.

"Well done, you," she said. "Now let's go mingle before you're called on to break up another fight or, god forbid, deliver a baby!"

With that and a flash of her famous dimples, the two of them moved off in a swish of crinoline and silk.

∽

An hour after the American Senator fought with the man who was obviously his daughter's bodyguard, Jean-Marc had made several circuits of the room, sampled all the edibles the event had to offer, and of course several glasses of the very good champagne. Except for one small thing left to do, he was ready to leave.

He spotted Claire across the room talking to one of the American embassy people. Her cheeks were flushed a pale pink, and a small smile tugged at the corners of her lips. She was always beautiful but particularly so tonight. And it was not just the gown that fit her curves as if it were a couture's mannequin, but in the animation and ebullience that he saw in her face. He would remember this night for no other reason than the sheer enjoyment of watching her face light up as she —normally so cool and even distant with strangers because of her affliction—enjoyed a night of lively socializing.

As he reached for another glass of Veuve Cliquot—after all, he would not be driving tonight—the band filled the ballroom with a lively melody. Immediately appreciative applause erupted. Jean-Marc turned to glance at Claire again, waiting for her to turn and look his way. He watched her talking and scanning the crowd for him. He smiled when she finally spotted him. When she did, they locked eyes and he held out one arm in silent invitation.

She politely broke off her conversation and found her way around the perimeter of the dance floor toward him, her gown seeming to float around her like a whirl of glittering stardust. She stood before him, breathless and blushing, her eyes glittering from the champagne, the music, the night. And him. He held his arm out and guided her towards the center of the dance floor. He could barely hear the music over the pounding of his heart.

In his mind, the crowd had melted away around them as he swept her into the waltz. His body moved effortlessly in time with hers, her body light and responsive to his every movement.

He leaned in close, his breath tickling her ear. "You never cease to amaze me," he whispered.

Claire looked into his eyes and smiled. As they danced around the room, Jean-Marc felt as if the world around them had disappeared until it was just the two of them.

In that perfect moment set to music with his love in his arms, nothing and no one else, had ever mattered before.

7

I'm pretty sure I'm going to remember that dance for the rest of my life. Especially the moment I felt Jean-Marc looking at me from across the room. When I turned and saw him, I felt a pull as strong as if we had been physically tied to one another.

Jean-Marc, in his tuxedo, and his molten eyes, seemed to fix me with a gaze that made me feel as if I was seeing him for the first time. That dance—our first ever—was a magical moment —with his arms around me and the music sweeping over us in a delicious wave of enchantment.

It occurred to me later that this was the first formal event that Jean-Marc and I have attended together as romantic partners. Our relationship has been so up and down—and honestly mostly down—that there are a lot of blanks in our timeline. We've not gone on vacation together or danced together. I've not met any of his family. We've not gone to a movie or a play together. On the other hand, we've shared some experiences that are one of a kind in the intimacy department.

Especially if you count murder as a fairly intimate experience which I have to say I do. Jean-Marc and I have been through life and death situations, the losses of both our spouses, betrayal and hurt. But we've also been there when the light burst through the darkness, and we were hand in hand when it did.

As I stood waiting for Jean-Marc to return with more champagne, I felt a zing of excitement shoot through me. It had been six months since Jean-Marc and I had gone into business together.

More importantly, it had been six months since the two of us had decided to reignite our romance.

In the middle of a conversation with a low-level embassy drone who I nonetheless thought might prove useful someday in my business, I saw Ethan heading my way. I made my apologies to the young American stateswoman and turned to him.

There was something about the way Ethan was looking at me that made me think he had more on his mind than just saying goodbye. His face was flushed, likely from too much drink, and I could see he had his coat room ticket clutched in one hand.

"Not leaving so soon?" I asked lightly.

He stopped in front of me, the bowtie to his tuxedo slightly askew. He seemed mildly out of breath.

"Yes, I'm afraid so," he said. "Early nights lately for me. But I did want to say again how sorry I was to hear about Bob."

"Thank you."

I remembered that Ethan and his wife Dilly had sent flowers when Bob died. My husband has been gone for five years now. I wondered mildly what Ethan made of the fact that I was here tonight with a man. It really isn't unusual in Paris for a woman my age to be seen on the arm of a man.

It's not like it is in the US where a woman over sixty with a boyfriend would qualify as banner news. I'm not saying people don't do it back home, but in my experience most women tend to call it quits when the man they chose in their twenties dies or otherwise leaves them to navigate old age on their own.

Ethan is a man of the world. He probably doesn't think anything of it at all.

He abruptly leaned over to kiss me on the cheek, and I felt him push a folded piece of paper into my hand. For a moment, I thought he'd given me his coat check ticket but when he pulled back, I saw he still had that.

"Later, yes?" he said pointedly.

His face was close and I could see the broken capillaries in his nose and the red veins in his eyes.

"Of course," I said, smiling, but confused since we hadn't made plans to meet.

We said goodnight and I watched him walk away, a little unsteady on his feet. I felt the note in my hand, and closed my fingers around it, hiding it, although I was not sure why.

Paris at night was always a thrill. It's like walking onto a stage surrounded by old world charm but alive with living style and beauty. And for me, that goes double when the streets are wet with rain. That night, after more dances than I can ever remember dancing in my entire life, Jean-Marc and I left the gala and walked across the Place de la Concorde to the room he'd booked at Hôtel de Crillon barely a block from where the gala was held at the US Club.

The cobbled, glistening streets of Paris were lined with statues and monuments by the sidewalks as Jean-Marc and I made our way back to his hotel.

It was a perfect summer night. The night sky was speckled with stars and the air was thick and warm. Even if it hadn't rained recently, I tend to think the night streets of Paris are always wet. That can't possibly be true, but it seems as if it's been true as far as I can remember, and I've lived here now for nearly four years.

From the outside, the Hôtel de Crillon is unsurprisingly as astonishingly elegant as it is renown, with its stunning white marble columns and arches. Inside, it is designed to take your breath away with marbled floors, gold-gilded walls, and enormous chandeliers.

We enjoyed a leisurely drink at the sumptuously furnished hotel bar—where I could not resist taking a few photos for my Instagram account until Jean-Marc reminded me that private investigators bragging about staying at the Hôtel de Crillon may not be a good look for our business.

While he paid the bill, I remembered the note Ethan had slipped me. I pulled it out of my beaded clutch, wondering why all the mystery? I seriously hoped he wasn't making a pass. In some ways it was extraordinary that my mind would even go there. After all, I'm sixty-five years old. But living in Paris has tended to erode the feeling so prevalent in the States that a woman loses her allure after fifty.

In Paris, I have been made aware on several occasions that my allure is evidently very much alive.

I unfolded the piece of paper and my brow creased with puzzlement when I saw that it had been hastily scrawled. He'd written:

Meet me at the Sofitel Hotel Faubourg. Tomorrow noon. Don't mention to Madeleine.

8

Désirée had been told to be there at midnight on the nose, not a minute sooner or later. She'd had to wander the hotel bar and then race to the elevator to make it up to the john's room in time—a very uncomfortable exercise with every man in the bar watching her as if she were about to self-destruct at any moment.

Or as if they knew exactly what she was doing there.

She adjusted the skirt of her tight, red dress and walked down the hall to the number on the room door she'd been given. The dress kept riding up and she was tired of the constant war of tugging it back into place. But it was her lucky skirt. Plus, of course the clients all loved it.

She was tired and was hoping for an easy job tonight. The caller had said it would be fast and tonight she needed fast. She pushed back a curl that had escaped from her glossy dark hair. She straightened her shoulders and knocked lightly on the hotel room door, glancing down the long hallway. It was a nice hotel—one of the nicest in Paris—and she'd never been here before.

She knew the doorman, at least by reputation, and he

would've already alerted security that she was in the hotel. In her experience, men made up their minds about you no matter how you looked or acted. It felt absurd but she'd been advised by the man booking her tonight to comport herself like a perfect lady. Her john was used to being with courtesans. Whatever that was.

When the door opened, she was met by a distinguished-looking gentleman, his silver hair and narrow glasses perched on the end of his nose giving him an air of sophistication. He studied her for a moment, his eyebrows pinched together in consternation.

For a moment, Désirée thought he might turn her away. She felt a throb of panic in her throat that she forced down.

"I'm Désirée," she said confidently, moving past him into the room. "You're waiting for me, I think, Monsieur?"

9

The next morning, I sat in the dining room of one of the most elegant hotels in the world and ate a breakfast that was everything I'd imagined it could be. Even the guilt of what I knew the night had cost Jean-Marc—two thousand euros for the room—couldn't stand up to the sheer elegance and luxury of the experience. Forget the one thousand thread count sheets, the all-marble bathroom, and the carpet underfoot so plush that you literally sank in on every step—the dining room alone was worth the cost of admission.

Here too it was all in white marble with crystal accents and mahogany furnishings, panoramic ceiling-high windows overlooking the Place de la Concorde no less, and fine silk linens adorning every table setting. The atmosphere in the room was quiet, with only the muted rustle of the wait staff as they moved between tables, and the soft tinkling of silverware and dishes.

Further completing the picture were fresh peonies, daffodils and extravagant moth orchids—arranged in brilliant crystal vases at each table—their heady perfume competing with the mouth-watering fragrance of just-baked baguettes and croissants—and all of it seeming to hover in the air like a cloud of breathless anticipation.

Talk about Cinderella the night after the ball! My feet still have not touched the ground.

"You were so beautiful last night," Jean-Marc said.

I smiled, tempted to ask how I was doing this morning but decided to let the compliment be a compliment.

"Thank you. I'd never seen you in a tux before. I think we need to do this more often."

He drank his espresso and signaled to the ever-attentive waiter. I'm pretty sure we had our own dedicated server. There was no way she was ever going to let us run out of *confiture* or engraved butter pats, so I was curious as to what in the world Jean-Marc thought he needed.

"Can you shut the blinds just an inch?" he said, indicating the slim gleam of sunlight that was hitting me at eye level.

So enchanted was I with everything, I hadn't even noticed the mild glare in my eye.

"At once, Monsieur," she said with an urgency that would rival most EMTs at a crash site as she swiftly turned and left.

Jean-Marc reached over and took my hand.

"Where were we?" he asked.

"You were commenting on my beauty, I believe," I said in mock seriousness.

He smiled and tilted his head as if considering me from a different angle.

"I am glad we found our way back to each other," he said.

For a moment, I didn't know what to say. It was very unusual for Jean-Marc of all people to give voice to the unspoken thought. And this was a thought that I believed was all mine.

"Me, too," I said.

I was surprised to be so tongue-tied. I'd known at least a year ago how I felt about Jean-Marc. That was right about the time that I'd chased him away—for good I thought. I'd had plenty of time in the intervening months to regret my tart tongue and to rue the loss of what I'd had but hadn't appreciated.

I'd vowed if I got a second chance with him, I wouldn't make the same mistake again. But now that a tailor-made moment was here to tell him just how much I cared, how much I in fact loved him, I found myself unable to find the words.

"The working together," he said with a smile. "I wasn't so sure."

I smiled. Our history had been a rollercoaster of highs and lows, but particularly when it came to working the cases that we inevitably did together. Or if not exactly together—since we'd always come at them from opposite sides of the fence—then at least at the same time.

Jean-Marc had been a by-the-book kind of police detective. And by that, I mean he knew every single rule he then systematically broke. It was a miracle he hadn't been ejected from the department or sent to prison long ago. But even then, I believed he was deep down, essentially a good man and a good detective, frustrated with the red tape of his occupation and with the unfairness of life—to him and the victims of all violence, including his late wife.

When Jean-Marc walked away from his thirty-year career at the Paris police department last summer—largely because of me—and eventually suggested we join forces as a private investigations company partnership, I'd wanted it as intensely as I also believed that it could only be a disastrous failure.

And amazingly, so far, it wasn't.

"What are you going to do about the note?" Jean-Marc asked as he smiled his thanks to the waitress and reached into the croissant basket.

"The note?"

"From the Senator? Are you going to meet him?"

I'd completely forgotten Ethan's cryptic note from last night. I sipped my coffee and made an effort to change mental gears.

"I suppose so. I mean, for curiosity's sake if nothing else. It's odd that he asked me not to say anything to his daughter, don't you think?"

"Probably means it's a sex thing."

I gave him a playfully scornful look.

"Sex isn't the only reason why he might not want her to know," I said. "He could be trying to protect her from something."

"*Oui*, from information about his perverted sexual peccadilloes that are about to become public."

I raised an eyebrow which I hoped he could translate as I would not honor that comment with a response.

"Why couldn't he just text you? Or call you?" he asked.

"Well, for some people of a certain age, those ways don't come naturally. He clearly has something sensitive he wants to discuss with me."

"Buy why *you*?"

"Well, I did tell him I'm working as a private investigator these days. It's probably business."

"Except he would have access to much higher echelon investigators than an old friend he bumped into at an embassy party."

"Well, we'll just have to wait and see, won't we?"

～

I hated to leave after breakfast, wanting the magic to last just a little bit longer, but I had a little boy back at the apartment and other responsibilities. Jean-Marc too, had things to do on this beautiful summer day in Paris. We made plans for dinner at my apartment later and after a moment of handholding and looking meaningfully into one another's eyes, we kissed and parted company on the street in front of the hotel.

I watched him stride away as I turned in the opposite direction toward the eighth arrondissement. As I did, I heard a ding come from my phone and dug it out of my bag to see I'd received a text from Geneviève asking me to stop and pick up bread on my way home.

I couldn't wait to tell her about the gala—the ball gowns, the opulence—and also Hotel de Crillon. I wondered if she'd ever been inside. Most people manage to at least go in for a drink at its impressive bar.

While I headed down the street to hail a taxi—I wanted to keep the Cinderella moment going for as long as possible and that did not involve a ride on the subway—I received another call and was surprised to see it was from Stanley Cole.

"Hello, stranger," I said, answering as I got in line at the taxi queue on rue Boissy d'Anglas. "I'm surprised to hear from you so soon. Last night was such a—"

"Claire, stop," Stanley said, his voice strained and thick with anguish.

Instantly, I stepped away from the taxi stand, my senses prickling with dread.

"Look," he said, "I'm calling everyone, so they don't hear it from the press first."

"What's happened?" I asked, my mind going to terrorist threats or attacks.

"It's...it's Ethan," he said.

I felt a cold hard weight press into my chest, and I stopped moving, clutching the phone to my ear. For a moment, I'm sure I stopped breathing.

"He was murdered last night in his hotel room."

10

I don't even remember the rest of my conversation with Stanley. He had no real information or details, beyond the fact that Ethan had died in his room sometime after the gala. It was entirely possible that Stanley was hoping that *I* might be able to tell *him* something, but he didn't ask and I'm sure my honest reaction of complete shock told him I knew less than he did. He did mention that the police weren't sharing any information with the embassy, which set my Spidey-sense to vibrating.

Why would the Paris police be cagey unless the death was suspicious?

Stanley said he had many more people to call so I let him go and quickly called Jean-Marc as soon as I found a bench. My legs were definitely wobbly and only partially because of all the champagne I'd had last night. I was so stunned, I couldn't even think straight. I just couldn't believe it was true.

Jean-Marc picked up on the first ring.

"You've heard?" he said.

I was astonished that he'd already heard but I didn't ask how. He still had many contacts inside the Paris police department. Maybe someone knew he'd been at the gala last night. There had been photographers taking pictures of all of us. Were the photos published already?

"What do you know?" I asked.

"Not much. I'll reach out to homicide after I hang up with you. But whatever it is, I'm sure the US Diplomatic Service will be handling it not the Paris police."

That was true. Now that I thought about it, I wondered why Stanley had referenced the Paris police when, like Jean-Marc said, Ethan was a US statesman so it would not be their jurisdiction.

"Okay," I said. "Just call me when you hear anything."

I sat back on the bench, stunned and sick, my happy delirium of just a few moments before gone like smoke wisps dissolved in the air.

∽

The restaurant where Députée Michel Leblanc sat the morning after the gala was a quiet, unassuming place, tucked away in a small corner of the city and at the moment surprisingly free of customers for the lunch hour. Michel tried not to think of how unusual that was and told himself he had grown accustomed to the idea that especially here—and certainly for his purposes—discretion was of the utmost importance.

The waiter led him to a table in a dark corner at the back of the restaurant and Michel sat down, observing his surroundings. He felt out of place here, but he understood the need for anonymity. He always seemed to attract attention despite his best efforts to keep a low profile. The person he was to meet today had hinted not too subtly at that very thing. He felt a flutter of heart palpitations at the memory.

Michel knew what the press said of him, particularly that unauthorized biography. He still wasn't sure how he was going to deal with that or, more specifically, with the double-crossing journalist author. The media twisted everything.

Yes, he was an influential man and he'd worked hard to create that illusion. But to have the label of *charm* presented as a method to catch people off guard was just a sheer misrepresentation of the truth. Fake news at its worst. He was merely very good at getting people to trust him. Surely, not a crime?

It was just that, lately, he seemed to be just as good at getting them to hate him.

He thought back to last night—if for no other reason than to attempt to calm his nerves while he waited. It had hardly been the triumph he'd been hoping for, but it wasn't a total disaster either. Like anything else, it could be managed. Whether by him or someone else. He needn't worry about that. He felt a moistness on his top lip and quickly wiped it away.

It wouldn't help to look nervous.

The waiter didn't come back and while Michel hadn't necessarily expected it—he wasn't here to dine after all—a drink would have been nice. He checked his watch and realized that it was nearly past time. More sweat popped out on his forehead, and he hurriedly opened up his cellphone and typed in the code to make the transfer.

Then he watched as a sizable chunk of his savings disappeared with a ridiculous swishing sound. He swallowed hard and put his phone on the table, willing his hands to stop shaking.

Suddenly the waiter appeared at his table and without saying a word placed a simple folded sheet of paper on the table. Michel took it in his hands, noticing how they trembled as he did, and unfolded it. Only the words *"Va t'en!"* were scrawled across the page.

Leave.

Michel looked up at the waiter, as if for some explanation, but the man had already turned and headed back toward the kitchen. Shaken, Michel gathered up his briefcase and his phone and stood up.

His contact would either reschedule the meeting or he wouldn't. In any case, Michel could do no more here.

As he wound his way through the empty restaurant toward the front door, his mind went back to the image on his phone of the three hundred thousand euros being transferred from his account.

He hoped it would be enough.

11

It was late afternoon, and Jean-Marc sat alone at Café Le Boule, the small café on Boulevard de Palais not far from the police headquarters on the Île de la Cité. The aroma of herbs and spices drifted in from the café's kitchen and mixed with a hint of cigarette smoke. The tables that surrounded him were filled with conversation and laughter.

He had already sipped his way through two glasses of white wine, regardless of the fact that it was nowhere near *apéro* time.

Claire hadn't asked him to reach out to his ex-colleagues but she didn't have to. He knew there was no way of getting any inside information on the Andrews case except through him. On the one hand, he swelled with pride at the thought of how useful he would be and how grateful Claire would be.

On the other, he had no strong sense of how his old friends would greet him. They'd been happy enough to go out with him for drinks last fall when the separation had been fresh. But that had faded in the months leading up to Christmas and then, in the New Year when Chantal Resnelle had taken his old position as *Inspecteur Principal*, it had stopped entirely.

Jean-Marc signaled to the water to order another drink and

frowned into the afternoon sun as it inched slowly downward over the cityscape.

He had been so busy creating his place in Claire's investigation business that he'd hardly noticed that his friends had stopped calling him. He may have reached out a time or two and they were too busy, and right after the holidays, that was entirely believable. However, even then, he'd had a gut feeling that perhaps there was something more.

This was the café they'd all adopted as their own. It was friendly to police—half the time refusing payment—and there was always the assurance of privacy at the interior tables.

All he wanted was to reconnect with them. And if it turned out that the murder at the US Club was something they wanted to talk about, all the better. He glanced at his watch. He was surprised nobody had shown up yet. Had they migrated to a different café in the months that he'd been gone?

Suddenly he saw two figures walking down the sidewalk toward the café. Both had the distinctive policeman's gait pounded into every cadet in the academy of the slight roll of the shoulder and the erect stance, the confident stride.

It was Colette Girard and Victor Durand. Both glanced idly around their surroundings. A cop is never really off duty, Jean-Marc thought with a grim smile. He knew them both well and for years. He stood up, making himself visible.

Colette spotted him first. The look on her face was frozen for a split second before she put her hand up to wave. Jean-Marc watched her speak to Durand out of the corner of her mouth. Then Durand turned and saw Jean-Marc. He too, waved.

They both kept walking past the café.

Jean-Marc sat back down.

So, it's like that, is it?

The rejection was brutal. They had definitely been walking toward the café. His stomach ground in bitterness. He was glad he'd made them reroute. He hoped they found a place who would gouge coppers instead of pandering to them. There were such places.

He couldn't help but watch them as they continued on their way until they were swallowed up by the crowds of commuters and tourists, Colette's tell-tale laugher finally mixing with the street noise until he was left totally alone.

Jean-Marc could still feel the sun's warmth through his light jacket, despite the growing emptiness inside of him. He stretched his neck to see if anyone else was coming down the sidewalk, but Colette would've phoned to alert the rest of them. He'd been a pariah before. It hadn't mattered before. Not really.

He pulled out his phone and scrolled through his contacts. He was tempted to delete Girard and Durand but decided not to overreact. Life was long. A slap in the face today could well be a handshake tomorrow. Although at the moment that didn't feel likely.

He saw Paul Olivier's number and called him. Paul had been a fairly close associate for years. They'd not been in the same division for the past five years, but they'd kept in touch.

"Fancy hearing from you," Paul said, answering his phone.

"Been busy," Jean-Marc said, warming to Paul's friendly tone. Whatever was going on with his old department, it hadn't filtered down to Paul. And if it ever did, Jean-Marc had hopes that Paul wouldn't catch it.

"So I hear. With Claire Baskerville. How's that working?"

Jean-Marc grimaced at the thought that he may have had a few post-Claire beers with Paul last summer where he'd been less than glowing about the future of his relationship with Claire.

"Things change," he said cryptically now.

"Obviously. Do you miss us yet?"

Jean-Marc smiled. "Not even a little. How are things there?"

Paul sighed.

"Look, Jean-Marc, if you're calling for info on the Andrews case, I can't help you."

Jean-Marc was dismayed that he'd been so easily caught. His determination to show Claire what he could bring to the table was making him careless.

"Can't I just call up an old friend?" he asked.

"You can," Paul said evenly, "as long as you don't try to pump that old friend for information on cases your department is handling."

"Perish the thought," Jean-Marc said. "Just a friendly chat. Meet me at Le Boule?"

"Can't do it. And even if I didn't need to get home," Paul said, "you should know that there is currently a fairly large and very black X by your name."

Jean-Marc frowned. "Resnelle?"

"You can't blame her. She's heard some of the old rumors about you."

"I was vindicated."

"Sure you were, Jean-Marc. But she wants the department to have a clean start. They all do. Upper level and linemen both."

"Really."

"I'm not saying it's worth our jobs to be seen with you, but it wouldn't be doing anyone's career trajectory any good. Let's leave it at that. Thanks for reaching out. I have to go."

Jean-Marc sat and stared at his phone for a few seconds before setting it on the table. He can't say that he wasn't totally surprised. He'd had a rocky status with the department for years. If it hadn't been for Chloe and half the department feeling sorry for him, he'd probably have been fired years ago.

Resnelle didn't know him. She had no reason to cut him a break. And now that he was gone, even more so. She wouldn't easily allow him in through the back door. Jean-Marc tried to tell himself he'd do the same thing if it were him.

Except he was trying not to lie these days. To himself or anyone else.

"Hey, haven't seen you in a while," a familiar voice called out.

Jean-Marc looked up to see Étienne Benoit striding toward his table, a grin on his face.

Étienne Benoit was a big man, unusual for a Frenchman, with blond hair. He was clean shaven, and his dark brown eyes darted around the room—the classic picture of the undercover cop which Étienne had been for years before finally taking a place on the vice team of the Paris Police department.

Jean-Marc felt a surge of relief followed by the unmistakable realization that because Étienne worked in vice, not homicide, he wouldn't have been on anyone's call list to warn him off the Café Le Boule today.

Jean-Marc stood up and the two men shook hands.

"Étienne," Jean-Marc said. "It's been a while."

"I hear you've gone into business for yourself," Étienne said as he signaled to the waiter to bring two more of what Jean-Marc was drinking.

"*Oui*," Jean-Marc said. "Better hours, better hierarchy."

Étienne laughed. "I hear you. Got any interesting cases or is it all cheating spouses?"

"It's mostly cheating spouses," Jean-Marc admitted. "My partner handles most of the problems in the Expat community, Americans and Brits."

"Right. Your ex-girlfriend, right?"

Jean-Marc decided he didn't need to go into details.

"Correct," he said. "It's working," he added with a shrug.

Étienne looked around.

"I'm surprised homicide isn't here. They normally own this place. Nice to have it to ourselves today."

"I imagine they're pretty busy with the case of the American Senator," Jean-Marc said.

"Well, they've got their suspect in custody so they're essentially just in clean-up mode now."

"And they have all the evidence they need to hold him?"

Étienne grinned at him.

"What is this, LaRue?" he asked good-naturedly. "Pumping me for inside info?"

"Just making conversation," Jean-Marc said but he grinned when he said it to let Étienne know that he wasn't far wrong.

"So do you know much about it?"

"Just what I hear," Étienne said as the waiter came and set two glasses of wine on their table.

Jean-Marc pulled out his wallet. "I'll get these."

"*Bon*," Étienne said reaching for his glass. "I guess that means you do want something from me."

"Nothing much," Jean-Marc said. "Just your company and if there's any departmental gossip, I'm up for that too."

Étienne frowned.

"Not much in vice that you'd be interested in," he said. "But I heard that the new head of homicide is kicking *derrière*."

"A real tyrant?"

Étienne waggled his hand.

"If you're asking, is she fair, you could make an argument for it. If you're asking, is she warm and friendly? Absolutely not. But the team doesn't hate her."

"Interesting. It's a feather in her cap to make an arrest so quickly."

"Don't think she's not making the most of it," Étienne said.

"Good for her," Jean-Marc said, wondering exactly how he was going to go about getting whatever information Étienne had out of him. He had the bare bones of an idea, but it had been so long since he'd done anything like what he'd need to do to implement it, he needed to take another long swig of his wine, nearly draining the glass.

"Monique and I are expecting again," Étienne said.

"Congratulations, Étienne. Give my best wishes to Monique. That's two, yes?"

Étienne nodded. "That makes a boy and a girl. I told Monique it's time to stop now that we have one of each."

"Sounds like a plan," Jean-Marc said. "Hey, remember that time out by Saint-Denis? We both nearly bought it that night. You remember?"

Étienne took a sip of his wine.

"You mean the night where you pulled me back just as the second gunman came around the corner?"

Jean-Marc shrugged. "Oh, well. All part of the craziness of that night."

"I haven't forgotten, Jean-Marc," Étienne said seriously. "You saved my life that night."

"You'd have done the same for me," Jean-Marc said. He knew it hadn't been subtle and he hated that he didn't feel that he'd had the time for a little more finesse.

The two of them drank silently for a moment and watched the people walk by the café. The lights had begun to come on down the boulevard de Palais, even though it was summer, and it would be hours yet before they were needed.

"Let me get the next round," Étienne said. "And maybe I do remember hearing a thing or two about the Andrews case that I picked up around the department."

"That would be great," Jean-Marc said. "Let's get some olives and they do a good *socca*, too. I'm a little peckish this far from dinner time."

12

I went through the rest of the day as if I were walking through a thick fog. The fact that I'd just seen Ethan made it all the more personal for me. I was dying to find out the details of what had happened but resisted texting Jean-Marc. I knew he'd call as soon as he knew anything.

Failing that, he was coming over for dinner tonight. We'd originally planned it to be a work evening. I'd found Gigi, the Matheson's wayward au pair living in Nice, and needed to sort out with Jean-Marc which of us would reach out to her.

Since it was Saturday, there was no school for Robbie today and thankfully my babysitter, Haley, was coming over to amuse the little monsieur. Haley had been helping me with Robbie since he was two years old. In that time, I'd seen her do a fair amount of growing up, too. After Saturday's visit, Haley was flying out to visit some college campuses in the US. She was too late for applications for the fall, but she had her heart set on leaving France after Christmas.

That was six months away and already I had no idea of what I was going to do without her.

I spent the rest of the morning cleaning house while

Robbie watched his favorite television shows. I've raised this child since he was four months old, and I have to say it's been the most exhausting and most extraordinary thing I've ever done.

I don't really count the years raising my daughter Catherine in Atlanta since I did that with hired help, nannies and babysitters. Although I had a husband in those days, Bob always came home too late from work to interact with his daughter, let alone help her with her homework.

That, of course, didn't stop Catherine from blaming me for the horrific secrets that came to light after Bob's death as if they were my fault.

Secrets that involved the conception of Robbie, actually.

As I dusted and cleaned, I looked constantly at my phone for any news at all about the gala murder but there was very little. Either the embassy had one hell of a public relations team—and of course they would—or somebody was keeping a media lid on the murder. In any case, I was in the dark.

By the time Robbie was getting tired of sitting indoors on a beautiful July day in Paris, Haley showed up and I was never so glad to see anyone. She had a special way with him, gruff and loving, and he of course adored her.

"We're playing *Mosquito!*" he crowed after Haley set up the game in the living room.

"Nice," I said as I made my way to the door.

My apartment has a special security function that prohibits people from getting into the building unless they know the security code. Long before I gave him the code, Jean-Marc had had no problem gaining access. I'm not sure I saw that as a positive harbinger at the time, but I do now. That and the fact that he is the only person I know who Izzy does not bark at when he knocks on my door.

I opened the door to him now with Izzy jumping silently at my feet. Jean-Marc's arms were full of two shopping bags—one of which I was sure contained wine and probably cheese since he never believes I have enough of either.

We kissed as he entered.

"Jean-Marc!" Robbie called. "Haley and I are playing the *Mosquito* game!"

"*Très bien*, Robbie," Jean-Marc answered as he brought the bags to the kitchen and began to set up for dinner.

I followed him into the kitchen as he brought out a small chicken and a package of mushrooms. They weren't covered in plastic, so I imagined he got them at some outdoor market. Knowing him, probably on the way to my apartment.

"*Coq au vin*?" I asked, as I pulled out a large, covered casserole and turned on the stove burner.

He turned and poured a measure of olive oil into the pan.

"*Pourquoi pas?*" he said. "Robbie loves it, *non*?"

I smiled, because Robbie was a little Frenchman at heart and he loved all food with equal relish. That is not something I can say about most American children who tend to turn their noses up at anything that isn't a fried nugget of some kind or coated in sugar.

Jean-Marc tossed a small package of pancetta into the smoking oil. And I brought down a bowl to get it ready for the salad Robbie and I've been eating with every meal this summer.

"Are you ready to hear the details?" Jean-Marc asked casually as he gave the sautéing pancetta a stir.

I sat on the kitchen stool near him and dropped my voice.

"How did you hear them? Was it from the people in your old department?"

I knew he intended to make contact with his former colleagues, but I also knew he wasn't sure they'd be willing to talk to him.

"Are you sure?" he asked, tilting his head at me. "Some parts are a little hard to hear."

I swallowed hard and nodded. "I want to know," I said.

He gave a glance to the living room to make sure that Robbie and Haley couldn't hear us.

"It seems that an escort came to Senator Andrews' room after the gala. When housekeeping knocked on the door the next morning, they found Andrews dead and the escort unconscious. The prostitute, a Mademoiselle Désirée Deschamps, was arrested for his murder."

I was glad I was sitting down. Jean-Marc gave me a concerned look which I waved away.

"They believe that Senator Andrews was incapacitated, tortured with cigarette burns, and then smothered to death with a pillow."

"Dear God," I whispered, feeling my stomach lurch in spite of my best efforts. Hearing that Ethan had died was one thing. Learning how was something else entirely. *Cigarette burns!*

Jean-Marc scooped the pancetta out of the pan and added the chicken pieces, using a tong to move them around the sizzling pan.

"So they think the sex worker killed him?" I asked.

"Evidently," he said as he began chopping carrots. "I might know someone who can get me a transcript of what she tells the police."

I cringed at how someone's civil liberties were about to be so effortlessly set aside. Hearing him say it, reminded me how not too long ago Jean-Marc would have been the first to scoff at such niceties.

"You said she was unconscious, too," I said.

"They both appeared to have been drugged."

"But she wasn't tortured?"

Jean-Marc cocked his head at me questioningly.

"But she still might have been left for dead, don't you think?" I asked. "Maybe the killer thought he'd given her enough of the drug. Otherwise, does it make sense that she would have been drugged, too?"

He shrugged, as usual, unwilling to commit to a speculation. As for myself, I honestly didn't know what to think of the scenario. But if the woman was supposed to have died too, perhaps police custody was the safest place for her.

"Anything else?" I asked.

"The room was ransacked, which goes with the evidence of his being tortured."

"The killer was trying to get information from him."

"Presumably."

I stood up as if suddenly with too much energy. More than ever, I could not help but wonder what it was that Ethan had wanted to say to me when he asked me to meet him.

Dinner was its usual hectic occasion when there's a six-year-old at the table. Robbie is a perfect gentleman most of the time, and absolutely well behaved, but he is still a child. Even so, because Haley was there, she retrieved the tossed olives and baguette crusts that Robbie had intended for Izzy and generally kept him contained and amused—not easy to do since he is enamored of Jean-Marc and hardly left his side.

I felt sobered by the details that Jean-Marc had told me about Ethan's death. I could sense that he'd hesitated to tell me at all since I'd known Ethan personally. So I attempted to put on a brave front.

But it's hard when someone you know—even if you didn't know them well—and someone with whom you just spent time is suddenly and brutally murdered. You'd think I'd be used to it by now.

Just when Haley had managed to get Robbie halfway to his bedroom after his bath, Izzy began barking like a fiend and ran to the front door. Again, unless it is someone who lives in the building—or Jean-Marc—an unexpected knock on the door shouldn't happen.

Jean-Marc's eyebrows shot up at me in question, but I just shrugged. I went to the door, holding the dog back with one hand. When I opened it, I let go of Izzy and stood up in surprise.

"I am so sorry to interrupt your evening," Madeleine Andrews said as she stepped into my apartment.

13

When Madeleine appeared, I hugged her and gave her my sincerest condolences and then excused myself to put Robbie to bed. But also, I needed a moment to think.

I left Madeleine and Jean-Marc in the living room with coffees. As I walked Robbie from the bathroom to his room I could hear the soft murmurs of their voices. By the time Haley helped me finally put Robbie to bed and then left herself, it was nearly ten o'clock.

After going downstairs to see the Uber driver with my own eyes who would be taking Haley home, I hurried back upstairs to join Madeline and Jean-Marc in the living room where Jean-Marc was plying her with wine. Her bodyguard had appeared at the door with her but had been sent to a nearby restaurant to wait until Madeleine called for him.

I put my hand on her shoulder as I came into the living room and sat down beside her.

"I can't imagine what you're going through right now," I said.

"Claire, you have to help me," she said, her eyes glistening with tears. "I was just telling Jean-Marc that what they're saying isn't true. A prostitute?" She shuddered. "I can't have my mother hear that!"

I nodded, as I took a glass of wine from Jean-Marc.

"He would never do anything like that to my mother! You have to believe me!"

"Yes, of course, Madeleine," I said, deliberately not looking at Jean-Marc. "Maybe she was just a friend."

"She wasn't a friend!" she said hotly, wiping the tears from her face. "She was a hired assassin!"

I frowned. I had only just learned that Ethan had been murdered. I couldn't help but wonder how Madeleine knew. I was fairly certain she hadn't gotten that information from the Paris police.

"You believe your father was murdered?" I asked.

"I know he was! And I know why, too. Did Dad tell you about the death threats?"

I shook my head and glanced again at Jean-Marc.

"Your father and I were really just acquaintances," I said.

"So he didn't mention them to you?"

"I'm sorry, darling, no," I said.

She looked as if she was going to cry again. I saw that Jean-Marc was frowning into his wine glass. I couldn't imagine what he was thinking.

"There's more," Madeleine said as she gulped down her glass of wine and pushed it toward Jean-Marc for a refill. "I'm pretty sure I'm next."

Jean-Marc stopped pouring midway and looked at her with surprise.

"You think you are a target?" he asked.

"I do. Just like Dad was. And for the same reason." She turned to me. "You probably don't keep up with politics back home but he's the author of this really controversial Senate bill.

I mean we're all so proud of him, but like I said, he's been getting death threats over it."

"What is the bill?"

"It's one that would make it illegal to use animals in any kind of scientific experiments anywhere in the US. Period," Madeleine said. "Dad felt so strongly about it."

"Okay, so, why do you think *you're* in danger?"

"I've commented all over social media on how important I think this bill is and how I'm determined to do what I can to help my father push it through."

I tried to pick my words carefully.

"And if your father wasn't killed because of the bill?"

"But he was!" She hesitated and looked down at her hands before rubbing her arms as if suddenly chilled. "And yesterday, someone sent me a note. In my room. I found it under my *pillow*."

I felt a rippling of chills down my own arms. Ethan had died from a pillow.

"What did it say?" I asked.

"It basically said I was going to die."

Madeleine took the wine from Jean-Marc and looked from one to the other of us.

"Do you have the note?" I asked.

"I flushed it. I know I probably should have kept it, but I was just so freaked out and it was so nasty, I just wanted to get rid of it. *And* someone's following me!"

"Are you sure?" I gave it a beat. "What does your bodyguard think?"

"Jimmy? He thinks I'm paranoid."

I tried not to look at Jean-Marc because I was pretty sure I knew what he was thinking: that this girl was hysterical and the idea that Ethan might have been killed because of wanting to support animal rights was absurd.

I tended to agree with him that her reasons didn't sound

like serious ones. But one thing was definite, and that was that Madeleine was afraid for her life.

"Have you talked to the police?"

"Yes, but since my father and I went our separate ways right after the gala, they didn't think I had much to tell them. And now with him being...being...m-murdered, I just know I'm next."

Madeline closed her eyes and let out a long, deep sigh, allowing the tears to cascade down her face.

"But you still have your bodyguard," I said.

She wrinkled her nose.

"For all the good he'll do me when it comes to saving my life! You've met him. He's a dolt. My father hired him as a favor to *his* father."

"What are you hoping I can do for you, Madeline? I'm not any kind of protective service."

"But you're a private eye, right? Isn't that what you told Dad last night? So, I thought you could find out who did this and expose them."

"The police don't tend to love involvement in their capital crime cases by private citizens," I said. "Have you talked to the embassy?"

"Mr. Cole, you mean? He's the one who told me *you* might be able to help. He has no idea what's going on. He keeps saying to let the police handle it."

I frowned. "What about the Diplomatic Security Service?"

The Bureau of Diplomatic Security was in charge of protecting senior diplomats abroad, and also handling all international criminal investigations. Most members were foreign service specialists and law enforcement officers. "I have no idea. Stanley says the US Bureau of Consular Affairs will contact next of kin but what good is that? *I'm* the next of kin and I already know what happened!"

She burst into tears, and I quickly put an arm around her and looked up into Jean-Marc's eyes which, for once conveyed an easily read message.

There was something here that wasn't quite right.

14

Later, after Madeline left, Jean-Marc and I sat in the living room drinking more wine. He didn't normally spend the night at my place because of Robbie but it was late, and I think we both felt we needed to be together after all that had happened.

"You cannot seriously be thinking of involving yourself in this case, *chérie*," he said to me as he draped an arm over my shoulders. "You must know that it will be a political hot potato, yes? It is a very high profile murder."

"Not that high profile," I said. "There's almost nothing about it in the media."

"That tells you how high profile it is. So much so that the media can be manipulated. Perhaps you should go through channels at the American embassy?"

I thought about that. My only real contact at the embassy was Stanley and the last time I talked to him he seemed fairly clueless. Plus, if it was true that the Diplomatic Security Service was investigating the death, there was really nothing I could do, and they were even more close-mouthed than the Paris police. I felt bad because I should have told Madeleine that straight out. As it was, I'm pretty sure I gave her the impression that I'd ask around and investigate on my own.

"I just feel so bad for her," I said to him as I rested my head on his shoulder.

"Of course. She has just lost her father. It is terrible."

We were quiet for a few moments and then I sighed.

"Did you still want to work on the Matheson case tonight?"

It was really too late, but there had been many times when Jean-Marc and I had worked into the wee hours. I was willing if he was.

"Do you have any news?" he asked, his eyebrows arching in surprise.

I sat up and turned to face him.

"I found Gigi in Nice," I said. "She's staying at an apartment of a friend."

"In Nice?"

Jean-Marc had lived in Nice after his wife died a few years ago. We were on a serious break at the time and he'd had a girlfriend down there.

"Do you want to go down there and confront her?" I asked.

"I thought our clients were paying us to find her," he said, frowning. "We should pass this information on to them."

"Do we really know what they'll do with the information?"

He raised his eyebrows.

"You suspect them of planning to do the girl harm?"

Brad and Lizzie Matheson were wealthy Americans living in Paris "for the fun of it" and not the kind of people I could easily imagine plotting the demise of a poor au pair. But still, I've been wrong before.

"I think we should tell them we've found her," I said. "But unless they report the theft to the police, we won't tell them where."

"They may not pay us."

I shrugged. "So be it. I never understood why they didn't call the police as soon as they knew she'd stolen the credit cards."

"Did you not?" Jean-Marc asked, arching an eyebrow at me.

I narrowed my eyes.

"You think Brad was screwing the babysitter?"

"I think he may not want to get her spilling her guts, as you Americans say, to the police who will then feel obligated to tell his wife what was revealed."

"Ugh. Why do all our clients have to be so grubby?"

"Nature of the business, *chérie*," he said and kissed me. "I loved dancing with you last night, by the way."

"Me too," I said, gazing into his eyes. "Clearly we need to get out more—and not just sitting in cars waiting for adulterers to make themselves visible from hotel room windows so we can get the money shot."

He laughed at the same time my phone began to ring. I picked it up and saw with surprise that it was my stepmother Joelle. I literally cannot think of any other time that woman has called me except the one time she set me up to have legal papers served at a café in the Latin Quarter.

"Hello?" I answered warily.

"I do not know what you think you are doing," Joelle said, her voice sarcastic and brusque. "But whatever it is, Madame Marple, stop it immediately."

"I don't know what you're talking about."

I could not imagine how in the world she knew that Madeleine had come to ask me for help. And then it came to me—Michel Leblanc. He probably had the girl's phone bugged.

Jean-Marc watched me, his eyes searching and keen as he listened to my side of the conversation.

"I forbid you to investigate the Senator's death," Joelle said.

"What?" I said. "You can't make—"

"And stay away from Députée Leblanc. Or else."

And then she hung up.

15

I sat on the couch, still holding the phone in my hands and was momentarily speechless after Joelle had hung up on me.

"She wants me to back off investigating Ethan's murder," I said.

Jean-Marc's eyes widened. "How did she know about it?"

"That is the million-dollar question, isn't it? Any chance her boyfriend might have planted a bug in my apartment?"

Jean-Marc glanced around the room, but I don't think he took my question seriously. Besides, I was joking. Sort of.

I stood up and eased the kinks out of my back.

"How dare she try to forbid me anything? Doesn't that sound suspicious to you? Another glass of wine?" I asked as I walked to the kitchen to pour two more glasses.

"Are you okay?" he asked from the living room.

I came back and handed him his glass.

"You know," I said, "it occurs to me that setting up a sex worker for murder is a pretty easy frame-up."

"Don't tell me you want to take *the prostitute's* case too?" Jean-Marc said.

"I think we already are, don't you? Helping Madeleine find out who killed her father would be helping Désirée."

"*Oui,* but that only helps if Désirée isn't in fact the killer. *Chérie,* are you sure you are taking this on for the right reasons?"

I frowned at him.

"What do you mean? A young, grieving American woman has asked for my help in the case of her murdered father—someone I actually happen to know."

"*Oui,*" he said. "But it was a case you were hesitant to involve yourself with until Joelle Lapin called."

"What difference does that make?" I asked, suddenly annoyed with his probing. "The point is the case, not why we're working it."

After that, even as late as it was, Jean-Marc insisted on going back to his own place after all. I didn't take it personally. We had a very good groove worked out and both of us were hesitant to upset the balance by seemingly trivial changes.

It works, let's don't break it.

After he left, and even as late as it was, I found myself antsy and unable to go to sleep. It was probably Joelle's call. Why did it mean so much to her? Was she worried about her new boyfriend?

I pulled down my laptop and instantly Googled *Michel Leblanc.* What I found was sickening but not surprising. There were media stories dating back ten years of Leblanc rumored to have blackmailed a rival politician with incriminating evidence, as well as another piece that suggested he might have received campaign contributions from a world-renowned shady billionaire.

There was more but there didn't seem any point in going further. The guy was a bully and probably corrupt. Joelle was welcome to him.

Did Leblanc ask Joelle to reach out to me to warn me off? It was hard to imagine Joelle as anyone's errand girl. But perhaps Leblanc had a hold on her. It was at least possible. I often thought that deep down Joelle must share at least some human characteristics with the rest of us.

While I had my laptop open, I shifted over to Ethan Andrew's web page. The landing page for the Senator looked expensive. It was designed with crisp, simple fonts to give an immediate impression of straightforwardness and trustworthiness.

I went to the pulldown menu titled *Events* and was immediately confused by a series of photographs showing Ethan, his wife Dilly, and Madeleine at a lavish DC party with the banner *Happy Retirement Senator Andrews* draped in the background.

My skin tingled ominously. I was shocked to see that Ethan had retired from politics the year before. I wondered if Madeleine could possibly *not* know that her father was no longer a senator. I wracked my brain to remember if Ethan had presented himself to me as such last night. One thing this news meant was that he was no longer eligible for Diplomatic Security protection, which was probably why he had his own personal bodyguard instead of Secret Service.

Knowing it was late and hating that I knew I was going to wake him up, I put a call into Stanley. He answered quickly and didn't sound one bit sleepy.

"I'm sorry to be calling so late," I said.

"I can't sleep anyway. I still can't wrap my head around what happened."

"I know. Listen, there's still no news about it anywhere. And I just got off Ethan's web page and saw that he'd retired. Does that mean the Diplomatic Service isn't investigating his death?"

"No, the Paris police are doing it," he said with a sigh. "They're just so difficult. Every time I turn around there's another point person. I swear they switch them up just to keep me guessing."

16

Before Madeleine left, I made a date to meet up with her the next day at a café on boulevard Malesherbes near her hotel. The police had cordoned off the whole top floor where Ethan and his group had been staying at the Sofitel Paris le Faubourg. Her new place, Hotel Fauchon, was only a dozen blocks or so from my apartment.

I can't imagine saying that sentence without quaking if I were still living back in Atlanta, but these days I can log twenty thousand steps just doing the groceries and enjoying a walk in the park and think nothing of it.

We arranged to meet at Le Café Delmas after Robbie and I got out of church Sunday morning. It was our routine after church to walk to Parc Monceau and then home for lunch, usually with Geneviève.

One thing I've learned this time around raising a child is that it is very important to maintain a schedule. Robbie is an even-tempered little fellow but even he can have a meltdown if too much of his routine gets rearranged.

Normally, though, he likes meeting new people, possibly

"Who are you working with?"

"At the moment, nobody. I hope they're at least givin[g] information, but I don't really know."

"How is she?"

"She's destroyed, Claire. I can't believe I had to tell h[er] the phone."

I made a mental note to call Dilly the next day. It wo[uld be] agonizing, and truthfully, I hadn't known her very well.

"So Ethan didn't have any diplomatic protection at all [when] he was in Paris?" I asked.

"No, he was here as a private citizen, so he didn't g[et the] benefit of the whole Secret Service thing."

"Does that mean he *doesn't* have a bill in congress? Be[cause] Madeline seems to think he had a controversial bill pendi[ng.]"

"I mean, I'm sure he still has friends in Congress and [has] got a favorite bill, I'm not saying he doesn't have enough [clout] to move the needle on it, maybe by working with s[pecial] interest groups or something? But he's a private citizen. I[t can't] be *his* bill."

That settled that. Ethan certainly wouldn't be targete[d and] murdered for a bill he had no real control over whet[her it] passed or not.

Would he?

"Do you know why he quit politics?" I asked.

"Honestly, I think Dilly pressured him. She wanted h[im to] relax and kick back because she was worried about his h[ealth.] Isn't that ironic?"

I couldn't help but think that the person I saw last [night] glad-handing at an international gala *without his wife* [was] frankly doing the very opposite of relaxing and kicking ba[ck.]

because most of his home life is just the two of us. He's extremely fond of Haley and Geneviève of course and also Jean-Marc. I thought back to the moment when my daughter Catherine came over in the spring to take her baby, little Maddie, back to the States.

Technically, Catherine is Robbie's half-sister although she is in her late thirties. There had been a time when she wanted to bring Robbie home with her and raise him, but her then-husband had forbidden it.

In the end, everything worked out as it should. I couldn't imagine anyone raising Robbie but me.

"Bonjour, Madeleine!" I said as Robbie and I walked up to the table where she and her bodyguard sat at the café.

The bodyguard, Jimmy, sat at the table, his acne-scarred face set in a permanent scowl as we approached. You didn't need to be particularly perceptive to want to steer clear of Jimmy, which I realized when both Robbie and Izzy detoured widely around him to greet Madeleine.

"Hello, little man," Madeleine said to Robbie, smiling broadly. "Your grandmother has told me lots about you."

"*Comme ça va*, Mademoiselle?" Robbie said happily.

"Speak English, darling," I said to him. "Miss Andrews is American like we are."

Robbie stuck out his hand to shake hands which from the look on Madeleine's face she seemed to think was as adorable as I did. I saw her put her hand on her tummy as she smiled at Robbie.

"I can't believe he's bilingual!" she said. "That is so cute."

"We don't normally stop at a café after church," I said to her. "Are you up for a walk to the park?"

Madeleine gathered up her purse and stood.

"Absolutely," she said. "It's a beautiful morning." She joined us on the sidewalk in front of the terrace while Jimmy flagged down the waiter to pay.

"Don't worry about him," she said as we walked on. "He'll catch up."

I felt like mentioning that that was likely not the best use of a bodyguard to have him running along behind her—especially if she was truly concerned for her safety. But I didn't want to say anything in front of Robbie, nor did I want to encourage any further fears from her on that score. I was simply not convinced she had anything to worry about.

The walk from the café on rue de Constantinople to Parc Monceau was pretty much a straight shot and of course, like most walking routes in Paris, absolutely lovely.

Parc Monceau was a beautiful, historic park located in the eighth arrondissement. Its stunning landscape is filled with magnificent fountains, sculptures, and colorful gardens–the perfect backdrop for summer picnics, family gatherings, and romantic strolls.

On sunny days, the park's cobblestone paths were dotted with people walking, laughing, and enjoying the pleasant weather. Despite its elegant facade, the park was a vibrant and lively place, bursting with life and energy

Because Robbie was with us, Madeleine and I were careful to keep our conversation neutral as we walked.

After a block or so, her bodyguard Jimmy did catch up with us, although he walked about five yards behind us. I couldn't help but notice that he was not quite out of ear shot.

As soon as we reached the ornate gilded gates of the park, Robbie called out the name of a friend of his and then turned to me with a hopeful look in his eye. As we were nearly inside the park itself, I gave the greenlight. He handed me Izzy's leash and took off at a run for his little friend Camille who was waiting just inside the gate with her au pair.

"I wanted to thank you again for seeing me last night," Madeleine said as we followed Robbie and Camille.

All around us the lawns were alive with activity: families

scattered across blankets, kids playing games and chasing each other, couples engaged in quiet conversation.

"Of course," I said. "I'm glad you came to me. How is your mother?"

She stared down at her hands.

"She's devastated. She was supposed to have come on this trip. I don't know whether to wish that she had or not. Would she have gotten killed too? Or helped prevent Dad dying?"

"There's no point in speculating," I advised gently.

Robbie and Camille had settled into throwing breadcrumbs that Camille's handler had brought into the pond for the park's ducks. Madeleine and I found a bench not far away where I could keep my eye on them.

"The police don't care anything about my father's political legacy," she said. "They barely even listened to me when I told them about the death threats."

I wanted to approach this next part of our conversation as delicately as possible.

"You know, Madeline, I saw on your father's webpage that he wasn't a Senator anymore."

She turned and gave me a strange look. "Did you think I didn't know that?"

"Well, you talk as if this bill of his—"

"No, no, no, no," she said impatiently, interrupting me. "You have to understand. Dad was the power behind the seated senator, Senator Tully. Without Dad, they'll drop it. Just you watch. They don't care about the poor monkeys and puppies being tortured to make sunscreen formulas!"

Her eyes shimmered with unshed tears.

"They just want something easy so they can take their money and go home. Yes, okay, fine. He may not have been a senator anymore, but he was more of a public servant than any of them!"

After a moment, she wiped her eyes, and I heard her phone ringing.

"Do you want to take that?" I asked.

She picked it up and looked at the screen and then put it away unanswered. "It's Henry, my fiancé," she said.

"Oh, I didn't know you were engaged. Congratulations."

It seemed a shame her fiancé hadn't made the trip to Paris with her. He could certainly have helped her weather this crisis a lot easier. I understood she didn't want to leave Paris until she could accompany her father's body back to America. But honestly, I thought it would be better for her as soon as she could get back to her family.

"Where is he?" I asked.

"Back in Atlanta," she said. "He's a social media content manager for Accenture."

I had no clue what that was, but I nodded anyway.

"I just wish I had some answers, you know?" she said and looked off into the distance watching Robbie and his little friend play. "I envy you so much. I envy your life."

"We all have challenges," I said.

She turned to look at me.

"I don't mean to be so self-centered."

"Don't be ridiculous. You just lost your father!"

"I know, but it doesn't help to focus on how it's affecting me every waking minute. That's not helpful."

"Don't be so hard on yourself."

"Are you close to your daughter?"

The question took me by surprise, and I hesitated.

"Yes and no," I admitted. "I wish we were closer, but Catherine is in a different space right now. In fact, she's angry with me."

"I can't imagine that. I'll bet you were an awesome mother."

I laughed.

"Well, you'll find out one day that sometimes what mothers

do for reasons that make perfect sense to them can make daughters hate them at least a little bit."

"No way. Why?"

I sighed. I really didn't want to burden her with more complications that the story of Catherine and her stolen frozen eggs might bring, so I made my sad story as brief as possible.

"Two years ago," I said, "Catherine and her late husband were storing their frozen eggs when Todd was murdered. Then later, the facility that was storing the eggs was broken into and the eggs were stolen."

Madeleine gasped and again I saw her put her hand on her stomach, telling me as clearly as if she'd announced it, that she was pregnant.

"What happened?" she asked fearfully.

I was impressed that she could tell that the theft itself wasn't the end of the story. I took in a long breath.

"I tracked down the perpetrator," I said. "And I retrieved one of the babies as it was born. Unfortunately, all the other eggs except one were not viable."

She sucked in a quick breath in astonishment.

"You got a baby from one of the stolen eggs? Your...your daughter recovered a live baby?"

"She did. We did. Unfortunately, because I thought Catherine was at the time in a very vulnerable place—after the loss of her husband and some other things that were going on —I'm afraid I didn't...tell her about the baby."

Madeleine's eyes widened and she looked away. I could tell she was trying to stay on board with thinking I was the super mom she'd already crowned me, but this bit of information was clearly making it hard.

"I was wrong," I said simply. "I should never have kept Maddie a secret from her."

"Maddie?" Madeleine snapped her head back and her eyes were wet. "The baby's name is Maddie?"

I nodded. "Short for Madeleine. Same as yours. Robbie named her after the French children's book."

We were quiet for a moment. The only sounds were the laughter and squeals of the children around the park.

"And Maddie is with her mom now?"

"She is." I felt a sudden lack of energy as I uttered the words.

"You miss her."

I smiled at her. "I miss them all. In addition to Catherine and Maddie, I have a nine-year old grandson, Cameron."

"I'm pregnant," Madeleine said as a tear trickled down her face and she quickly wiped it away.

"Congratulations," I said warmly, reaching out to take her hand and squeeze it. "That's the very best news."

"I know. I was so happy when I found out. Henry and I both are." She looked again in the direction of Robbie and Camille. "Only now all I can think of is that my father will never meet his grandson or granddaughter."

"Yes," I said, trying not to think of my own grandson off in the world somewhere, unfindable. "That would, of course, be very hard."

17

The smell of burned coffee and caféteria food lingered in the air along with the clacking sound of keyboard keys and the quiet chatter of the detectives in the background.

The walls of the uncarpeted hall Jean-Marc walked down were covered with posters about missing persons, unsolved murder cases, and cold cases, plus ancient admonishments to do better: *Do not Forget: You are the Job.* Then there was that old favorite: *The Victim is the Victim.* Jean-Marc had never really understood that one, but he imagined it had made sense to the department back in the eighties when it was penned.

The bullpen was the largest room on the floor. Its walls were made of bone-white tiles. There were a few desks, but no cubicles, no offices, and no sections. Just one big open room. Two lines of folding chairs faced a large white board. In spite of the fact that the building was located on the Île de la Cité, the room had no windows.

The better to concentrate on the lowest stratum of humanity, Jean-Marc thought grimly as he passed the room on his way to Étienne's cubicle.

Several familiar faces looked up at him as he walked the aisles of his old department. Colette Girard and her partner Victor Durand—once good friends of his, Jean-Marc thought—studiously avoided greeting him as he passed. He had been tempted to walk over to their desks and put on a big show of being great friends. But in the end, they were dodging him for a reason—a reason that had to do with their jobs and their current boss. Jean-Marc wouldn't make it more difficult for them.

He'd texted Étienne earlier about the possibility of getting a copy of the hotel surveillance footage from the night of the gala. Étienne said he thought he could get it, but that Jean-Marc would definitely owe him for the favor.

"You'll have to save my life twice for us to be even after this," he'd joked.

But now, Jean-Marc was sorry he hadn't told him he'd meet him back at Café Le Boule. He'd known this was going to be bad, but there was something irrational and insistent deep inside him that had made him want to poke the bear.

Speaking of the bear...

Just as Jean-Marc passed the final cubicle in the hall that led from homicide to vice, a tall woman with a severe expression stepped out into the hall and blocked his way.

Chantal Resenelle wasn't attractive, but she had a presence. Jean-Marc would give her that.

She had a sharp jawline with cold blue eyes and a stern mouth that Jean-Marc could not imagine smiling. She wore a black leather jacket, short to her hip, dark slacks and a white button-down shirt.

"May I help you, Monsieur?" she said tartly.

Jean-Marc knew that she knew exactly who he was. Pretending not to was beneath her. Or, more likely, it was a stalling tactic because she wasn't sure how to handle the situation.

He touched the Visitors badge he'd been given at the front desk.

"I have an appointment with Étienne Benoit," he said.

"Why?" she asked, crossing her arms.

"It has nothing to do with you," he said as he spotted Étienne at the end of the hall looking trapped. Jean-Marc watched as Étienne grabbed his jacket and hurried around the corner, disappearing from sight. Jean-Marc didn't blame him. It had been a mistake to come.

"I'm glad to hear that," Resnelle said. "And frankly, I'm glad you came in today so I could tell you to your face in front of witnesses that if I hear of you attempting to get one of my people to give you information on any case we're working on, or if I hear of you approaching one of my witnesses, I'll arrest you for obstruction."

She turned to look at the rest of the department personnel, all of their faces turned to watch the confrontation between her and Jean-Marc.

"Everybody clear?" she said loudly.

There was a general murmuring before Resnelle turned back to Jean-Marc.

"You've been warned, LaRue," she said as she stepped out of his path.

18

That afternoon, after dropping Robbie and Izzy off with Geneviève back at the apartment, I headed back out to catch the Metro from my neighborhood station, Saint-Augustin. Sunday is a special day for both me and Robbie, and I try very hard not to let anything derail our Sundays. But after talking to Madeleine I was determined to talk to a few people who might have seen something that night.

I honestly wasn't sure how much of Madeleine's belief that she was in danger wasn't a natural reaction to the trauma of losing her father to murder. Plus, I knew that involving myself too much to look into this case could only upset the Paris police department—something I tried regularly not to do.

On the other hand, if there was a chance that something I found out might help ease Madeleine's mind about what had happened to her father, it was worth my effort—and it was worth my Sunday.

With no commuters to deal with on the weekend, and fewer tourists even in summer because of the fact that there were so many shops and restaurants closed on Sunday, I had a very quiet ride on the Metro with few people in the car with me. I arrived at the train station nearest the hotel within thirty minutes.

The Sofitel Paris le Faubourg on rue Boissy d'Anglas was an easy two block walk from the Concorde Metro station. Because it was Sunday, I was a little dressed up. But honestly, many women wear dresses or skirts in Paris—much more than in the US. I think the thing that I enjoy about it is that there's such a sense of occasion when you wear a skirt or a dress. You have to wear proper shoes for one thing. And then you have to have a bag to match the shoes. Most days, especially since Paris is such a wonderful walking city, I wear comfortable shoes. Before I moved to Paris, I didn't know you could own comfortable shoes that weren't ugly.

As I approached in the light of day and from a distance of a block, the hotel looked understated yet Instagram-worthy and elegant. I'd never stayed there myself and since I lived in Paris there was no reason to. But I knew it was expensive. Not expensive like the Hôtel de Crillon, I thought with a smile. But still, for most people very pricey.

I walked up the marble steps to the entrance. A portly gentleman in his mid-sixties with a thick mustache, dressed in a smart dark uniform with gold epaulets stood at the door. When I approached, he immediately opened the door for me.

"Bonjour," I said pleasantly.

"Bonjour, Madame."

"My name is Claire Baskerville. I was wondering if I could ask you a question."

"If you are staying with us, Madame Baskerville," he said, "our concierge inside will be happy to assist."

"That's all right. I wanted to talk to you."

"*Moi?*" he said easily, not appearing at all surprised.

"I suppose the police have already talked to you at length," I said.

"Ah. The Senator. No, Madame, the police have not spoken with me."

"Oh, well. I'm a friend of the Senator and also a private investigator."

The smile on his face began to fade. Inevitably this was the effect my announcing my occupation to people tended to have.

"I am not sure how I can help you," he said, almost sternly, his eyes beginning to scan the street, perhaps in hopes of someone coming to the hotel so that he could ditch me.

"Just a few questions, Monsieur..."

"Beldon," he said.

"Monsieur Beldon," I said, still smiling. "Can you tell me when the last time was that you saw Senator Andrews?"

He flushed. It was clear he didn't want to talk to me about this.

"I...he came back from an event at the US Club around eleven o'clock. I cannot be more accurate, I'm afraid."

"Was he alone?" I asked.

"Yes."

I wasn't sure how long his patience with me was going to last. The problem with asking questions of people like doormen, maids and waiters, is that you really don't know what you want from them until you talk long enough asking questions until something valuable pops up. It wasn't the best way to expect success.

I dug out the photo I'd printed out back at the apartment of Désirée from her Facebook page. It was her profile picture and showed only an attractive dark-haired woman with no hint as to her occupation.

But the minute I showed it to Monsieur Beldon, he snorted in disgust.

"Do you know this woman?" I asked.

"*Non.*"

"Have you seen her before?"

"She was here that night," he said.

This of course was not very exciting information since Désirée has never denied she was here. Obviously, she was here. She was arrested here.

"So you saw her go into the hotel?"

"*Oui.*"

"Alone?"

He hesitated again. "*Oui.*"

I didn't bother asking him if he saw her come out, because of course *everyone* saw her leave—through the news network *France 24* if they weren't there to see it in person. In handcuffs.

"How is it you know someone you've never met before that night?"

"I don't have to see a cow to know it's a cow. Often the smell is enough."

Lovely.

"I am very busy, Madame Baskerville."

"I know and I don't want to keep you, Monsieur Beldon. One last question. Was there anything that happened that day or maybe even the day before that was unusual, would you say?"

"No."

"Really? Nothing unusual at all? That seems unlikely for a hotel that commands the reputation and prestige that the Sofitel le Faubourg does."

He jerked his head as if to relieve the tightness of his collar and then looked down the street.

"There was one thing," he said. "And after I tell you, I really must not be seen chatting while I am on duty."

"I understand totally." I felt a definite breathlessness at the prospect that he was about to reveal an important tidbit to me.

"The evening of the gala, Senator Andrews asked me where he might go to buy a cigar."

I felt my shoulders deflate. Maybe I should define the word *unusual* for him?

"Okay," I said.

"He was already dressed for his evening, so I spotted him easily when he came down the street on his way back to the hotel..."

He pointed down the long block from the hotel. "I was preparing to ask him if he found the *tabac* when a smaller man came out of the alley. They argued heatedly for several long moments before parting."

My senses lit up at hearing this.

"Could you hear what they were saying?"

He shook his head. "*Non*, but it was intense. I thought it might come to blows."

Ethan had an altercation with someone before the gala!

"Can you describe this man?"

He frowned and seemed to spot someone over my shoulder. I heard people coming up the sidewalk, clearly heading for the hotel.

"He was hairless," Beldon said, which I thought an exceedingly odd description. "Short in stature and wearing a tuxedo."

So someone also going to the gala.

"Was this person French?" I asked.

"He spoke English," he said with a shrug. "I was too far away to tell anything beyond that."

Already his attention was turning to the approaching guests.

"And you have no idea who...?"

"I have seen him in the hotel on multiple occasions," he said as he turned to reach for the door in readiness of opening it for the advancing hotel guests. "I believe he is the man from the American Embassy."

19

I walked away from the hotel with my head spinning. Could the person that the doorman had seen arguing with Ethan be anyone but Stanley Cole? And if that was true, why hadn't Stanley mentioned the altercation he'd had with Ethan? The doorman seemed to think it was not a trivial disagreement.

After getting as much from the doorman as I thought possible, at least for the moment, I decided to avail myself of the hotel's public restrooms before hoofing it back to the apartment. When I emerged, I thought briefly about staying for lunch when I saw Joelle Lapin, my stepmother, marching across the lobby toward me. She moved with grace and poise, her every move deliberate and calculated very much like the woman herself.

For an older woman, she was still devastatingly beautiful and commanded attention. The dress she wore hugged her frame, accentuating her perfect figure. She walked toward me, her face luminous. One would almost think she was happy to see me.

"What are you doing here?"

"Free country," I said haughtily, knowing how much it would anger her.

"I thought we had this discussion," she said hotly. "You are not to involve yourself in this. You are not to embarrass me by harassing Michel."

I looked around the lobby in mock confusion.

"Do you see me harassing him?"

"Let me be clear. I require you to stay away from him. I am warning you."

"I see that you are. Why did you pretend not to know Ethan Andrews at the gala?"

"How dare you? You think everyone is a liar just because you are?"

"Look, Joelle, I can find out the answer," I said. "It'll be more unpleasant for you if I'm forced to talk to your neighbors, your ex-work colleagues and the like. Or maybe his wife Dilly knows the truth?"

"You are despicable. Only an American would root around in the mud to dig up as much filth as possible."

"Well, I say if you're wallowing in the mud when I'm trying to find answers, so be it."

She looked like she wanted to hit me. I have to say there was a time—in fact most of my relationship with Joelle—where I have tried very hard to get her to like me or at least to stop detesting me. But hate is like love. It's passionate and it's often illogical and certainly unreasonable. Of course, I'm sure from Joelle's point of view, her reaction to me was entirely reasonable.

She'd been married to my stepfather who decided for reasons nobody could understand to leave the bulk of his wealth to me and not her. French inheritance laws make that a default situation, but I was no blood relation to Claude Lapin. Joelle had every reason to expect she would get all the goodies. So when it didn't happen that way, she lost, among other things, the beautiful Haussmann apartment that I now call home and that *she* had loved and lived in for a decade.

I would've been happy to have been all magnanimous and rejected the settlement but at the time, thanks to my deceased husband, I was broke and homeless. Claude had very much saved my bacon.

I was not in a position to be magnanimous at the time, but later, in a moment of madness or bravado I did offer her the apartment back which she rejected out of spite. I was intensely grateful that she wasn't able to take it as a gift from me. While I could probably have afforded to rent another place to live now, it wouldn't be right around the corner from all my favorite cafés, walking distance to my church, or a short Metro ride away from the Latin Quarter where I go all the time. I know that doesn't make me sound very unselfish, but there you have it. One of the benefits of getting older is that you can see yourself as you really are, flaws and all, and accept yourself.

And this particular personal flaw meant I was not prying my hands from my lovely Haussmann apartment in the fashionable eighth *arrondissement* for some crappy condo in the thirteenth. Stepmother guilt or not.

My phone rang then, and I couldn't have orchestrated it better since the sight of Joelle's face as I answered it—right in the middle of our conversation—made her go purple with outrage. Which of course was a bonus.

It was Jean-Marc calling.

"Hey," I said. "What's up?" I smiled at Joelle and held up a finger as if to indicate I would only be a minute.

"I'm at the *Palais Bourbon*," he said. "Shall I see where Michel Leblanc was two nights ago?"

"Seriously?"

This was unexpected since the last time we talked, Jean-Marc had not seemed keen on our doing anything with this case except staying as far away from it as possible.

"Yeah, absolutely go for it," I said, trying to tamp down the excitement in my voice. "Talk later."

I hung up and faced my stepmother.

"Want me to leave Leblanc alone? Then tell me why you pretended not to know Ethan."

She clenched her teeth, her eyes boring into me with loathing.

"It was only a couple of nights ten years ago," she bit out.

"While you were married to Claude?"

"*Va te faire foutre*," she spat.

I was impressed she used the *tu* form to cuss me out. Her face was flushed with fury as she turned on her reptilian Manolo Blahniks—nearly toppling over in the process—and stomped as much as one can in five-inch heels across the lobby toward the exit.

I watched her go and thought about the fact that I'd just made a deal with her that I wouldn't interview Leblanc while at the same time giving Jean-Marc the greenlight to go ahead and do just that. Amazingly, I didn't feel at all guilty about lying to her. Not a bit.

Honestly, right now, all I felt was a pleasant shot of self-esteem that I was finally not dancing to that woman's warped tune.

20

Jean-Marc hung up from Claire and turned to face the Palais Bourbon, on the right bank of the Seine, across from the Place de la Concorde. A massive neoclassical building covered in white stone, the structure was designed in the Italian style, its roofs hidden by balustrades invisible from street level. The building housed the *Assemblée Nationale*, the lower house of the French Parliament.

Leblanc was a legislator of the National Assembly,

After Jean-Marc's disaster at the police station he'd walked out, the back of his neck burning with the eyes of old comrades and associates—and with Étienne not answering his phone, Jean-Marc had been determined not to end the day on such a sour note.

Claire would be astonished to know how much he wanted her to be impressed with him, to appreciate his contribution to the business. He knew she loved him. He wanted more. He needed her to respect and admire what he could do. What only he could do.

As he approached the grand marble staircase on the Rue de la Université that led to the building's impressive entrance, he couldn't help thinking it looked more like a medieval castle, made of dirty, weathered stone, blackened with age, sitting atop a hill overlooking the rest of Paris, than the private palace it had been built as in 1722.

He'd made his appointment with Leblanc posing as a member of the Paris police. He had no doubt that if he were called on it, he'd be promptly arrested at the very least—especially after Resnelle's threat earlier. But Leblanc was a politician first and he'd not immediately default to causing a problem if he could avoid it.

Jean-Marc had to admit he had no real lead that would suggest that Leblanc was involved in the Senator's death. He was just ticking names off a list. Names of people who'd been around the Senator during his last hours. Names of people who'd been at the gala or at the hotel—both of which included Leblanc. It wasn't much to go on, but it was a start.

When it came to questioning him, Jean-Marc knew he'd have to be careful while at the same time try to hold the man's feet close to the fire. He wouldn't get anything out of him by flattering or soft-soaping him. Which was just as well, since he didn't have the stomach for that anyway.

He took the elevator to the third floor which opened up immediately onto an expansive and palatial lobby whose marble floors echoed the sound of his footsteps as he walked to the receptionists' desk.

There was no one else in the waiting room. Situated on polished wooden side tables beside thick-stuffed leather sofas were small display cases showing a variety of antiquated coins and gems.

"*Oui*, Monsieur?" said the receptionist, a stunning red head with flawless skin.

"Jean-Marc LaRue to see the Députée," Jean-Marc said.

"He is waiting for you," she said, getting up and walking to the massive double doors at the end of the waiting room.

Jean-Marc was pleased to have kept the man waiting. Sometimes it was the little things in an important interaction that shifted the balance of power.

The receptionist opened the door and ushered Jean-Marc into the room. Dark, mahogany bookshelves lined the walls. A massive, hand-carved desk sat at the center of the room. Ceiling to floor velvet curtains billowed behind it against the backdrop of enormous bay windows that looked out upon rue Aristide-Briande.

Michel Leblanc stood up from his desk but made no move to approach Jean-Marc or to extend his hand. A small, balding man, Leblanc could be charming, Jean-Marc knew. After all he was a politician. He had strong features, in spite of his short stature, but his chin was too pointed and while Jean-Marc could imagine he might be called interesting-looking by others, to him he looked sinister.

But maybe that's because I know so much about him.

"Do I know you?" Leblanc said, frowning as if trying to place Jean-Marc.

Jean-Marc glanced around the room at the long credenza holding dozens of ornately framed photos, most of famous people posing with Leblanc. Jean-Marc couldn't detect a single personal photo or evidence of family

"I saw you at the gala on Friday," Jean-Marc said as he seated himself in a leather tufted chair across from the desk. "With Madame Lapin."

Leblanc's face stiffened.

"Leave my personal life alone, LaRue," he said. "Yes, I remember you now. Your cheap ploy to misrepresent yourself didn't fool me. What do you want?"

"Ethan Andrews was a colleague of yours," Jean-Marc said. "I was wondering how you might benefit from his sudden death."

Leblanc snorted.

"I should have you thrown out of here," he said with a sneer. "I barely knew Andrews. Is that all?"

"Did the police ask you where you were that night after the gala?"

Leblanc bared his teeth, his lips curled over them in nearly canine aggression.

"How dare you question me like this! I know what your game is, LaRue." He jabbed a button on the side of his desk. "And if I hear a word about the Pardeux Committee showing up in any media outlet anywhere in Paris, I will sue you for slander. You don't have the Paris police department backing you up now. As a private citizen I can have you sent to prison for decades. Do I make myself clear?"

His doors swung open but, instead of the beautiful young receptionist a pair of burly thugs wearing suits much too small for them approached Jean-Marc, cracking their knuckles as they came.

Jean-Marc stood up and turned toward the door. The two men let him pass but fell into line behind him as he walked out of Leblanc's office.

Jean-Marc smiled at the pretty young receptionist as he was escorted out of the lobby and into the elevator where one of the men reached in and punched him hard in the stomach, dropping him to his knees. As the doors closed, and fighting for breath, Jean-Marc found himself actually grinning.

The fact was he'd just gotten a fairly significant lead from Leblanc—one he hadn't known about before now. Claire would be pleased.

When you add that to the fact that Jean-Marc was pretty sure he'd ruined the statesman's afternoon, it was a very good day's work all in all.

21

That night, I made a point of having a quiet night in with just Robbie. He was a compliant child for the most part and complaining was not a part of his DNA, so it was up to me to notice when I'd been taking advantage of his good nature and needed to put him back into the center of my world.

I made a quiche for dinner, partly because Robbie loves quiche and partly because I love the way the scent of it baking fills our apartment. The building my apartment is in is more than two hundred years old and, while quite small and sometimes noisy from knocking radiators and street noise, I don't think I've ever felt more at home in a place.

I am consciously aware of wanting our apartment to be Robbie's refuge from the world when he comes home from school or play. As such, I've furnished it with plush rugs, soft couches and chairs and lots of color in the paintings I've found in galleries and flea markets.

After dinner—which we ate in front of the TV on trays—we played a card game he likes, and I tried hard not to win every time. Then, I had him bring our dishes into the kitchen and fill the sink with sudsy water while I ran Izzy downstairs to the courtyard for her last call of the night.

Then, I let Robbie wash while I dried the dishes. Then while he brushed his teeth and got into his pjs I put away leftovers in the small fridge.

There are times when I literally cannot recall what my life was like before these all-important nighttime rituals. Tucking him into his bed, reading to him until I see his eyes grow heavy, then kissing him goodnight, usually with Izzy curled up beside him on his bed. It's about as perfect as life can be.

If I ever take a moment to think about how Robbie came into my life and how much he means to me now, I would end up marveling at how strange and even ridiculous life is.

By the time I came back into the living room and poured myself a glass of wine, I was ready to call Jean-Marc and debrief with him on our separate days.

"*Chérie,*" Jean-Marc answered when I called. "How was your day?"

I loved hearing his voice, so smooth and warm with so many hidden depths—even through a telephone wire.

"I had an interesting day," I said. "But I can't wait to hear about yours. How was Leblanc?"

"A sly fox and twice as vicious. But he mentioned something we need to look into. He seemed to think I was there to question him about something called the Pardeux Committee."

"I'm on it," I said, opening up my laptop while I was still on the phone with him. "Anything else?"

"He's an extremely unpleasant fellow. I can't imagine how he keeps getting re-elected."

"It's not the people who elect him, is it?" I said as I typed *The Pardeux Committee* into my Google search function.

"True," Jean-Marc said. "Now you."

"Well," I said as I watched my laptop struggle to connect to the Internet. "I talked to the doorman which was mostly boring except for one little thing. It seems he witnessed a rather heated exchanged between Ethan and Stanley Cole on the night of the gala."

"Interesting."

"I know, isn't it? I guess I can understand why Stanley might not have mentioned that to me. But I'm going to have to have a little conversation with him to see what that was all about. And then I ran into Joelle. In fact, when you called me today, I was in the middle of facing off with her."

"Oh? How did that go?"

The little spinning ball on my computer just kept spinning until I finally gave up. My Paris apartment was a dream in every way but occasionally it did have major skips in Wi-Fi connectivity. I'd have to try it again later.

"It went pretty well, actually," I said. "She tried to bully me as per usual. But not only did I not cave, I found out that she pretended not to know Ethan because they'd had a one-nighter with him years ago."

There was silence on the line.

"Jean-Marc?"

"Do you believe her?"

"Well," I said, hesitating. "It's not the sort of thing most people would be happy to have publicly known. Why do you doubt it?"

"Because it is so...*évident*. It sounds like a lie to me."

I shook my head, but I was smiling. The French. Truly, so different from us.

"Well, I believed her," I said.

"I thought you said the Senator was the very paragon of Southern honor?"

"Did I say that?"

I was pretty sure I hadn't and so chalked up Jean-Marc's comment to his innate jealousy which was sometimes flattering but usually just annoying. "But even if that's true—and

I do think Ethan was a good guy—people can make mistakes."

"I am surprised to hear you say that, *chérie*."

I definitely thought the conversation was starting to veer off into a different area.

"In any event," I said. "It explains why Joelle pretended not to know him."

"Okay."

His comment annoyed me since it was so clear he did not accept her explanation and it bothered me that he thought I was being gullible. It's true that in the past I have had a problem standing up to my stepmother, but I really felt like I'd made strides in the opposite direction today.

"I talked to Brad Matheson," Jean-Marc said, referencing one of our expat clients.

"Oh?" I said. "How did that go?"

"He admitted he'd been sleeping with the au pair."

I gave a snort of disgust, but Jean-Marc continued.

"He is happy to simply cancel the credit cards and let the matter go. He said he will deal with his wife."

"Good luck with that," I said.

"And he wired our fee into our account."

"Good job," I said. "Remind me again, how do we meet all these sleazy clients we get?"

Jean-Marc laughed.

"I thought they might be a nice break from all the runaways and the people skipping out on their bills," he said.

And murder, I thought but didn't say.

After that we talked for a few moments more before signing off. Later, after showering, flossing, brushing my teeth and slathering my usual collection of oils and unguents on my skin, I went back online—this time from my bed—and was able to connect with the story I'd tried before. What I found slowly but surely woke me up as if I'd ended the evening with a double espresso.

It seemed that Leblanc had been publicly removed from a prestigious cabinet group, called The Pardeux Committee, for what the article referred to as "less than savory" behavior. After having already read about the rumors of his other supposed misdeeds, that didn't shock me. But when I read further into articles about the Pardeux incident I was surprised to see Senator Ethan Andrews's name linked to the story.

With growing excitement, I clicked on the link, *US Senator testifies in Pardeux Scandal,* where it was revealed that Ethan was instrumental in getting Députée Leblanc removed from the esteemed committee.

My eyes widened. Some sources reported that Leblanc was lucky to have kept his seat in the French Senate.

I leaned back into my pillows, stunned and now fully awake. Just when I had been vaguely wondering why Jean-Marc had chosen to question Leblanc in the first place, some things became clear.

In fact, that was the moment it occurred to me that if Michel Leblanc was the kind of person to hold a grudge, this particular insult might well be something he'd wait years to avenge.

22

The next morning, after dropping Robbie off at his summer camp for the day, I met Stanley outside the police station on the Île de la Cité. Normally, this is a beautiful area of Paris at any time of day—a little crowded with tourists, but so beautiful that you can see why someone decided to build a gorgeous cathedral there. Not to mention, a few hundred souvenir and sandwich shops.

"Thanks for meeting me, Claire," Stanley said. He looked wrung out from the heat of the day, even though it was barely midmorning. His eyes were bloodshot and I thought I detected stubble on his chin.

"I should be thanking you," I said. "There's no way the *Inspecteur Principal* of the Paris Police would agree to see me if not for you. I can't believe you managed to score an appointment."

"Well, my office did," he said as he opened the door of the building.

Inside was a bustling cacophony of noise and activity. The discordant clang of metal desks and the ringing of phones filled the air as did the smell of musty sweat and cigarettes.

The commotion of activity in the reception area was a steady pulse, and a reminder of the daily grind involved in keeping the streets of Paris safe. When our turn came, we were led down a long hallway. We passed pods of police officers talking to each other and also to handcuffed individuals, as well as to lawyers discussing various cases. The room radiated a palpable sense of urgency, purpose and despair.

We were brought in to see Superintendent Resnelle herself and I'm sure that was due to Stanley and the clout of the American Embassy behind him. Although I hadn't worked with her before I was sure she wouldn't have gone out of her way to extend in professional courtesies to me. She must know that Jean-Marc LaRue was working with me now. And I couldn't imagine that would work in my favor.

After formal introductions, Stanley jumped right in with why we were there—a uniquely American habit that the French don't tend to love.

"We need information about Ethan Andrews' death," Stanley said, his voice wavering slightly. "We've heard that there are some suspicious circumstances surrounding it."

The *Inspecteur* snorted derisively and then spoke condescendingly.

"I'm not sure what you're expecting me to say," she said. "It is not our policy to share proprietary information with civilians."

"We are not civilians," Stanley said stiffly. "I represent the United States of America. The American embassy has a duty to the family of the victim to learn all the information related to this tragic, unfortunate event."

I watched Resnelle fold her arms across her chest and look down her nose at Stanley. I could have told him that evoking the US of A was not going to be his best approach here.

"We just want to get the facts," I said reasonably. "The family deserves that."

Resnelle's expression hardened.

"I have nothing else I can tell you," she said in a clipped tone as she picked up a file and tapped its edge on the desk as if she were done with us and ready to move on.

"Wait," Stanley said, biting his bottom lip. "What about the CCTV footage in the hotel hallway? Could we see that?"

"There is no CCTV footage," Resnelle said, standing up to encourage us to do the same.

"He means the personal surveillance cameras," I said, knowing that the hotel wouldn't have CCTV which was a state-controlled system. "Surely, there were cameras in all the hallways of the hotel?"

She looked at me, coldly. I know she wanted to say that she was unaware of any—thereby shutting me down—but she probably didn't want to admit that. She scowled at me, instead.

"That footage will not be released until after we close our case," she said.

"And there's nothing else you can tell us?" Stanley pressed. "The embassy was told that we would be kept apprised, but nobody has contacted us."

"Then there is nothing new to tell you," she said with a shrug. "Now if you will excuse me. I have much to do today. *Merci, Monsieur et Madame.*"

She pointed to the door. Beyond causing a scene, there wasn't anything we could do
except leave.

"I can't believe that woman," I said with frustration as we walked back down the hallway toward the main reception area. "It's like she doesn't want to help us at all."

"Or she's in someone's pocket," Stanley muttered.

I thought about that for a moment. It wouldn't be an outlandish idea to discover that the head of the *commissariat de police* was bought. But it would sure make our job a lot more difficult going forward.

As we stepped out into the sunshine, both of us blinking against its brightness, Stanley sighed.

"Now, what?" he asked. "I'm supposed to report to my boss. And what do I tell Dilly?"

We began walking in the general direction of the Crypte Archéolgique. The morning glare had burned off, but it was still very bright. It was a discouraging start to the day, although my hopes hadn't been that high for getting information from Resnelle. Jean-Marc was pretty tight-lipped about her, but I thought that was because he didn't want to badmouth his replacement. I made a mental note to ask him if he thought she could be bought.

"And there's nothing more the US Embassy can do?" I asked.

"Beyond notifying next of kin?" Stanley said sadly, shaking his head.

We passed a popular café, one I knew from Jean-Marc was frequented by a lot of the police. I searched the tables for a familiar face but didn't recognize anyone. Still, it was too early for lunch.

"Do you have the contact information for Roger O'Connell?" I asked.

"Ethan's bodyguard?" He opened his phone to begin scrolling through his contact numbers. "I don't think he's left the country yet. Why?"

"I'm just hoping to talk to someone who might know something about what happened that night."

"I think I heard Ethan gave his man the night off."

I frowned. That would explain why O'Connell wasn't at the gala as Jimmy was—or anywhere near Ethan's room at the time of the attack. Stanley texted me a contact number for O'Connell.

"Thanks," I said. "Let's pop in here, do you mind?"

We stood in front of a small not very busy café on the boulevard St-Michel.

"I've got time," Stanley said.

We found a table on the terrace and ordered coffees although I'd already had too much caffeine.

"There's something I need to ask you, Stanley," I said with a heavy sigh. "And I hate to even bring it up."

He looked weary, his shoulders slumped in defeat. I'd seen him in plenty of different situations over the years—and most of them stressful because of the kind of work I do and the reasons why he'd need me—but this morning he looked really drained.

"Claire, just ask," he said. "We're both looking for the same thing—an answer to what happened to Ethan. You can't hurt my feelings. They're already destroyed."

"The doorman at Ethan's hotel said he saw you and Ethan arguing on the sidewalk in front of his hotel."

"Me and Ethan?" He frowned. "The night of the gala?"

"He said you were both in tuxedos. And that it was very heated."

"No way," Stanley said firmly. "Are you kidding? I had a lot riding on that night. My boss was there, and my boss's boss was there. Why in hell would I be arguing with Ethan?"

I shrugged helplessly. "I'm just telling you what the guy said he saw."

Stanley sat across from me, his shoulders hunched, his eyes misty. He didn't look guilty. He looked frankly heartbroken.

"Well, he's wrong." He shook his head and then straightened up as if something had just occurred to him. "Did he describe me or identify me?" he asked.

Now *that* was an interesting question.

The waiter came and deposited our espressos on the table and departed without a word or eye contact. The fact is, with my face blindness, it wouldn't have occurred to me—until

Stanley pointed it out—that the description of a guy who was short and balding and dressed in a tuxedo might easily have been someone else entirely. In fact, now that I thought about it, I hadn't realized how much Stanley and Michel Leblanc resemble each other.

I felt a wave of relief. The whole idea of Stanley and Ethan arguing hadn't made sense. Not just because they were friends, but also because I'd only ever seen Stanley completely affable if not deferential to most people. The idea of him raising his voice just wouldn't gel.

But Michel Leblanc? Now *that* I could believe.

23

The café on rue de Bourdeaux was nestled between two cobblestone-flanked buildings, its entrance surrounded by ivy-covered walls. The outdoor seating area was brilliantly illuminated by the bright morning sun. Between the sunlight and the delicious aroma of freshly-brewed coffee Jean-Marc felt a rare sense of well-being that he had to remind himself was unfounded in reality.

He put his hand up to wave when he saw Étienne standing at the entrance to the terrace scanning the cafe for him.

Jean-Marc didn't think meeting up at their usual place where all the city's cops tended to gather would be a very good look for Étienne—which he'd made abundantly clear by bolting out of the office the day before. Nor would it bode well for Jean-Marc. He wasn't sure if his former friends were just determined to give him a wide berth or if they were actively supporting Resnelle in her campaign against him. He didn't want to push it, and he really didn't want to know which of his pals were now adversaries.

"You're skating close to the line these days, LaRue," Étienne said as he took a seat at Jean-Marc's table. "The whole department knows that your American girlfriend came in this morning with some flunky from the American embassy demanding answers. Resnelle has been breathing fire ever since. Are you sure this is worth it?"

"I wouldn't blame you if you decided not to do this," Jean-Marc said, hoping the man had enough pride not to take the bait.

"Resnelle doesn't tell me what to do," Étienne said, puffing out his chest. "The others might jump like tics on a hot plate when she barks, but she doesn't bother me."

"Glad to hear it. What do you have for me?"

Étienne signaled to the waiter to bring him a coffee.

"Well, depending on which side of the fence you're on," he said, "will determine if what I found out is good or bad news. Are you seriously trying to defend the hooker?"

"She's not our client, no."

"So it's the daughter you're working for?"

Jean-Marc was surprised Étienne knew about Madeleine, but he shouldn't have been. Étienne was a detective. He was naturally curious—which was one of the reasons he was so good at his job—and he would have kept his ears open. In fact, that was the main reason he was of use to Jean-Marc.

"Yes, she came to us to get answers about her father," Jean-Marc said.

"I'm pretty sure she's not going to like what I found."

"Well, the truth is often disagreeable, but not knowing is usually worse. What do you have for me?"

"First I've got proof that the victim called the hooker that night to arrange the appointment."

Jean-Marc was surprised and he must have looked it.

Étienne's eyes widened.

"There's a record of it on the victim's phone," Étienne said. "Did you seriously think there was a possibility the vic *didn't* call the girl up for sex?"

"I was trying to keep an open mind," Jean-Marc said.

This was terrible news. If Senator Andrews had in fact called to have the girl come to his room, it eliminated the one possibility that Jean-Marc and Claire were hoping they could use—which was that Andrews had been set up by his killer.

How did that work if he'd actually called the girl in? Was it possible she was the assassin after all?

"Well, in that case, you're a better man than I am," Étienne said with a laugh as he pushed a jump drive across the table.

Jean-Marc picked it up. "What's this?"

"Let's call it part two of the biggest thank you that you now owe me. It's a copy of the surveillance footage taken from the hallway on the floor of the victim's room that night."

Jean-Marc very nearly did a fist pump in the air.

"How did you get it?" he asked.

"Don't ask. And don't get too excited. Let's just say if you're hoping to find the prostitute innocent, this isn't going to help your case."

Jean-Marc tucked the jump drive into his jacket breast pocket and extended his hand to his friend.

"*Merci*, Étienne. I won't forget this."

"Picking up the coffees today would be a start," Étienne said with a grin.

24

After parting company with Stanley, I called Adele Cote, one of my closest friends and one of my first friends in Paris, to see if she could meet me at Le Petit Chanson, one of my new favorite cafés in the Latin Quarter.

A forensic tech thirty years my junior, Adele and I met my first summer in Paris when the simultaneous tragedies of her brother's and my husband's murders coincided. Because the DNA laboratory she worked for was often called in to relieve the heavy forensics workload of the Paris homicide division, Adele frequently—and very conveniently for me—had proprietary information on various criminal cases.

Knowing someone who is a forensic tech was a lucky break for me and my work, although I tried hard not to take advantage of our friendship too much. Today, however, I was almost desperate to get some inside information that might spawn a lead or two.

Le Petit Chanson had a terrace facing the street and a view of the popular and always mesmerizing boulevard St-Michel.

The café makes an onion soup that I swear can solve world problems.

It was a beautiful day. The sun was full out which is always one of the best times to be sitting on a terrace of any Paris café. I closed my eyes and tilted my face skyward to let the sun caress my cheeks. Living in the city as I do, I rarely get a chance to get much sun except for when I'm sitting in a café.

My phone rang and I instantly frowned. Adele was a busy girl—both professionally and socially—and we often had trouble finding time to meet face to face. When I saw her name on the screen on my phone, I knew she was going to cancel on me.

"Hey," I said as I answered.

"I am so sorry, Claire," Adele said. "It's just not possible today, you know?"

"I understand," I said. "You've got a lot on your plate."

Just being young, attractive with a demanding, prestigious job and a singles-life in Paris would be enough to fill up most people's dance cards, I reasoned.

"But I do have a little something for you," she said. "The post-mortem on the Senator?"

"Really?" I said with excitement. "That's great."

"I'll email it to you, yes?"

"Oh, Adele, that would be amazing," I said. "Have you had a chance to look at it?"

"No time. I mentioned that I didn't work this case, right?"

"Yes, I know. This is great, Adele. I definitely owe you dinner."

"I will take you up on that, *mon amie*! I'm sending it now. It's twenty pages but I'm just sending the summary, okay?"

"That's great."

"I have to send it in two separate emails though."

"That's fine."

"*Á tout a l'heure*, Claire," she said signing off.

I leaned back in my chair and then signaled the waiter to order *pommes frites* while I kept one eye on my phone for the emails from Adele. It occurred to me that, since Adele wasn't coming, I might see if Jean-Marc could meet up instead and we could go over all that we'd learned.

We also had three other cases in varying stages of completion and as much as I wanted to devote all my time to solving Ethan's murder for Madeleine's sake, I knew we couldn't just drop our other clients in the meantime.

By the time Jean-Marc strolled up to my table an hour later, I'd had lunch, my first glass of wine for the day, and made several pages of notes on one of our cases involving the teenage girl of two American expats.

The girl had run away twice and both times I'd tracked her down and given the information to her father, who then went and retrieved her, once from Berlin and the other time from Marseille. She'd just left a third time and I felt that I needed to frame a letter to her parents saying that I was honor bound to tell the police at this point.

I had no indication that the girl was in any way abused. I'd spoken to her teachers and also to her friends—what few she had—and interviewed her parents in depth. Sometimes, even as much as you love them, kids just act contrary.

I didn't know what was going on, but the third time was the charm as far as little Casey was concerned. What I was doing with her parents wasn't working—or at least it wasn't stopping Casey from fleeing. Now it was time for the professionals to step in. And by professionals I meant mental health.

Adele's emails hadn't come through, but she'd texted me that she'd gotten caught in a meeting and had to push off the time when she could send them. I nearly just texted her to "photograph and text them!" but she was doing me a favor and pushing her to do it on my timeline wouldn't be appreciated.

In that way, the French were no different from anyone else.

Jean-Marc kissed me in greeting and settled into the chair opposite me.

"Have you eaten?" I asked as I gestured for the waiter again.

"I have," he said.

When the waiter walked up, Jean-Marc ordered a glass of white wine.

"How did you hear about this place?" He looked around the terrace with an approving look on his face.

"One of the influencers I follow on Instagram raves about it," I said.

He frowned at the unfamiliar word, and I laughed.

"Never mind," I said. "How was your morning?"

"Fruitful, I think," he said. "And yourself?"

I shook my head.

"Adele couldn't make it," I said. "But she's sending me a copy of the postmortem."

Jean-Marc's eyebrows shot up.

"I know, I know," I said. "I didn't ask her how she got it. Half the time I feel like I'm a CIA agent instead of a private investigator."

"There does seem to be some definite overlap," he said with a slight smile on his lips.

"Your contact from the department?" I prompted.

"Étienne, yes. Although he's not in homicide, he has access to information."

"Great. So?"

"You're not going to like it."

I felt my heart sink.

"He said the Senator's phone records reveal he did call the escort service and ask for someone to come to his room," Jean-Marc said.

"Seriously?" I said, disappointment lacing my voice. "He called for the hooker?"

"I'm afraid so."

"Specifically, Désirée?"

"That I don't know. They really just have a record of the call and the time it was made, not the content of the conversation. But of course, why else would he call an escort service?"

"Yes, yes, especially since an hour later an escort showed up at his door. No, you don't have to know the content of the conversation to guess what was said. It's just really disappointing."

"One other interesting note is that the hooker claimed to the police that she didn't have sexual relations with the Senator."

"Somehow I think I already knew that," I said. "Ethan wasn't like that. I'm still having trouble believing he called her in the first place."

He pulled out a jump drive from his jacket and placed it on the table.

"And then, there's this," he said.

"Oh my gosh, is that what I think it is?" I asked.

A shiver of anticipation ran through me, and I was tempted to hug him.

"It's a copy of the hotel video footage from Ethan's floor on the night."

"How in the world did your guy get this?" I asked, as I reached down to pull my lap top out of my briefcase next to my chair. "And what did you promise your guy for this?"

Jean-Marc laughed.

"I'm sure there will be quid pro quo," he said. "But Étienne is honorable. It won't be a kidney or anything. Now that you mention it, he has a new baby. Perhaps a gift would be in order."

"A gift is definitely in order," I said feeling a giddy breathlessness as I inserted the jump drive in my laptop. "Maybe two."

"Étienne said to go to about hour twenty-one," Jean-Marc said. "There's nothing but an empty hallway before then."

I cued it up to the time Jean-Marc suggested and positioned the screen so that we could both watch. At around eleven-thirty that night, the video showed Ethan walking down the hallway toward his room.

Ethan's gait was unsteady and heavy as if he was weary. After the night he'd had, I thought remembering his altercation with Madeleine's bodyguard, that was not surprising.

We watched him enter his room. Thirty minutes later, Désirée walked down the hallway from the bank of elevators. She looked a little unsteady on her high heels. She glanced down the hallway before knocking on his door. The door opened and after a few seconds, she entered.

"Étienne said there's nothing after that until housekeeping shows up at around seven in the morning."

I fast forwarded through the long night until I saw a pair of maids pushing a janitorial cart down the hallway to the room. I watched as they knocked, and then entered. Within seconds, they ran out of the room and down the hallway.

"When was the murder called in?" I asked as I fast-forwarded the video again until I saw a hotel security guard running down the hall, followed twenty minutes later by two police officers.

I didn't need to see the rest which would show homicide, a crime scene team, and a series of detectives traipsing in and out of the room, until finally Désirée was escorted out of the room in handcuffs. And the body was removed on a draped gurney.

"I guess I was hoping to see someone come into the room after Désirée," I said.

"I know."

"This is pretty damning for her."

At that moment my phone dinged, and I picked it up to see that the first page of Adele's email had just come through. The waiter returned with Jean-Marc's wine and, before opening the email, I handed my phone to Jean-Marc while I ordered chicken tacos. I'd eaten lunch but found I was still hungry.

When I turned back to Jean-Marc, I held out my hand for the phone, but his face looked grave. My throat tightened as a chill ran down my spine.

"You're not going to love this," he said as he handed me my phone. "Adele's email says that forensics confirmed that Ethan definitely had sex with her."

25

"I don't believe it," I said, as I reached for my phone and skimmed the first page of the forensic report that Adele had sent. My heart sank to the soles of my shoes.

"But Désirée said they didn't have relations," I said as I read and re-read the report, trying to get a different result from what I was seeing.

"Sorry, *chérie*. It appears she was lying. DNA evidence trumps testimony every time."

"Maybe she doesn't remember?" I asked as I looked at him. "I mean, she was drugged after all."

He shrugged. Jean-Marc had been a policeman for a very long time. He was much more inclined than I was to believe the worst of someone. He'd seen too much in his thirty years on the job to prove that humanity didn't typically improve with age.

I read the rest of the page, my heart growing heavier as I did. The report was very specific that Ethan's semen was found inside Désirée. Plus, the drug that was found in both their systems was the same—a common drug used to enhance the pleasure of the sexual act. When taken too much, it can be lethal. This confirmed to me that Désirée was lucky to be alive. Did that mean it was a suicide attempt on her part?

"So the whole thing was an accident?" I asked, more confused than before I'd read Adele's email.

"Cigarette burns don't really feel very unintentional."

"Good point. But then who drugged whom?"

"The detectives will say that Désirée drugged them both. She drugged him to incapacitate him and her to give herself an alibi for the killing, but she misgauged the drug dosage for herself."

I snorted in disbelief. That just sounded mad to me. Why would she torture him first? If she truly did, what was she trying to find out? I scanned the document again. It didn't mention if Désirée's DNA had been found anywhere else in the room. But wouldn't it have been if she was the one who'd performed the room search?

"There are some holes," Jean-Marc said. "I can't imagine what the homicide detectives know that we don't. But there must be something we're out of the loop on."

"You mean because they haven't released Désirée," I said. "No offence, Jean-Marc, but you know very well that the desire to enhance case clearance rates can sometimes drive a cop to draw outside the lines."

I hated mentioning this well-known fact to him since if there was a definition of the phrase *bent copper*, I fear that a photo of my darling boyfriend would definitely show up. Jean-Marc had rehabilitated since those days, but he definitely knew the temptation of taking the short cut, the easy bribe, the low-hanging fruit.

"I know the people I worked with in the department are all dedicated law enforcement officers," he said tightly.

"I've made you mad."

His gave me a flat look and folded his arms stubbornly across his chest.

"No, Claire. You have every right to say the things you do. I admit I did some bad things in my career."

"Jean-Marc, please stop. This isn't about you. Can't you just imagine that it's possible that otherwise decent cops might try to take the easy way if it was offered to them?"

"Is that supposed to make me feel better? That you think corruption is okay?"

"I just don't want to fight with you."

Something passed across his face, and he seemed to have come to a decision because he reached across the table and took my hand.

"You're right," he said. "Let's don't fight. We don't know what the police are thinking, and we don't know why they are holding someone who to us seems like a less than ideal suspect."

I felt a flush of relief that he'd been willing to move the spotlight off his past crimes and keep it focussed where it needed to be—on the current Paris homicide department detectives.

I'm not saying that Jean-Marc isn't loyal to his old workmates or his old department. He definitely is. But he's also worked very hard to be a different person from his days of bribe-taking and I can see how it would go against the grain for him to accuse someone else of that.

Honestly? Seeing him struggle with that is partly the reason I loved him.

My phone dinged again and, eager to remove myself from our intense conversation, I picked it up and scanned the second page.

"What is it, Claire?" Jean-Marc asked.

I looked at him and then at my phone again to make sure I was seeing what I was seeing.

"You're not going to believe this," I said feeling a numbness spread through me.

I handed him my phone, still seeing the words on the screen in my mind.

"They found DNA on the pillow used to kill Ethan," I said, feeling the excitement begin to ramp up inside me. "You'll never guess who."

He looked up at me, astounded. "Madeleine's bodyguard, Jimmy?"

26

Now *that* was a shocker.

"Can this be true?" I asked in bewilderment, reaching for my phone. "It means they have somebody's DNA besides Désirée's on the murder weapon. But they're still holding her for Ethan's murder?"

Jean-Marc took a sip of his wine, but I could see his mind working. I was sure he agreed with me, at least silently, that this had to be a case of police corruption—if not incompetence.

"Why would the police ignore DNA evidence?" I asked. "Unless someone high up wanted Désirée out of the picture? Is it possible she slept with someone powerful who's now embarrassed by what she could say about them?"

Someone like Michel Leblanc?

Jean-Marc gave me a skeptical look but that didn't discourage me. There had to be a reason why the Paris police wanted a prostitute to take the fall for a murder when they had actual evidence against someone else.

"What was Jimmy's DNA doing on the pillow? How in the world can that be explained away?"

"I don't know, *chérie*. But you saw the hotel video. Nobody else went into Ethan's room that night."

I stared at him for a moment. Something was flickering around the edges of my brain. I reached for my laptop and clicked on the surveillance video footage again.

"It's not going to show you something new, Claire," Jean-Marc said wearily. "Ethan came into the room and then Désirée. And nobody else came into the room until housekeeping went in the next morning and discovered both of them—Ethan dead and Désirée unconscious. There is no way Jimmy could've gone in during the time in question."

"But his DNA!"

"I know. It doesn't make sense," Jean-Marc admitted. "Unless his DNA somehow got on the pillow *before* the gala?"

"On Ethan's pillow?! What possible explanation could there be for Jimmy's DNA to be on Madeleine's father's bed pillow?"

"But you can see on the video that he does not come into the room at all that night. The video clearly shows only Désirée entered the room."

"Where did Étienne get this video?"

"You think it was doctored?"

"I don't know. At the very least I think we need to talk to Jimmy again."

I watched the footage again where Ethan disappeared into his room and then fast forwarded until Désirée showed up.

"Look! Right there," I said pointing at the video. "She's wobbling."

Jean-Marc turned the screen around to face him and squinted.

"Can you see? She's unsteady on her feet," I said.

"Maybe she stopped and had a drink."

"One drink shouldn't have her wobble like that."

"So what are you thinking?"

I closed the laptop with a satisfying click.

"I think she was drugged before she ever got to Ethan's room."

~

The harsh afternoon sun streamed through the giant plate glass window, bathing everything in the office with a golden light. The man sat at his desk, looking out at the street below. From this vantage point, he could see people scurrying about, going about their day-to-day activities—as if unaware of the magnificent architecture that surrounded them.

"I don't want to hear excuses," he said acidly into the phone he was holding to his ear. He glanced around his office, too upset to focus on any one thing for longer than a few seconds. This conversation was long overdue and now that he was finally having it, he didn't know why he'd hesitated. "I want an accounting."

"I don't know what you want me to say."

"I want you to tell me why something that was supposed to look like suicide ended up a murder case!"

"Why do you care as long as the cops are happy with who they have?"

"I care," he screamed into the phone, spittle flying, "because that was not what I instructed you to do!"

"Look, calm down. The job got done, didn't it?"

"Sloppy! The job got done *sloppy*! And the police are still investigating!"

"What are you worried about? You're the last person they'd think had anything to do with it."

"No thanks to *you*!"

The sigh on the other end was arrogant and even contemptuous.

"Look, was it perfect? No. But it could've been a whole lot worse."

"Why was the hooker left alive?"

"I don't need this BS. Mistakes were made, okay? But how else were we going to explain Ethan being tortured with no sign of anyone else in the room? It worked out!"

"It did not work out, you idiot! The hooker had no reason to burn Ethan with cigarettes! Did that ever occur to you?"

"I thought the cops might think it was some kind of kinky sex thing."

"You're an idiot!"

Suddenly the phone disconnected and, for a moment, he just stood at his desk, his mouth opening and shutting as if he was about to say more—disbelieving that he'd been hung up on. Finally, he turned to look out at the view of the Paris street below him and took in a long breath to regain his composure.

Red and white checkered awnings fluttered over the terrace of the café tables across the street. Flower boxes, filled with blood-red geraniums, perched on windowsills and along the black wrought iron Juliet balconies on the building across from him.

The sun peeked through a hole in the cloud cover, setting the street momentarily aglow against the ancient, cobbled streets.

He turned away from the sight which usually filled him with awe, took in another long breath and flung his phone across the room.

27

I'm not sure what my discovery about Désirée's likely drugging before her appointment with Ethan meant—especially when added to the fact that Jimmy's DNA was found on the murder weapon even though there was no sign of him on the hotel video.

I know Étienne was a friend of Jean-Marc's, but I needed to know how he got his hands on that video. The fact was it wasn't a CCTV which is next to impossible to tamper with. But I know for a fact that altering a private video is no problem at all.

As Jean-Marc and I walked down boulevard Malesherbes on our way to our meeting with Madeleine at her hotel he was very quiet.

"Look, Jean-Marc," I said. "I'm not saying your friend is a bad guy…"

"I'll take it to Gilbert this afternoon," he said.

Gilbert worked for a service we often used for surveillance equipment. Gilbert would be able to examine the video to see if it had been altered in any way.

"It doesn't mean you shouldn't trust Étienne," I said.

"Claire, stop," Jean-Marc said, flushing and clearly trying to keep control of his temper. "We will find out if the video is to be trusted and go from there."

I knew him well enough to know when to let things go.

We continued walking toward the Hotel Fauchon where Madeleine had moved after the third floor of the Sofitel hotel had been turned into a crime scene,

Half the time when I'm walking around Paris I feel like I'm on a Hollywood movie set. I never get tired of seeing all the beautiful French architecture around me, and in Paris that can range from jaw-dropping palaces to medieval washhouses.

I loved the feeling of the sun on my shoulders through my cotton dress. I tend to believe that everyone who lives in Paris is in tune with the weather, as if the sun is the city's true beacon. Today the skies were clear, the sun bright and warming gave me a lift as I walked down the street.

Hotel Fauchon is on the corner of rue de l'Arcade and boulevard Malesherbes, and like so many architectural buildings in Paris, its presentation is designed to take one's breath away.

I couldn't help but notice that Madeleine had moved to a much more expensive hotel than where she had been staying with her father. The building was neoclassical in style, featuring a rounded *porte-cochère*. From the street it looked like a castle made of stucco and limestone. I have always loved this hotel and often recommend it to visiting friends. Well-heeled friends, I might add, since the hotel was easily a thousand euros a night. Or more. To put it in context, we passed the Hermès Paris store on our way here as well as the Dior boutique.

When Madeleine opened the door to her room I was immediately struck by the grandeur of the room, complete with plush furniture that had been carefully positioned to frame the view of the Eiffel Tower which was visible through the floor to ceiling windows.

But after all she had gone through, I didn't have the heart to judge her for the expense. If a little bit of comfort and pampering helped, and you could afford it, by all means, do it.

"Hello, Claire," Madeleine said as Jean-Marc and I stepped into the room.

I gave her a brief hug and looked around the room.

"No Jimmy?"

"He...he's running a personal errand," Madeleine said.

I glanced at Jean-Marc who nodded.

"I'll wait for him in the hall," he said, stepping back into the hall and closing the door behind him.

I followed Madeleine into the salon and sat on one of two velvet sofas. The late afternoon light flooded the space through the tall windows, bathing us both in a soft glow.

"I'm so glad you could come," Madeleine said. "I've had some thoughts about who I think is out to kill me and I wanted to share them with you."

Knowing that there was every chance that the person who was out to kill her—if there really was someone—was her own bodyguard Jimmy, I only nodded. She seemed fond of the man. These things must be approached delicately.

"It seems to me," she said, but then broke off as her phone which was face down on the coffee table between us began to vibrate.

She picked it up, looked at the screen and then pushed the button to dismiss the call.

"I can step outside," I said. "If you want to take that."

"No, it's only Henry. I talked to him for hours this morning. He's so worried about me and honestly, it doesn't help. If he were here, that would be one thing. But with all his fretting, he's only making me more anxious."

"I'm sure he's also worried about the baby," I said.

She put a hand on her stomach and smiled wanly.

"The baby is fine," she said. "I'm only four months along and he's safely padded inside me."

"Enjoy the feeling," I said. "Because once he's out in the world, it's a never ending project to keep him safe. The worry never ends."

"That's what my mother says," she said and then her smile dropped. "My poor mother."

"Have you talked to her?"

"I have. I feel so helpless being this far from her, but I really think I can do more from Paris than back in Atlanta. Besides, she's got my Auntie Flo with her."

I was glad to hear that Dilly wasn't alone.

Her phone dinged, indicating that the caller had left a voicemail. Madeleine glanced at the phone and smiled.

"Honestly, Henry is everything Dad ever wanted for me," she said. "He's smart and ambitious but not too ambitious. He wants a family and he's crazy about me."

"That would be every father's dream for a beloved daughter," I said.

She nodded, her eyes misting.

"I know. I'm so lucky. Especially since I was a little wild in high school. But Henry saw past all that."

"How did you meet him?"

"My Auntie Flo introduced us at a gallery opening in Atlanta a year ago. We've been together ever since."

She picked up her phone and smiled fondly at it as if thinking of the call she would make to him later after I'd left.

"How has everything else been?" I asked.

Jean-Marc and I had already decided we would not tell Madeleine about the pillow with Jimmy's DNA on it. Jean-Marc wanted to interview Jimmy separately.

Those intentions were scuttled with Madeleine's next sentence.

"Why is Jean-Marc out in the hall waiting for Jimmy?" she asked. "Has something happened?"

I debated lying to her, but quickly decided that was not the best way forward.

"There was a report that Jimmy's DNA was found in your father's room. Do you know why that would be?"

Madeleine frowned and thought for a moment.

"I don't, honestly. He's always with me. Maybe it's a mistake?"

I shook my head. "DNA doesn't lie."

"Well, there has to be another explanation. Because Jimmy and my dad barely even talked to each other. Honestly, I think Jimmy was a little afraid of him which is absurd since Jimmy's this big hulking dude. Did I mention that when my dad hired him, he did it because Jimmy's dad was an old school friend of his?"

"I think you did mention that," I said, wondering if Jean-Marc had intercepted Jimmy in the hall and was even now questioning him.

"Well, it seems he had a problem when he was in high school."

I snapped my attention back to her. "What kind of problem?"

"He wasn't charged, mind you, so I think that tells you something about the validity of the accusation."

"What was he accused of?" I asked.

"Try not to judge him too harshly," she said. "Remember, he was never charged."

I knew what she was going to say before she said it.

"Some girl accused him of rape."

28

Suffice to say, I was floored by Madeleine's revelation that Jimmy had been accused of such a crime—and also that it didn't seem to bother her that he had. She appeared so convinced that he'd been railroaded or that the girl who'd made the accusation had an ulterior motive for wanting to hurt him, that she wouldn't even hear of the possibility that her bodyguard might be dangerous.

After that, she begged off from the rest of our visit, citing a hair appointment in the salon downstairs. I got the impression that she was eager to call Henry back.

As I walked to the door, she lightly touched my arm.

"Please give Jimmy the benefit of the doubt," she said.

"I'll try," I said.

We hugged briefly and then I stepped outside where Jean-Marc was still waiting as Madeleine closed the door.

"We need to find Jimmy ASAP," I said as we hurried down the hallway. "Madeleine just told me he was accused of rape in high school."

Jean-Marc pressed the tips of his fingers against his temples as if he felt a headache coming on. "And her father hired him as her bodyguard?" he said in disbelief.

"Well, Madeleine said her father believed that the girl who accused Jimmy was lying."

"*Incroyable!*"

"I know there must be more to it. But with no police record, short of flying to Dayton, Ohio, and tracking down the girl, there's no way to know the truth."

"And possibly not even then."

I felt the same as Jean-Marc—unsatisfied and mildly confused—and more certain than ever that Jimmy had killed Ethan.

As Jean-Marc and I crossed the street in front of the hotel, preparing to go our separate ways, we stopped long enough to attempt to process what we'd learned.

"She needs a security detail," Jean-Marc said.

"How is that going to happen?" I asked. "Unless it's us?"

For whatever reason, Madeleine did not think that Jimmy was a threat to her or anyone else.

I'd met people like her before and usually, like Madeleine, they were young and naive. It didn't make the situation any less frustrating.

"What do you think? Is she deluded?" Jean-Marc asked, shaking his head in amazement.

"I don't know what to think," I said. "She seems incredibly naïve to me on a lot of different levels. I mean, she says she's afraid for her life, but she's got a rapist as her bodyguard."

"Alleged rapist."

"Oh, spare me," I said. "Smoke, fire."

"I am not knowing this American idiom."

"Basically it means Jimmy raped someone. So what next? We need to talk to him now more than ever."

"Correction. *I* need to talk to him."

"That works too," I said wearily.

After Jean-Marc and I went our separate ways—he to wait at the hotel to intercept Jimmy—and me to go back to the apartment to spend some quality time with Robbie, and possibly to try to manipulate a few old friends into a favor or two down at the police department.

I went home by way of the Monoprix, Paris's premier supermarket and all-round shopping emporium to get ingredients for tonight's dinner. I've learned I can find pretty much everything at Monoprix—from cashmere gloves to mascara and of course groceries. It has a pretty fantastic bakery, too.

As I walked down its wide, colorful aisles putting various dinner ingredient items in my basket, I found myself reflecting on the fact that Jean-Marc didn't tend to talk much about his old pals at the station. While I knew he'd reached out to a few of them, I also knew this Étienne Benoit was not someone with whom he usually spent time. That told me that the others had either turned their backs on Jean-Marc or been in some way warned off him.

I spent some time in the bakery section of the store selecting a baguette for tonight's meal as well as a couple of *pains au chocolat* for Robbie's breakfast in the morning. It was still amazing to me even after all these years that the bakery section of a chain Paris supermarket could rival most freestanding bakeries in any American city.

As I pushed my grocery cart down the aisle I thought if Chantal Resnelle, the new boss in Jean-Marc's old position, was feeling insecure about Jean-Marc's even peripheral involvement in the case, it would explain why we were getting absolutely no help from an official source.

Jean-Marc's involvement in this case, it would explain why we were getting absolutely no help from an official source.

I couldn't make his old friends talk to him about the case, but I might be able to come in through the back door.

I stood in line at the cashier's and reflected back on the fact that six months ago, I'd nearly succeeded in getting a perfectly nice man killed who had, up until then shown a romantic interest in me. While that experience had understandably cooled his interest, I knew David was an honorable man and as long as I was not trying to talk him into climbing onto a Paris rooftop with a convicted killer, he might be talked into helping me again.

David Fontaine was a public defender for the police department. If he wasn't handling Désirée's case himself, he would know who was.

I paid for my purchases, wishing I had my canvas grocery chariot with me, and made my way down boulevard Haussmann toward my apartment. I seriously hoped that it was David who was defending Désirée. First, because he was such a good guy—and a very skilled legal defender.

And second, because I knew how to get a favor out of him—even if it *was* his preference never to lay eyes on me again.

29

Jean-Marc waited outside Madeleine's hotel on boulevard Malesherbes until he saw the bodyguard start to approach and then turn and begin to retrace his steps in the opposite direction. Jean-Marc followed him until the man turned on rue de Laborde.

All of Jean-Marc's senses went on high alert.

Rue de Laborde is Claire's street.

A part of him had been hoping that Jimmy was meeting with someone, but when he turned on Claire's street, all Jean-Marc could think was that the man had to be casing the neighborhood for some nefarious reason.

Jean-Marc slid behind a parked delivery van on the street and watched as Jimmy darted down an alley off Laborde in the direction of what Jean-Marc knew was a small, hidden park.

Frowning, Jean-Marc walked quickly to the alley in time to see Jimmy reach the end of it and stride toward the park. Jean-Marc followed and saw the bodyguard settle onto a park bench in front of a nonfunctioning fountain, one ankle crossed over his knee and pull out a packet of cigarettes.

Jean-Marc made a sound of disgust. He walked over to him,

making no more effort to be secretive. Jimmy looked at him in surprise and sat up straight before looking around the park as if wondering if there was anyone else about to pop out of the woodwork.

"That must have been humiliating when the senator publicly chastised you at the gala," Jean-Marc said as he faced Jimmy, his arms folded across his chest.

"Give me a break," Jimmy said sourly. "Are you following me now?"

"To me," Jean-Marc continued, looking around the park with a casual air, "it looked like he knocked you on your ass."

"Didn't bother me."

"I was there. You looked like you were about to hit him back."

"Well, you're wrong. It didn't mean anything."

"I think it did mean something," Jean-Marc said. "I think you were humiliated. I think you were looking for a way to pay the old man back."

"You're crazy," Jimmy said as he puffed on his cigarette. Jean-Marc could see his nails were bitten to the quick.

"I'm told by Paris Homicide that your DNA was found in the senator's room. Can you tell me how that happened?"

Jimmy stopped smoking. "You're lying."

"They said your DNA was found on the pillow that was used to suffocate the senator."

Jimmy whitened visibly.

"You're lying," he said again, licking his lips. "You got no evidence! I was never in his room!"

Jimmy stood up and snatched up his jacket where he pulled out the pack of cigarettes although he hadn't finished smoking the one in his hand. Jean-Marc hated the fact that he was not privy to whether the brand of cigarettes used to torture the senator was known. Jimmy threw away his lit cigarette and lighted another and glared at Jean-Marc.

"I understand you had a little brush with the law when you were younger," Jean-Marc said.

"You talking about that stolen car?" Jimmy sucked hard on his cigarette and shrugged. "It wasn't me who stole it, it was my cousin, and he went down for it."

"No, I'm talking about the sexual assault accusation made against you when you were in high school."

Jimmy frowned as if trying to remember. Jean-Marc got the impression he wasn't acting.

"I don't know what you're talking about," Jimmy said finally.

"A girl didn't accuse you of rape when you were in school?"

Jimmy burst out laughing.

"Only about every day! But nobody who'd have the nerve to go to the cops."

The rest of the interview was just as frustrating and revealed virtually nothing. For a man of relatively low intelligence, Jean-Marc noted, Jimmy had done an adequate job of avoiding answering Jean-Marc's questions.

As he left the park where they'd met up, Jean-Marc thought back to the moment where he'd briefly considered threatening Jimmy to get him to reveal more of what he was sure Jimmy was not telling. He'd given up on the idea but not just because Jimmy outweighed him and was forty years younger.

Claire thinks I've changed.

I'd like for her to go on thinking that for as long as possible.

~

My evening was stress-free and pleasant. I did think of Madeleine from time to time, and of course, her poor mother, but generally, I allowed myself to relax and just enjoy being with Robbie. We played a few games, talked about nothing important, and watched an hour of television together after dinner. Robbie then took his bath and I read to him for an hour before taking Izzy downstairs to wet the courtyard pavers. When I came back upstairs, I toyed with the idea of calling Catherine.

I was pretty sure that it was seeing Robbie snuggled down in his bed which triggered the impulse. When I looked at him, so happy and safe and secure, I just couldn't help but be reminded that there was a child somewhere out there in the world who shared my DNA and who was lost to me, possibly forever. I have tried that thought on for size so many times in an attempt to get used to it—knowing how much it would relieve both Jean-Marc and Geneviève if I could believe it—and I found that I can't. Not yet anyway.

I knew I was just delaying making the call to David. If he was going to be rude to me or cuss me out or just turn me down flat, at least I would have tried. I poured myself a glass of sherry and called him.

Ten minutes later, feeling the flush of delight at the result of my call, I settled down in the living room with the television on mute to await Jean-Marc's call. I'd been trying not to anticipate his report on interviewing Jimmy and I found, now that he was due to call, that I was very eager to hear what had transpired.

He called within minutes of my hanging up with David.

"*Allo, chérie,*" he said. "Is the young Monsieur asleep?"

"Like a log," I said, knowing the idiom would make no sense to him. "How'd it go with Jimmy? Did you confront him with the evidence of his DNA on the pillow?"

"He denied being in the senator's room."

I groaned. Without a confession from Jimmy the information of his DNA was useless to us since the police had it and were ignoring it.

"Did you learn anything else?" I asked.

"He was surprised about the pillow with his DNA."

"Maybe he thought he was more careful than that."

"I don't know. He looked genuinely perplexed as to how his DNA could've gotten on the pillow."

"It's hard to tell with people like Jimmy," I said. "Stupid people always look a little perplexed all the time. What did he say about the rape charge?"

"He said he'd be surprised if any girl had the nerve to actually go to the police to report him."

"So he didn't deny it?" I let out a breath of frustration. "Poor Madeleine. I hate that she trusts this jerk. I wish we could get her away from him somehow."

"When is she planning to return to the States?" Jean-Marc asked.

"As soon as the police release Ethan's body."

"That could be weeks."

"Not at the rate they're processing the crime," I reminded him. "Things move pretty quickly when you're manufacturing your own evidence to support your case."

"We are not sure they are doing that, *chérie*," Jean-Marc reminded me. "What else did you do tonight?" he asked, clearly trying to change the subject.

"As a matter of fact, I haven't been idle."

"Does that mean you made dinner?"

"Ha ha. *Très droll*. I did actually, but more importantly, I set up a call for later tonight with Désirée Deschamps."

There was a brief hesitation. "How did you manage that?"

"Not to worry. Suffice to say my life savings are still secure and I didn't have to pledge any first-born children."

"I'm impressed."

If I could read anything into a phone conversation where you can't see the person's face and a foreign language which I'm not all that good at reading face to face, I'd say that *impressed* was not what Jean-Marc was feeling.

I was sorry to have leapfrogged over him—if that's what he thought I did—but speaking directly to the suspect that the police have in custody was essential for moving our investigation out of the land of fantasy into the direction of a real working theory. I knew Jean-Marc knew that. But I also knew he didn't love how I'd managed it without him.

Men. The French version is just like the American version, only—like everything else about them—more so.

30

I'd set the call up for nine o'clock that night. David had been understandably unhappy to hear from me, but I like to think since it turned out that Désirée was his client, he was a little less unhappy that I was interested in interviewing her.

We'd worked together fairly well, David and I, last Christmas—until the whole killer-swinging-a-golf-club-at-his-head debacle—and I think he saw before that, that I was professional and competent. And of course well-meaning. And passionate—if something of a lunatic.

Besides, David knew that the evidence was well and fully stacked against his client. The DNA evidence alone would burn Désirée and any chance she had of ever seeing life outside a prison cell. If there was a hope in hell that he could save her from a life sentence, well, I was that hope. And for a good guy like David, that hope balanced out the fear that this time I might somehow manage to yet get him killed.

My phone rang at precisely seventeen hundred hours. When I picked up, I was informed by a robotic voice that I needed to accept or decline a call from an inmate of the Paris Police Detention Center.

"Accept," I said. "Hello? Madame Deschamps?"

"My solicitor said I needed to talk to you," a sultry but sullen voice said.

"I thank you for speaking with me, Madame Deschamps," I said formally. "I don't know if Monsieur Fontaine told you, but I'm hoping to find evidence to help your case."

She sighed on the other line and said nothing.

"First of all, Madame Deschamps," I said. "The police are saying that the victim's DNA was found inside you. Can you explain how—"

"That is bull shit! I told my solicitor that. The police are trying to frame me!"

"So you're saying you did not have sex with Ethan Andrews that night?"

"No, we did not have sex."

"Are you sure?"

Désirée let out an impatient huff.

"Don't you think I'd *know* if I'd had sex?"

"Presumably."

"So you think I'm lying?"

"Look, Madame Deschamps," I said. "I don't think that at all. But the facts remain that DNA evidence of Ethan Andrews' semen was recovered from your body. Is there any way that sex could have happened, but you don't remember it?"

Désirée let out a helpless sigh. "I guess. If he was weirder than I thought."

"But you yourself didn't notice any...evidence of this on your body?"

"I had a lot going on at the time, you know? When I woke up, I had people screaming and slapping cuffs on me. I think I can be forgiven for not noticing something like that!"

This was just all too bizarre. I should've asked David before

I talked to her to see if he thought she was telling the truth. Hell, maybe she did kill Ethan?

"Why would he assault me when I was unconscious? He didn't even expect me when I showed up. When I demanded my money, he got angry. So you're suggesting he saw me unconscious on the bed, and changed his mind?"

"Is it possible you had sex and then passed out and can't remember?"

She was silent for a moment.

"Maybe," she said reluctantly. "I have to admit, lots about that night is just one big empty space."

"Do you remember getting the phone call and going up to his room?"

"Yes, of course. I remember him answering the door and then being angry when he saw me."

"Because you were late? Or because you weren't the kind of woman he was expecting?"

"No! Angry because he wasn't expecting anyone at all!"

"But he let you in anyway?"

She paused. "I may have pushed my way in. The hotel doesn't like people like me loitering in hallways."

"What else?"

"I remember talking with him for a few minutes and then feeling sick all of a sudden and then just...blackness."

"And you seriously don't remember having sex with him?"

"I told you! No!"

Claire frowned. So, Ethan supposedly called a sex worker, then denied having called her and refused to pay her, but then supposedly drugged her, and when she was out cold, had sex with her unconscious body?

It was one thing to imagine someone you knew and respected calling for an escort. That was disappointing but it was a whole different thing to believe he'd try to cheat the woman out of her money by drugging her and having sex with her limp body!

"Do you smoke?" I asked.

The cigarette burns were a particular gruesome bit of Intel that Jean-Marc had managed to winkle out of his contacts. When matched with the destroyed room, they suggested a very ugly picture indeed.

"Okay, yes, I smoke. But I would never burn someone!"

"Even if they asked you to?"

Désirée gave a snort of disgust.

"I know sex workers don't enjoy the highest regard from the public," she said. "But I have never met anyone who thought it was a turn-on to be burned with cigarettes!"

I had to admit. Absolutely none of it made sense.

31

After I'd hung up from Désirée and spent a few moments debriefing with David, I made a few notes in my notebook about the conversation to go over with Jean-Marc tomorrow. I honestly wasn't sure what to make of the whole thing. Without being able to see the woman face to face, it was hard to determine if she was telling the truth. But David was a good judge of people and he seemed to believe her.

After checking on Robbie to confirm that he was fast asleep —again, alongside Izzy—I went into the kitchen to make myself a cup of tea and try—even as tired as I was—to see if there was anything that sprang to mind that might point the finger in a direction *other* than Jimmy.

Or Michel Leblanc.

It was great to have suspects, but at the moment the only two I had also had serious questions that needed answering.

Why would Leblanc want Ethan dead? I granted that the Pardeux Committee had been humiliating for him at the time but that was nearly five years ago. Otherwise, since they were senators from two different countries, they really didn't have much interaction—at least not formally.

I considered the idea of talking to Joelle again, perhaps to pump her for information but quickly discarded the thought. Joelle was as wily as a mental patient and very smart. Any attempt to get information out of her would undoubtedly end with her pulling all my secrets out of me.

And then there was Jimmy who was unlikable and whose DNA was found on the murder weapon but who, in every other regard, was too boorish and stupid to have pulled something like this off. I would've thought.

He had a sort of motive—the altercation at the gala which was at least more recent than Leblanc's—but it was still weak as far as motives went.

Looking at my notes of the phone call with Désirée I found myself writing down Roger O'Connell's name. I had no reason to suspect him, but he *had* been close to the senator, and it didn't feel right to ignore him. I'd know more after I talked with him.

After I looked at just about everyone who was near or connected to Ethan, I had to honestly reconsider Désirée. The fact was, she was in the room. Plus, the DNA indicated she did have sex with him, and she did survive. I had no idea how clever she was but if one was going to kill someone, pretending to be a victim yourself was a classic and often successful ploy.

On the other hand, I trusted David's intuition about her. I wished I could meet her myself.

Who else did that leave?

I briefly thought of Madeleine because it went against the grain for me to let anybody off the hook at this point in my investigation. But patricide is a whole different kettle of fish to your garden-variety homicide. And the way I saw her and her father interact at the gala showed a relationship that was, if not particularly intimate, at least caring.

And again, my personal assessment was that Madeleine's grief at losing her father was real.

That also left the question of whether or not she was really in danger. During our conversations, she'd hinted at the possibility that she might want to pick up the flag after her father's death in some of the causes that were close to him. It was possible, if Ethan really had been killed because of his passion for animal rights, and if Madeleine had made public her intention to back his bills, she might well be in danger too.

I rubbed the bridge of my nose, truly and finally ready to leave it for the night. I went to the bathroom to brush my teeth and get ready for bed, when I heard my phone ding from where I'd set it on the kitchen counter.

Assuming it was Jean-Marc texting to say goodnight which he'd lately gotten in the habit of doing, I went into the kitchen, noting my teacup that I'd forgotten, and picked up my phone.

I stared at the text message. It wasn't from Jean-Marc.

<*The baby was born at Église Clinic in Basel. They have answers for you there.*>

32

Jean-Marc strode down the rue de Balzar fighting the fury and impatience he'd been trying to hold off for the past thirty minutes. It was well past ten o'clock by the time their video expert Gilbert had gotten back to him.

He stopped before the small boarded-up establishment on the corner of boulevard de Port-Royal and Boulevard Saint-Marcel. It had been a favorite bar of his in the old days.

The Chloe Days.

He grimaced and kept walking. The street was lined with eclectic shops and cafes, now closed at this time of night.

Not even getting drunk was going to obliterate this feeling in his stomach, the one he'd gotten when Gilbert told him that the video he'd dropped off with him had been edited.

Jean-Marc ground his teeth in fury as he thought back to the moment he sat at Café Le Boule, when everyone else in the department had walked past him, avoiding him. Was it just a coincidence that Étienne had shown up? Or had that been deliberate? How did he get a hold of the altered video? Was he somebody's patsy?

Or was Jean-Marc his?

He felt heat flushing through his body as he continued down the street with Gilbert's words ringing in his head.

"Yeah, man, the video stopped recording at right past midnight. It picked up again around six the next morning."

A gap of six hours? How is it he and Claire hadn't realized that? Oh, that had been easily answered, too.

"They just edited in six hours of blank hallway, maybe from the night before."

Basically, there had been a six-hour gap, from right after Désirée walked into Ethan's room until just before the housekeeping staff showed up. Six hours. Plenty of time for someone to come in after Désirée, kill Ethan, and leave again.

"Hey! Look where you're going!" a man snarled at Jean-Marc as he shouldered into him hard on the sidewalk.

"Sorry, sorry," Jean-Marc said, tucking his head to continue on to his apartment.

The good news—someone was trying to make it look as if Désirée was the killer, which had to mean there was someone trying to protect themselves.

The bad news— Étienne had lied to him. Why? For money? From whom? Was it someone within the department who didn't want him investigating the case? Or who didn't care just as long as he got it all wrong?

He reached the security door of his building and punched in his code, jerking open the heavy iron grill door and slipping inside, careful to make sure it clicked behind him. They'd had a couple of thefts recently, mostly of the older residents. They weren't paying attention and someone followed them inside.

Jean-Marc hurried across the stone courtyard to the door of his apartment building and took the elevator up to his floor. Every now and then he remembered what it had felt like to have a house in the country with the garden and the long winding driveway. Eventually it had only belonged to Chloe. And then she'd died there.

He jerked open the security door of the elevator when it reached his floor, hoping the sound and the motion would knock the morbid thoughts out of him. He'd tried calling Claire earlier, but her phone was off. He didn't blame her. It was late and she was doing a lot lately. Let her get her beauty sleep.

He went to his apartment door and inserted his key when his phone vibrated in his jacket pocket. He pulled it out and saw it was a call coming from none other than Étienne himself. Jean-Marc grunted and answered the phone as he pushed open his front door. He'd been wrestling with whether or not to confront the bastard, or to use him to find out who was trying to throw them off the scent.

"*Allo*," he said. "Étienne?"

"Bonsoir, Jean-Marc," Étienne said, his voice strained.

"I'm glad you called." Jean-Marc moved into the kitchen and tossed his keys onto the counter. "I wanted to thank you again for the video. That was a big help."

"I'm glad, Jean-Marc," Étienne said. "But I'm calling to tell you I think I'm done. I'm getting a little worried about sticking my neck out."

"Oh?"

"I think I'm making people suspicious. I have a new baby. I can't afford to lose this job."

"Sure," Jean-Marc said. "No worries. I appreciate what you've done for me up to now. You're a true friend, Étienne. I won't forget it."

"Okay. Well. Great. See you around, Jean-Marc. Good luck with everything."

Jean-Marc disconnected. He heard the regret, even remorse in the man's voice. And the guilt. He didn't know if whoever was prodding Étienne from the other side was getting more dangerous or if Resenelle had had a word with him.

In the end, it didn't matter. He would deal with Étienne down the road. Life was long and there would come a time.

Jean-Marc went to his window and stared out for a long time. Unlike Claire's apartment his windows looked out on a partial brick wall of the building next to him. There was a sliver of blinking lights visible—a reflection from the street activity down the block. He'd rented the place when he came back to Paris from Nice two years ago. He'd rented it when he had only his salary and not a single *sou* more to his name.

He felt a wave of bitterness as the thought about his career, his friends over the years, the supervisors he'd kowtowed to, and the criminals he'd rubbed shoulders with. He felt his stomach tighten. He went into the kitchen and opened the refrigerator although he wasn't really hungry, and it was too late anyway. He pulled out a half-full bottle of Chardonnay and poured himself a glass before bringing it back to the room that served both as his living room and dining room. He found himself sorry he'd not bothered to get a television set.

He toyed with the idea of calling Claire again but not seriously. He wouldn't wake her. After all, on top of a full-time business, she was raising a child. He shook his head at the thought. There wasn't much she couldn't do. And she never complained.

Why couldn't it have been him to have set up the phone call with Désirée? Or who could've given her authentic Intel instead of this misleading pack of lies? He felt a fury tingle through his shoulders. He knew Claire respected him. He just didn't know why.

His phone vibrated again, and he picked it up, hoping it was Claire. It was an unidentified number.

"*Allo?*" he said.

"Monsieur LaRue?" a hoarse whispered voice said.

Jean-Marc sat up straight, his heartbeat steady, but his chest tightening in anticipation.

"My name is Bruno Debuille. I...I work for Michel Leblanc. I was wondering if I could...talk to you?"

"We're talking now," Jean-Marc said.

"It would be worth my life if my boss knew I was talking to you," Bruno said, his voice thick with fear. "But you need to know something about him."

"I'm listening."

"He...he got my sister pregnant and then pretended not to know her," Bruno said bitterly.

"That is unfortunate."

"She killed herself." Bruno's voice was choked with anguish. "I want him to pay but he owns the police. You're my only hope."

"What do you have on him?" Jean-Marc asked, reaching for a notebook on the coffee table.

"I can't say over the phone. But it has to do with the American Senator."

"Leblanc was involved with that?"

"Up to his lying, murdering little neck."

Jean-Marc felt a flutter of triumph. "When can you meet?"

"Tonight?"

"Where?"

"Do you know the *Petit Blanc*?"

"I do. Thirty minutes?"

"Monsieur LaRue, it is essential for my safety that no one knows what I—"

"Yes, yes. No one will know it was you. What you're about to tell me...can it be proven with evidence?"

"Oh, yes," Bruno said bitterly. "And testimony."

"I'll see you there."

Jean-Marc hung up and glanced at his watch. He'd barely be able to make it to the bar in thirty minutes. But he knew the man would wait for him.

Nothing like revenge to make you brave enough to take down the big fish.

He grabbed up his keys and turned off the ringer on his

phone, jamming it into his jacket pocket. He hurried down the stairs and then out into the courtyard, his mind whirling with how he was going to be able to tell Claire he'd found a weak link in Leblanc's defenses. After the humiliation of the Étienne fiasco, he needed this nearly as much as poor Bruno did.

He hurried to the outer security door and wrenched it open, stepping out onto the sidewalk, his mind buzzing with jubilation at finally catching a break. He glanced again at his watch and tried to decide whether he should grab a taxi or call an Uber.

Suddenly, hands reached out and wrenched him off the sidewalk into the side alley. He smashed up against the wall but stayed on his feet, turning and raising his fists to face his attacker.

Attackers. Plural.

Their faces were hidden underneath hoods. They were both dressed in leather jackets, jeans and beaded chains. Jean-Marc noted the thickened muscled arms, and the menacing glint in their eyes.

"Going somewhere, LaRue?" one of them said with a laugh. Then he changed his voice to mimic that of Bruno Debuille. "Oh, please don't tell anyone I called you."

Jean-Marc's stomach tightened with fear and self-loathing. He'd been had. One of the men pulled out a pair of brass knuckles and slipped them on, slamming his fist into his own meaty hand.

"Yeah, the boss thought this message should be delivered in person."

They closed in on him from both sides.

33

A last-minute flight from Paris to Basel, Switzerland wasn't cheap, but it was available and for that I was grateful. By the time I got to the CDG—after rushing downstairs to beg Geneviève to move upstairs to be with Robbie—the terminal was a maze of people, running, languidly walking, and even sleeping. In my mind, they all seemed to move like one amorphous blob, almost like a school of fish, darting and weaving to get to their respective destinations.

The security lines were long even at this time of night. The smell of coffee wafted down the wide hallways and because this is France the scent of garlic drifted down to from the many concession stands along the terminals' walkways.

I sat at my gate and looked through the huge plate glass window onto the runway with its colorful landing beacons and bright runway lights. I forced myself to close my eyes and take a long breath and block out the look on Geneviève's face when I'd told her what I was doing.

I knew she thought I'm crazy, but I also knew that up until tonight I had zero leads for finding the baby born earlier this year from Catherine's stolen egg. I couldn't live with myself if I just walked away from any possibility—no matter how crazy—that might lead me to him.

I tried to block out the general commotion around me of the planes, roaring and shaking the glass as they took off, of people talking on their cell phones and the ocean of noise that crested and receded in my brain.

I needed to stay focused. I needed to think of nothing else but my mission. The mysterious text message had definitely come from someone who knew about the frozen eggs, and my desperate search for the male baby born from one of them. That would have to mean Abd-El-Kader or perhaps the surrogate mother herself. It mattered little to me which one it was.

An hour later, I was airborne watching the tips of the wings of the plane glowing in the moonlight, as it soared through the night sky. Instead of a window, I had some overly dramatic movie playing on the screen in front of me, but it was of my choosing. I needed distraction, not moody thoughts as I stared out into the cosmos.

The flight attendant brought coffee which I drank since I knew I would be up all night.

I watched the lights of Paris glittering beneath me, and I thought of Robbie asleep in his little bed, snug and safe. I couldn't do any less for the lost baby, for my little grandson, born somewhere in the world, who was sleeping somewhere in the world without his family.

I took in a breath and tried not to get overly emotional. I would need all my strength to do whatever the next day might demand of me.

Was I just going for information? Or was it possible I might actually find the baby? And if that happened, then what? Was I prepared to kidnap him? To fly him across international borders? I hadn't thought any of this out. I just knew I needed to find out more about where he was.

The stars twinkled over the patchwork of fields and towns as the plane descended steadily.

At some point during the flight, I'd resolved that I was not going to continue to refuse to name him. Once I got him safely back home, Catherine could rename him whatever she wanted. But I was no longer going to refer to him as *the frozen egg that got fertilized* or even *the baby*. He was alive and out there and real. For now, until I can hold him in my arms and Catherine says differently, I'm going to call him John. I struggled to stop the tears that threatened. My throat closed up as I fought them.

Hebrew for *Beloved of God*. It was a strong name. Maybe the strongest.

And he'll need to be strong.

I made my way through the Basel International Airport at half past four in the morning. found a kiosk with a few seats and ordered a *pain aux raisins* and a strong coffee. I planned to go straight to the taxi stand outside the airport for a cab that would take me to the L'Église Clinic.

While I sat drinking my coffee at the kiosk, waiting for the clinic to open at seven, I used my cellphone to go to the clinic's website where I discovered that it was a private maternity clinic, and very likely the place where my grandson's surrogate had given birth.

I'm coming, Baby John.

Once in the taxi and on my way, I watched the streets fly by in an early morning blur from the Flughafenstrasse to the Metzerstrasse. It took less than thirty minutes to arrive at the address I'd given the cab driver. When he pulled up to the curb, I stared up at the front of the clinic.

The thought that there was someone inside who might know something to help me find John made my heart beat a little faster.

The sky was grey, and there was a slight chill in the air as I stepped out of the taxi to make my way up the cracked sidewalk. The building was old, its bricks crumbling which I thought odd for a modern clinic. It's true that many buildings in Europe are very old, but hospitals and medical facilities are almost always exceptions.

I noted that there was a garden overgrown with weeds to the side which I thought unusual for an upscale birthing clinic. I continued up the path toward the front door and was within a few feet of it when a figure stepped out of the shadows of an alcove that framed the doorway.

At first, because I was so focused on the answers I was hoping to get—or possibly even finding John himself—that the fact that a man was standing in front of me, masked and hooded, didn't immediately make sense to me.

Before I could process what was happening, he rushed at me, his arm raised above his head.

A crowbar in his hand.

34

I screamed and ducked out of the way just in time. The man stumbled on the broken pavement but caught himself and turned, aiming the crowbar at me again. But the stumble had given me time.

I scrambled backward on the sidewalk, flinging my purse in his face in desperation.

That alone shouldn't have stopped him. I raced back into the street, praying there were people there. The taxi was still parked at the curb. I jerked the door open and jumped inside, locking the door behind me. When I looked out the window, my heart pounding in my throat, I saw my attacker fleeing across the side garden.

My purse still lay on the sidewalk with its contents spilled out.

"Everything is okay, Madame?" the driver asked me.

I took in a breath and unlocked the door.

"Wait here," I instructed him.

I stepped out of the taxi and looked around before slowly venturing back up the sidewalk. All my money, my passport, my cellphone—it was all there, strewn across the walkway.

My heart was still pounding as I gathered up the contents of my purse, one eye out for the direction my assailant had run.

So, not a robbery.

I stood up, my purse in my hands, and squared my shoulders. I motioned to the taxi driver to go on. Then I turned and walked up the steps of the clinic, knowing without a shadow of doubt that I was going to find precisely nothing that had anything to do with my lost grandson.

An hour later after spending the morning interviewing the director of the clinic, I was one step closer to realizing what a total and complete fool I'd been.

The clinic itself was a gleaming facility of white and gold, its floor tiling and walls accented by sparkling glass and silver accent pieces in a beautiful Scandinavian-styled lobby. Underneath it all was the clinical scent of alcohol, cleaners, and soap. Underneath that, chlorine disinfectant and bizarrely, a faint fragrance of strawberries.

The clinic director, Madame Gezelle, had worked at the clinic for a decade. With her trim figure, expansive mouth and sharp eyes, she struck me straightaway as nobody's fool.

Unlike me.

According to Madame Gezelle, there was no record of a baby born at the clinic in the past year who was connected to Abd-El-Kader or to anyone in Dubai or the Middle East. It was true that Madame Gezelle might have been lying to me, but in my experience, bald-faced lying is not a skill many people possess.

I thanked her and left the clinic, exhausted, shaken, bitterly disappointed but possessing one absolute conviction. And that was that the man who'd attacked me and who'd left my money, passport and phone untouched on the sidewalk when I'd flung them at him, was not a mugger.

Which meant his attack on me was not at all random.

35

I spent a good deal of time on the flight home beating myself up for having fallen for the mysterious text message sending me to Switzerland. Who would do this? Who would lead me to Switzerland into a trap? For what possible reason?

I thought of Abd-El-Kader. I'd met him two years ago and found him handsome, icy and ruthless. Even though in the end he'd allowed me to take Maddie after she was born, he'd done it for his own selfish reasons, not because he cared about appeasing me or doing the right thing.

He was the one who'd stolen Catherine's eggs and fertilized them with his own sperm. He was of course my first suspect for having sent the text to me. But this didn't seem like his style. For one thing, he lived in Dubai and was extremely powerful. He didn't need to send me back-off messages like this. Honestly, it would be easier to just have me killed.

Unless that's what my attacker intended?

But no, having a purse flung in his face was not enough to deter your typical assassin. He'd been sent to deliver a message, yes, but not a lethal one.

But if not from Abd-El-Kader, then who?

By the time I landed at CDG and turned my phone back on, a stream of text and phone messages showed up. Some were from Madeleine, but the vast majority from Jean-Marc. Honestly, I felt a shiver of guilt at not immediately calling him, but only a series of frantic messages from Geneviève would have galvanized me to respond immediately. Since Geneviève hadn't called, I could safely assume all was well with Robbie.

Since I didn't have carryon and there was no need to stop at baggage claim, I made my way through the terminal to the taxi stand outside. Normally, I would've taken the Metro to the eighth arrondissement, but I didn't feel like being jostled with a crowd of pushy Parisians on their way to work.

As I settled into the back of the taxi, I texted Geneviève that I was back and would see her shortly and then I called Jean-Marc. I figured, with any luck, he wouldn't know I'd been out of town. I hadn't been gone that long.

Before I put the call in, my mind revisited the mystery of who could have sent me on this wild goose chase and the idea —for some reason—popped into my mind that it might be Michel Leblanc.

I tend to pay attention to thoughts that just self-generate seemingly without triggers since I think they are prompted by my subconscious thoughts. Often, I'll come up with a lead with no real substance or evidence to support it and then go looking for reasons for it, and voila! I end up finding the reasons to support the theory.

It doesn't always work but I'd learned to trust my instincts. I gazed out the window of the cab as urban Paris passed by. The weather was still fine, clear and promising to be a hot June day. Speaking of trusting my instincts, I just couldn't imagine Jimmy Dodger, semi-thug and amateur bodyguard, having the clout or finesse to have been involved with my Swiss escapade.. Besides, how would he even have known about my search for the baby in the first place?

Leblanc, on the other hand, would at least have access to any kind of information there is. My search for Catherine's stolen eggs had not been a secret in the last two years. Besides, Joelle was well acquainted with the whole sad story—firsthand even. It would be completely like her to tell Leblanc about my search for the stolen eggs so he could use it against me.

Plus, he would have the connections to hire someone to ambush me outside of France.

Satisfied that this was at least a practical possibility and one I'd need to explore further—since if he was trying to sideline me or warn me, what was he afraid of if not that I might get close to information surrounding Ethan's death?—I put the call in to Jean-Marc. He answered on the first ring.

"Where have you been?" he said sharply. "I've been calling you all morning."

Instantly, I could tell by the tone of his voice that he wasn't merely peeved.

"What is it?" I asked feeling the dread creep over me. "What's happened?"

"Madeleine was attacked early this morning."

36

I had the taxi take me from the airport straight to Madeleine's hotel. After I paid him, instead of going inside, I walked down the block to the café on rue de la Pépinière where I'd arranged to meet up with Jean-Marc first to discuss what happened to Madeline.

The café was not very far from my apartment, so I knew it well. It was small but always inviting with a myriad of different tables and chairs. The street outside the café was bustling with people, vehicles, skateboarders, scooters and bicycles.

Jean-Marc was seated at one of the terrace tables. I waved, knowing I was in the doghouse with him. He sat waiting for me, his posture erect and stiff. My steps slowed as I approached and saw the bandage across his nose. A deep cut bisected his lip, and one eye was puffy and dark.

It's hard to see such harm done to anyone but when you see someone you love—someone whose lips you've kissed and whose jaw you've caressed—well, let's just say, I almost felt as if it had been done to me, too.

"Jean-Marc," I said, my voice soft with horror. "What happened?"

He held up a hand forestalling any questions.

"Later," he said. "It's not related to the case."

There was something about the way he said it that made me know it was a lie. I don't know how I could tell that or why he would try to prevaricate. Maybe he was just so angry with me that he couldn't allow me the outrage and concern that any girlfriend deserved.

"We'll get all the details of the assault against Madeleine when we meet up with her," Jean-Marc said, his eyes cold and refusing to look at me. "But basically, she went out to get a bag of macarons at Ladurée on rue Saint-Honoré last night, not realizing it would be closed at ten at night, and a man stepped out of an alley."

"Where was Jimmy?"

"Unclear."

"And?"

He shrugged. "That's all I know other than the fact that she escaped her assailant with minor injuries. Do you want to tell me now where *you* were?"

I swallowed hard in embarrassment. Jean-Marc and Geneviève had been right all along. I *wasn't* rational when it came to Baby John. I'd essentially lied to them, turned off my phone to prevent them talking me out of it, and plunged head-first into what could have been a real disaster.

Because I had already imagined the scenario of Jean-Marc and Geneviève getting word of my death, and then imagined how they would be forced to tell Robbie and what would then happen to him, Jean-Marc didn't need to scold me. I was already blaming myself for my stupidity.

I looked at my hands and said nothing.

"I had Gilbert examine the video footage that I got from Étienne," he said gruffly.

"That was fast."

"He said it had been altered."

I sucked in a quick gulp of breath. "Altered, how?"

"He said the section of video after the time Désirée went into the Senator's room had been replaced with a stretch of video taken some other time, likely the day before."

"This means someone else went into Ethan's room after Désirée," I said.

"Well, we knew that didn't we?" Jean-Marc said briskly. "Otherwise, Désirée had to be our killer and we never believed she was."

I could see he was angry, but I wasn't sure it was about the video. Probably it was a combination of my going radio dark for the last twelve hours and him being taken in by someone he considered a reliable contact if not a friend.

"Okay, so this is good," I said encouragingly. "Someone is trying to cover up what he did."

"Clearly someone powerful," Jean-Marc pointed out.

"Yes, possibly," I said, a little more doubtfully. I wasn't sure how much leverage or power someone would need to turn off the hall camera. But then again, it would need to be turned back on before the housekeepers showed up. And the captured video would then have to be edited to make it look as if it was a continuous feed.

I hated to ask my next question and thankfully, Jean-Marc didn't make me.

"We should consider discounting all the information that Étienne told me," he said.

"He told us that Ethan called for an escort service," I suggested.

"Yes, but on the other hand, there is proof that he and Désirée had sex," Jean-Marc said. "So possibly that was the truth. In fact, in my experience, most liars mix their lies with a little truth," Jean-Marc said bitterly.

"Will you confront Étienne?"

"Probably."

We were silent for a few moments longer until I didn't think I could bear it another second.

"Look, Jean-Marc," I said with a sigh. "I'm sorry, okay? I thought I had a lead, and I went for it. I made an error in judgement."

"A lead on the Andrews case?"

I realized then that he already knew that my absence and lack of communication had nothing to do with the case. He would have called Geneviève as soon as he couldn't reach me, and she'd have told him where I went.

"Look, I'm a fool, okay?" I said miserably.

He didn't speak for a moment which seemed to adequately underscore his agreement.

"How did it happen?" he asked finally.

"I got a text," I said.

"Show me."

I opened my phone and scrolled down until I found it and handed my phone over. He read it and then handed it back to me.

"I don't know what's wrong with me," I said.

He pointed to the nasty abrasion on my elbow.

"Yes, it was all a setup," I said with a sigh. "Someone was waiting for me at the clinic."

"I do not know what to do with you, Claire," he said.

I knew he was upset when he used my first name instead of the endearment *chérie* that he normally called me.

"You are being warned off," he said. "You see that, yes? The question is, was it about the stolen embryo or the Andrews case?"

I looked at him and felt a shiver of hope. If, instead of Leblanc or whoever Ethan's killer was, it was the people who had John who'd sent me the text message, it might mean I was getting close to finding him. Why else would they attempt to trap and then thwart me? It was a warning, yes, but also a sign that I was on the right track!

Jean-Marc tossed down a few euros for our coffees and stood up.

"Let's go," he said. "Madeleine is waiting. If I were you, I'd have a decent excuse for why nobody could get in touch with you for the last twelve hours."

He walked to the edge of the terrace, hesitated as if considering going on ahead, but then stood and waited.

37

Madeleine met us at the door of her hotel room with a black eye and her arm in a sling. She burst into tears as soon as she saw me. I felt so bad about having let her down that I nearly did too.

As soon as I saw with my own eyes the evidence of my incredibly stupid, selfish, insane folly, I began to rethink the possibility that it was someone connected to the baby who'd sent the text to me. It made more sense that someone wanted me off the playing field on the Andrews case.

But did it make sense that Madeleine was attacked because I was out of town? There was no way I could've prevented what happened to her even if I had been in town.

"Come in," Madeleine said, her face pale.

Jimmy was lounging in the living room with one leg looped over the couch arm as if he lived there. His beady eyes narrowed and followed us as we entered the room.

"So where were *you* when all this was going down?" I asked him archly, feeling my anger transfer to this duplicitous cretin.

"No, Claire," Madeleine said hurriedly. "Jimmy's the one

who saved me! He was a half block behind me and when he saw what was happening, he scared the guy away."

I gave Jimmy a malignant look. As far as I was concerned, if your client has a black eye and a broken arm, you didn't do your job. Or maybe he was only a half a block away because he'd set the whole thing up?

Jean-Marc and I sat down in the living room.

"I'm so sorry this happened to you, Madeleine," I said. "Did you call the police?"

Madeleine looked at Jean-Marc and then back at me.

"Do you think I should? I thought you guys could handle it."

I wasn't sure what she thought Jean-Marc or I could do. We certainly couldn't look through the police data base or dust the alley for fingerprints. Even if we could, how could we possibly track down the man who attacked her?

"Did you get a good look at him?" Jean-Marc asked.

She shook her head. "He was wearing a ski mask."

I turned to Jimmy.

"Why didn't you go with her? Nobody would've attacked her if you'd been walking beside her instead of skulking in the shadows behind her."

"Claire, please," Madeleine said. "This isn't Jimmy's fault."

"What are you implying?" Jimmy said to me, swinging his leg off the couch arm, his face flushed with anger.

"I think I'm being pretty clear," I said acidly. "Your job is to protect her. Are you aware that she believes herself to be in danger from the people who killed her father?"

"Wait," Madeleine said. "So you don't really think I'm in danger?"

The look she gave me was one I might imagine on a puppy's face who'd just had its dinner snatched from him. Jean-Marc stood up and took me by my bad elbow to get me on my feet.

"She's not saying that," he said sternly, more to me than

Madeleine. He nodded in her direction, telling me to remove her to the kitchen so he could question Jimmy alone.

"Madeleine," I said, "can we make coffee? Do you mind?"

She looked surprised and then stood up, holding her sling carefully by her side.

"No, not at all," she said as we moved into the kitchenette.

∽

Jean-Marc looked around the hotel room, noting that the walls were adorned with copies of paintings by French Impressionists. However, the most arresting sight of course was the window that allowed a glimpse of the Eiffel Tower.

"Man, who cleaned your clock?" Jimmy said with a laugh. "They really worked you over, didn't they?"

Jean-Marc turned to Jimmy who was once more lounging among the plush pillows and throws on the sofa and forced his expression to remain neutral. The beating he'd endured at the hands of Leblanc's goons had been thorough but that hadn't been the humiliating part. After a trip to the emergency room for his broken nose and cuts, he'd had all night to recognize that it had been his ego that had made him take the chance that had ended in the ambush.

Nothing hurt worse than knowing you've been a fool, he thought. Not even two cracked ribs and a broken nose.

"But then there is you," he said to Jimmy. "And you are the hero of the hour, yes? Can you tell me how you rescued her? I am very interested."

Jimmy sat up straight and rubbed his hands together in anticipation of telling his story.

"Well, it was my afternoon off and I was just going to go do some stuff when all of a sudden I see Madeleine with this guy down the block. So I run after them and yell out, 'Leave her alone!' and then I let him get away off and because I wanted to make sure Madeleine was okay."

Jean-Marc stared at him. There was absolutely nothing genuine about that outburst. It was as forced and rehearsed as if he'd been reading it from a script.

"So you never saw his face?" he asked.

"I saw it when I punched him."

"You hit him?"

"Sure, I did. Twice! Once in the face and once in the stomach!"

He is going off script.

"What did he look like?" Jean-Marc asked.

"Huh?"

"His face. You say you punched him in his face. Can you describe him?"

"I'm not good with faces."

"*D'accord.* Was he white? Black? Old? Young?"

"He was black and young. Skinny with a big Afro."

He's making this up.

"I see."

"And tats. And a big scar down his cheek."

"Sounds like a scary guy. What was he doing with Madeleine?"

"What do you mean?"

"I mean, was he trying to snatch her purse or was he trying to drag her into the alley?"

Jimmy scratched his chin and looked dumbfounded. Whoever had coached him had left out the answers to those questions.

"Never mind," Jean-Marc said, now starting to believe that if there *had* been an assailant, he was probably somebody Jimmy knew well.

"Remind me again," Jean-Marc said. "What street was it?"

Jimmy frowned. "Rue something," he said. "Maybe that road with the big tower?"

As soon as Madeline and I stepped back into the living room with a small tray of four coffees (she'd insisted on making one for Jimmy too), I could feel the tension snapping in the air between Jimmy and Jean-Marc. I don't know what Jean-Marc had asked the bodyguard, but whatever it was, it had made the younger man very uncomfortable.

Jean-Marc took his coffee but as Jimmy reached for his, Jean-Marc stopped him.

"You won't be needing that," Jean-Marc said. "In fact, your services are suspended. Pack your bags. Don't leave France, and give me a number where you can be reached."

"You can't do that!" Jimmy said angrily, standing up to face Jean-Marc but pointing at me. "It's not my fault she went to Switzerland on a wild goose chase and Madeleine nearly got mugged!"

I turned to him.

"How did you know that?" I asked.

"Oh, bug off," he snarled.

"I think she's asked a very good question," Jean-Marc said. "How did you know she was in Switzerland?"

"I don't know what you're talking about!" Jimmy said, looking guiltily from me to Madeleine.

"What are they saying, Jimmy?" Madeleine asked shrilly. "Do you know something about what's going on?"

"I don't know anything!" he said loudly, almost desperately. "I only know you tried calling her a thousand times and she didn't answer her phone."

"Was it you who sent me the text telling me to go to Basel?" I asked him.

"What? No! You're out of your mind!"

"Then how did you know where I was?"

He took an agitated step toward me, his eyes drilling into mine, his fists balled up at his side.

"Back off, lady," he snarled.

Jean-Marc was between us in a blink of an eye. What happened next was blocked from my sight by Jean-Marc's body —such that I only heard the sound of a fist hitting hard flesh and then the building-shaking thud of Jimmy's body as it hit the floor.

38

The rest of the visit was hardly what I'd call constructive. Madeline was even more upset than she had been moments before, torn between wanting to administer to Jimmy and to apologize to Jean-Marc who was rubbing his fist like he'd just punched a brick wall. With the size and solidity of the man he'd just decked, that was a pretty fair assessment.

I was clear on two things at this point. One was that Jimmy was not to be trusted and the second was that Madeleine really *was* being targeted. Which, I have to say, I hadn't seriously believed up to now. But after her experience with the attacker in the alley, it was finally becoming clear to me that she might have a point about someone wanting to harm her. I was glad I realized that before it was too late.

Make that three things. Something was going on with Jean-Marc. He was angry and he was using Jimmy as a convenient excuse to get that anger off his chest. Something told me the thing he was angriest about was the bad Intel he'd gotten from his friend Étienne. Or possibly it was my flying to Basel in the middle of the night without telling him. A toss-up, really.

As soon as Jimmy was on his feet, Jean-Marc escorted him out into the hall while I helped Madeleine pack her bags. After Jimmy admitted he knew where I was last night, I was nearly jumping out of my skin with the need to question him more completely.

He knew about Switzerland.

Is he working for Leblanc?

If that was true it meant that the text I'd been sent really did have nothing to do with finding Baby John. I forced down the disappointment of that theory the best I could, at least for now.

But Jimmy still hadn't admitted to sending me the text. Neither would he explain how it was he knew about it. I couldn't imagine my being sent on a wild goose chase to Switzerland could seriously be connected to Madeleine's attack in any way.

Whether I was in town or not wouldn't hardly have affected the attack happening one way or another. But then why was I sent that text message?

"I don't want to be a burden," Madeleine said shakily as she watched me place her things in a suitcase.

"You're not," I said. "Did the hospital give you something for pain?"

She nodded her head toward the bathroom, and I went in and scraped all her toiletries and pain pills into her cosmetic bag.

"Are you sure we need to do this?" she asked. "I feel terrible about Jimmy."

"Jimmy is not your friend," I said firmly as I came out of the bathroom.

"But he saved me," Madeleine said in a fretful voice.

Or he wanted you to think he did.

"He knew I'd been sent on a wild goose chase to Basel," I said. "Maybe he even set it up himself. And he refuses to tell us the truth."

And that's before we even talk about the fact that his DNA was found on the murder weapon that killed your father.

"Wait. You don't think Jimmy had anything to do with my father's death?"

She looked at me, her eyes wide with fear and vulnerability. Incredibly, I could see she still wasn't ready to entertain the notion.

"It's early days yet," I said. "Let's see where all the leads go first, okay? Meanwhile, I want you to stay with me at my place, okay?"

It would be crowded with two extra people, but I couldn't hole up in a hotel room with Madeleine because of Robbie. He needed his routine and I needed to try to keep his life as normal as possible.

Sometimes when I look back on my reasonings for the things I did, I just want to laugh.

Unless I start to cry first.

39

That night felt like a symphony of love and laughter in my apartment. I know that sounds corny, but it was true. First, the exquisite aroma of the dinner Jean-Marc was making—roast potatoes and chicken—wafted into the living room and seemed to wrap around each of us, drawing us in and comforting us.

I sat on the couch with Madeleine who was watching Robbie with complete delight as she continually touched her stomach. Robbie of course was intent on showing our visitor every toy and game he owned. But even so, his laughter and good mood—in spite of the reason that Madeleine was with us for the night—seemed to fill the apartment with a comforting family feel that is difficult to create with just two people.

As Jean-Marc cooked, I watched him also begin to relax and his anger at me soften so that by the time we all sat down to dinner like one big family, he was smiling and teasing Robbie as usual. Even better, there was at least one glance in my direction—even if it was accompanied by a stoic smile—that told me I was forgiven.

As it turned out, after we'd split up earlier while I took

Madeleine back to my apartment, Jean-Marc had a fairly successful afternoon. The husband of our client had indeed shown up at his apartment that afternoon with the French teacher of one of his daughters. Jean-Marc photographed the two of them going into the apartment and then left.

The photos weren't enough to prove infidelity, but they would provide our client and her lawyer with ammunition to hammer out divorce details that favored her. I was glad we'd done what we were being paid to do, but again, I found myself feeling queasy about the manner in which we had to do it.

Jean-Marc had literally hidden in the bushes to catch the man doing what his heart had told him to do. Now that may be my romanticized version of the situation but it's how I keep my sanity. As far as I'm concerned, a serial adulterer gets what's coming to him—loss of wife, and children, and hopefully, income. But if the marriage had grown cold? If he'd truly fallen in love with someone else? Who am I to be the instrument that punished him for a matter of the heart?

I shook my head to try to dissipate these thoughts, which in the end, didn't benefit me or the profession I was in. When I'd called his wife earlier this evening to report our successful findings, she'd hardly been happy about the photographs which I then emailed to her.

It's a funny job when you do your job properly yet it results in your client weeping in bitter disappointment and self-recrimination.

Later that evening, after Madeleine had gone to bed in Robbie's bedroom, Jean-Marc was snoring on the couch, and Robbie was sound asleep in my bed with Izzy by his side, I found I couldn't sleep. The more I thought about what was bothering me in particular, the more I realized it was the fact that Jimmy had somehow known about my search for Baby John. I racked my brain as to how that could be.

It was true that I'd mentioned the stolen egg situation to Madeleine. She was the obvious source for Jimmy knowing about it. But there were other possibilities too, especially if Jimmy was at all connected to the criminal element as I suspected he was.

On the other hand, I hadn't kept my search a secret this past year. I'd never have gotten anywhere if I hadn't been vocal and very public about asking questions that might lead me to find the baby.

I decided to discount the idea that Jimmy was working for Leblanc. I'm not sure how that made sense since I was relatively sure Leblanc had his own thugs and didn't need to hire any visiting American ones.

Bottom line, at least at this point in the game, there was no telling *how* Jimmy had come by the information about Catherine's stolen eggs and the fact that I was looking for Baby John. But even an idiot could see that it was an obvious tool to use against me.

I shivered as I thought about the man with the crowbar waiting for me at the clinic. Being killed out of the country would've made finding my killer all the harder. I'm sure Jean-Marc would've tried his best to track him down but, in the end, it would've been just one more unsolved homicide chalked up in the books. I shook this morbid and ultimately useless thought from my head and opened my laptop for a little late-night research.

First, I scrolled through more wrongdoings by Leblanc that had been suggested in the media but for which he'd never been charged, and I began to see a picture that seemed to show he surely had someone in the police in his pocket. Aside from a logical assumption, given what I was seeing online, there was of course no real evidence for that. And I didn't have the time or inclination to do the work necessary to pull at the threads to see what came unraveled. Especially not with Jean-Marc on board in the agency. If Leblanc's creature was someone Jean-Marc knew or, God forbid, a friend, it would not be worth the benefit of finding out.

At least not for me and my relationship with Jean-Marc.

After reading page after page of pretty much the same thing, I switched over to looking at Ethan's webpage since I hadn't drilled down very far before tonight. A person's webpage—especially a celebrity or political figure—is not where one might go to find the truth. I knew that. Every page on Ethan's website would have been scoured and sanitized until it was only a political copywriter's vision of what the ideal candidate might say or believe in.

After confirming that that was indeed all I was finding on Ethan's website, I did a broader Google search for him, as I had with Leblanc.

What group was the opposite of PETA, I wondered? Could there be a group out there that was the anti-woke cognate of people who felt animals didn't have rights or protection from deliberate pain?

I opened up an Internet browser again and googled for *PETA* and then *anti-PETA*.

I got very little. It seemed there was no group that was comfortable publicly announcing their desire to hurt animals.

Good thing, too.

There were plenty of people who were in favor of animal testing for reasons of health and medical benefits to people, and there were a few religious nut cakes out there happy to rant about how animals didn't have souls.

While I was looking, I remembered Jean-Marc's reaction this afternoon when he'd insisted he interview Jimmy instead of me. It had been nice to see him get all protective of me. Last January when we first decided to work together, I'd wondered—worried—how that would work. Both of us had such different styles and backgrounds. The crooked Paris cop and the free-wheeling American PI.

It shouldn't work. It doesn't at all on paper. But it does work.

On top of that, the working arrangement gave us copious built-in opportunities to spend time together, time we needed to help repair our relationship.

I turned back to my laptop. I was getting nowhere with my idea of an anti-PETA group. I switched back to Ethan's webpage because I remembered an area on it for comments. Perhaps an irate constituent had written in? It wasn't much to go on, but in my experience, leads can be found in the least likely of places —and can blow a case wide open.

When I opened up Ethan's webpage, I typed *animal rights bill* in the search bar.

And nothing came up.

Frowning, I typed in *animal experiments for science bill*.

Again, nothing.

What the heck? If this was a favorite bill of his, wouldn't he be shouting it from the rooftops—or at least from his own webpage? I went to the side navigation bar that held the past six months of Ethan's *Letters to the People*.

I went back a full six months and skimmed every blog post, but I found absolutely nothing on animal rights or animal testing. What I did find was page after page of passionate diatribe —very nearly a screed—on the urgent need for the US to ban the use of nonrenewable energy sources.

I went to the search bar and typed in *energy sources*. This time, the page quickly populated with article after article on the subject of banning fossil fuels and other nonrenewable energy sources.

I stared at the first article that came up, an article from a vetted, respectable source, my mouth falling open in shock. Once I had the germ of the subject—which I hadn't had before —I put it into the search function and page after page came up.

I rubbed the base of my neck in confusion.

Did Madeleine lie to me about this? Why? Is it possible she doesn't know?

She seemed so passionate about her father and this bill. How could she have gotten this wrong? But what sense did it make to lie about it if that's what she did?

Banning fossil fuels might possibly be considered controversial, although it certainly wasn't a new idea and wasn't likely to get enough support to seriously threaten anyone.

This meant that Madeleine had gotten everything completely wrong about what her father was doing.

Or that she was lying.

40

The next morning, I decided to let Madeleine sleep in. She was exhausted and I could tell from how pale she was that she was also still in a certain amount of physical pain. I covered the kitchen table with an array of breakfast foods, croissants, jam, a couple of *pains au chocolat*, and a heated carafe of coffee and wrote her a note telling her I'd be back before lunch. Then I scribbled down my phone number although I knew she already had it.

Today was one of the French school system's many unexplained school holidays so I would need to drop Robbie off at Geneviève's for the morning. Jean-Marc had already gone out to run a quick errand and would meet me later. Robbie who had Izzy on a leash waited for me in the hallway as I locked up before going down to Geneviève's apartment.

Geneviève was in the doorway with her little dog Mignon whom she'd gotten last year when its owner, one of the apartment residents, had died suddenly.

"We shouldn't be too long," I said to her as Robbie and Izzy ran into her apartment. I hated taking advantage of her. I knew she adored Robbie, but she was eighty-five years old and last minute babysitting is not what any eighty-five-year-old signs up for. At least Haley should be back in another week. I hadn't really spoken to her since my mad dash to Switzerland and I knew I needed to.

My goal today was to interview Ethan's bodyguard Roger O'Connell with Jean-Marc. After that, I'd bring lunch back to Madeleine and collect Robbie, while Jean-Marc finished up another case of a cheating spouse we were working.

I met up with Jean-Marc on the corner of rue de Laborde.

"Madeleine okay?" he asked.

"Still sleeping."

We headed down rue de la Pépinière, I glanced at him out of the corner of my eye. His face still looked pretty bruised, in fact it looked worse today than it had yesterday. I know he was angry at me yesterday but I'm pretty sure his refusal to tell me how he got the beating had more to do with his pride than anything else.

"I really would like to know how you got your nose broken," I said.

"It was a couple of Michel Leblanc's goons," he said.

I gasped and stopped walking, but Jean-Marc didn't stop so I had to hurry to catch up to him.

"Jean-Marc, that's terrible! Why?"

We stopped at the crosswalk facing boulevard Haussmann to wait for the light to cross. He lightly touched his nose.

"He is a powerful man who is not used to people interrogating him or making veiled threats."

"You made veiled threats?"

"Actually, I'm not sure how veiled they were."

"But sending his henchmen out after you!"

I felt my blood pressure rise just thinking about it.

"It might mean nothing in connection with the murder.

Leblanc is a proud man and not used to being spoken to in the way that I did."

"What a bastard."

We crossed the street and joined the scrum of people heading to the subterranean entrance of the Saint-Augustin Metro.

"Any thoughts about Jimmy?" I asked, knowing he would not want to linger on the topic of his beating.

"I wonder if he was the one who put the idea into Madeleine's head that she was in danger," he said.

I frowned. "For what purpose?"

"To keep her dependent on him? Maybe he was afraid she'd fire him after her father died."

"I don't know. Seems pretty sophisticated for someone like Jimmy."

"I don't think whatever he's up to, he's up to it alone."

I felt a chill at his words.

"And we have no idea who his accomplice may be," I said.

"I think it's more boss than accomplice," he said. "Jimmy doesn't strike me as the guy pulling the strings."

My thoughts went back to Michel Leblanc, but I didn't say anything. We had no proof. And even if we did, it appeared that the Paris Homicide division was uninterested in hearing about such things.

"I found out something interesting last night," I said to him as we stood on the platform waiting for the southbound train.

"Oh?"

"I was doing more research about Ethan's bill. You know, the one that Madeleine thinks is why he was killed?"

"And?" he said, scanning the subway crowd as if looking for snipers or pick pockets.

"I learned that while it was true that Ethan was advocating for a bill, it wasn't about using animals in scientific experiments. It was about banning the use of nonrenewable energy sources."

"How very strange."

"I know. I mean, it's mildly controversial, but certainly nothing anybody would get killed over, especially someone who's no longer in any sort of position of power. I guess it makes me doubt that it was his political agenda that got him killed."

"What are you saying?"

"Well, for starters, I'm wondering how it is that Madeleine doesn't know this?"

"Maybe she does."

"Exactly. In which case my real question is, why did she lie to me and say his bill was about animal experiments?"

We made our way down the wide stairs to the train platform.

"It sounds as if you have things to discuss with her," he said ominously.

41

The Hotel Cambon, where Roger O'Connell had moved to after the Sofitel Hotel was much less grand than where he and Ethan had been staying. But since this was Paris, it was still amazing in its own way, plus it faced the Tuileries gardens. So, not too bad.

The lobby was small but with a floor inlaid in pale white marble with gold flecks and punctuated by four arches with columns of matching marble.

O'Connell was waiting for us at a back table at the hotel bar where he sat with an International Herald and a cup of coffee. He stood up as we approached.

I'd not met him the night of the gala and hadn't thought anything of the fact that Madeleine had had her bodyguard there that night, but Ethan didn't. If what Stanley said was true, O'Connell was off duty that night.

We all shook hands and Jean-Marc and I sat at his table.

"So how long are you staying in Paris?" I asked as Jean-Marc signaled to the waiter to bring two more coffees.

O'Connell was burly and not terribly tall, but he had an engaging smile and a hint of mystery in his green eyes that in any other context might suggest he was playful or at least had a good sense of humor. He wore a plain blue t-shirt over jeans, and I detected a faint scent of tobacco which told me he'd just had a cigarette.

"I'm not really sure," he said. "I thought I should stay in case the police want to talk to me, but so far they haven't reached out."

I gave Jean-Marc a side glance. The fact the police hadn't even talked to the victim's personal bodyguard was egregious in its ineptitude.

"My condolences for your loss," I said.

Instantly, his eyes filled with tears, and he briskly wiped them away. Although he was a few years younger than me, I recognized the type, especially in America. Roger was a tough guy with a heart of mush. I could see him doing the difficult tasks necessary to keep the Senator safe and by the fact that he winced as he moved in his seat, I imagined that over the years that had cost him. But I could also see that he'd loved Ethan and losing him was nearly as painful for him as it was for the Senator's family.

"I still can't believe it," he said, shaking his head and staring into his coffee.

"What will you do now?"

He sighed heavily.

"When I get back home? Probably retire. I'm a little long in the tooth to apply for bodyguard jobs when there are so many young bucks around."

"Like Jimmy Dodger?"

He made a face.

"I will never understand why the Senator hired him for Maddie," he said. "You know the man has a record?"

"It's sealed," I said. "So technically he doesn't."

"*Technically* doesn't cut it when it's your own daughter, you know?" he said lifting an eyebrow at me.

"Did you tell the Senator that you disagreed with his decision?"

He let out a breath and I watched his shoulders deflate.

"I could speak my mind with Ethan. He knew what I thought. But honestly, he might have been right."

"About Jimmy?"

He nodded. "He's been with us for over a year now and I have to admit I might have been wrong. He's been okay. I don't know if the sex accusation against him was true or not but yeah, I think he'd do anything to protect Maddie."

"And that's pretty much what you want in a bodyguard," I said.

"Monsieur O'Connell," Jean-Marc said as he finished his coffee. "Can I ask where you were the night of the gala and why you were not there?"

"I wanted to be," he said with a grunt. "The Senator wanted me to take the night off."

"Any particular reason?" I asked.

He laughed.

"That's how he was. He wanted me to enjoy Paris. There's not a day goes by I don't hate myself for not being on duty that night."

"What could you have done really? You don't sleep in the same room with him, do you?"

"In my heart I know I let him down."

He tightened his jaw in an attempt to get control of his emotions. I didn't want to torture him any longer than I had to. But as we were getting ready to leave, I thought of one more question.

"Did you know anything about the Senator's political interests?" I asked. "Madeleine seemed to think he had a bill to protect animals in scientific experiments."

He shook his head.

"I know he cared a lot about the people in his district. I'm not surprised if he was into animal rights. He owned dogs and horses in his childhood in south Georgia. But I didn't really stay in tune with the politics side of things, so I couldn't tell you which bill."

"Okay, thanks," I said. "Absolute final question. Do you know if the Senator met up with Michel Leblanc while he was in Paris?"

Roger frowned as if trying to remember.

"I don't know," he said finally. "If he did, it wasn't while I was with him."

"Would he have ditched you to meet him privately?"

"No way," Roger said. "But if he really wanted to talk to the guy he wouldn't have to slip away from me."

"Why is that?"

He shrugged. "Because Leblanc was staying at our same hotel."

42

Following our interview with Roger, Jean-Marc and I debriefed on the corner of rue de la Santé which led to the street of the flat of the newly separated husband of one of our clients. Jean-Marc was planning to stake out the place to discover if said husband was meeting with anyone other than the two daughters the couple shared.

As I've mentioned before, what I do for a living is grubby work, but someone must do it and, fortunately for me, Jean-Marc doesn't seem to mind.

"So what do you think?" I said. "Don't you think it's suspicious that Joelle didn't mention to me that she and Leblanc were at the same hotel as Ethan that night?"

"We should've known. We should've checked that."

"Sure, but without a police credential, was the hotel really going to show us their guest register? Especially a minister in the French government?"

Jean-Marc blew out a frustrated breath and rubbed the back of his neck, a gesture I have seen from him many times over the years when he was trying to figure out where to go from here.

"We can't just let Leblanc off the hook," he said finally.

"Jean-Marc, he's already given you a warning."

The last thing I wanted was for Jean-Marc to approach Leblanc again. He hadn't just been roughed up by Leblanc's men, he'd been pummeled. All I could think was that it was the kind of thing someone would do who had something big to hide.

Like murder.

"He had means and motive," Jean-Marc said. "Plus, now that we know the hotel surveillance video is fake and that he was staying at the hotel, it means he had opportunity too."

"Maybe he also has an alibi," I said.

Jean-Marc looked at me, his eyes narrowed. "Your stepmother?"

"She was with him. And she's been trying to warn me off."

"Do you think she might support his alibi even if it isn't true?"

I shrugged helplessly.

"I don't trust her not to lie, if that's what you're asking," I said.

We stood there for a few more moments longer but when it became clear that no more clarity was coming from rehashing our interview, we went our separate ways.

Jean-Marc headed down rue de la Santé and I turned and headed back to the Metro station to take the fifteen minute train ride to my neighborhood station, and Poulet Tikka, a favorite Indian restaurant of mine which was only a few blocks from my apartment. I called in an order of butter chicken and veggie korma so that it was ready for me when I got there and then went immediately to Geneviève's apartment to pick up Robbie and Izzy.

My personal take on Roger O'Connell's show of grief over losing Ethan was that it was genuine. I'm a pretty good judge of people and my initial assessment of Mr. O'Connell was that losing his employer had hurt him on several different levels, including his ongoing employment.

Being a bodyguard or personal security for someone meant being a part of that person's life in a very intimate way, often offering not just protection but companionship too. Ethan and Roger had been together for a long time. They were both Southern. While I didn't get the chance to see them interact, there was no doubt in my mind that they were friends as well as employer and employee.

Gut instinct counts for a lot in my business and especially because of my disability I've honed my ability to accurately assess a person. I hadn't expected much in the way of a lead from talking to Roger, but I'd been surprised to learn that Leblanc had been at the hotel that night. Now I just needed to confirm what floor he'd been on.

When I got to Geneviève's apartment, Robbie was happily watching television and, since Madeleine hadn't called me in any kind of distress, and because I really felt like I'd been taking advantage of Geneviève lately, I took some time to debrief with her.

I settled in on the couch as Geneviève finished making coffee and brought in two mugs with a plate of profiteroles from her kitchen.

"So, Monsieur Robbie says you have a full house these days?" Geneviève asked with an arched eyebrow.

"Yes," I said. "A new client of ours had an altercation in the street yesterday and was pretty badly shaken up. It's just for a night or two."

"Robbie said Jean-Marc spent the night too?"

"He did. On the couch, yes."

After that I filled her in on Madeleine's story. With Haley out of the country, I couldn't be sure I wasn't going to need to rely on Geneviève for childcare a few more times in the coming days. The least I could do was keep her in the loop.

"I am sorry for her," Geneviève said, her expression suddenly distant and still.

While she was referring to Madeleine losing her father, but always on the edge of Geneviève's emotions these days was the sadness she bears due to her own family situation. Although widowed after many happy years of marriage, she has twin sons, one married and living in the States who called infrequently and who she rarely saw, the other with whom she was totally out of touch with.

Knowing Geneviève as I do, and what a purely loving person she is, I find the whole situation so incredibly sad—when I'm not royally pissed off about it.

"Do we have to go back yet?" Robbie asked me, his bottom lip sticking out in charming appeal. "My favorite show is about to come on."

"*Mamie* has things to do, Robbie," I said.

"It's all right," Geneviève said. "If he wants to stay, I'm happy to have him."

"Are you sure? He can watch his show upstairs in our apartment."

"No, it's fine. Esmé and I love when Robbie and Izzy come to visit," she said with a smile for the child.

As if on cue, little Esmé barked and wagged her stubby tail.

"Okay," I said. "But are you hungry? I've brought butter chicken."

"I already ate," Robbie said, already turning away to focus on his show in the other room.

I turned to Geneviève. "Are you sure you don't mind?"

"Positive."

Right then her phone rang, and she got up to answer it. When I realized she would be talking for a few minutes, I pulled my laptop out of my satchel. I didn't want to rush off as soon as Geneviève had agreed to babysit a little longer, but her chatting on the phone gave me a moment to check on something before I went upstairs.

I was still upset about Leblanc's goons roughing up Jean-Marc and was determined to call the man to task on it somehow. The fact that he was connected to Joelle only made the idea of it all the sweeter.

Thinking of Joelle made me think again of her reason for her pretending not to know Ethan. The more I thought about it, the more I began to question her answer to me. Because the fact was, when Ethan had walked up to us and greeted her, he'd been enthusiastic, not ashamed or wary.

If what Joelle said was true, his treatment of her at the gala did not make sense.

I tabled those questions for the moment, instead reminding myself that Joelle of course knew all about the stolen embryos. If Leblanc had mentioned to her that he'd prefer I was removed from the playing field somehow, Joelle would know exactly how to do that.

As for Députée Leblanc himself, from the few things I read on the Internet, he definitely had the kind of power—and the ruthless ambition that went with it—to set up an attack on me in a foreign city. Some things I'd discovered in my Internet research were probably not too far off base for most politicians but when you're neck deep in a murder investigation, it can make you look askance at even the most innocent rumors.

The tabloid headlines I'd found from the past decade had connected Leblanc's name with allegations of police corruption, rumors that he took money from government reserves to fund his lifestyle, and charges of taking campaign contributions from a disreputable, possibly criminal, billionaire—all unfortunately unproven and unsubstantiated.

Smoke, fire.

Geneviève came back into the living room just when I realized I should get the food upstairs before it got cold.

"Sorry about that," she said. "An old friend."

"No worries," I said, standing up. "I need to get upstairs anyway. I'll be down in an hour to collect them."

"That's fine," she said as she walked me to the door.

"Bye, Robbie!" I called. "See you in an hour!"

He didn't respond but I'd hardly expected him to. I turned to climb in the ancient elevator that I normally don't bother with. I think it was retrofitted into the building sometime back in the 1930's—definitely pre both wars—and I'm not sure that wasn't the last time it saw any kind of maintenance. As it was, my apartment was only one floor up and I usually walked it regardless of how tired I was.

Today, for whatever reason, I decided to risk plummeting to my death rather than haul two bags of curry thirty steps up a set of stairs. As soon as I got in the elevator, I was about to hold my breath and begin praying when my phone rang, and I saw it was Jean-Marc.

I wasn't expecting to hear from him until later this evening, so I pushed the elevator button for my floor, and accepted his call.

"Hey," I said. "Everything okay?"

"Yep, just calling to see how your houseguest is."

"I haven't seen her since you have," I said. "I'm just getting home."

My stomach tensed as the elevator began to rattle and shudder noisily before moving.

"Do you want me to come over tonight?" he asked.

I rode the elevator up, counting the seconds until we reached my floor.

"Absolutely," I said. "If that's okay."

"Shall I pick up dinner?"

The elevator made a jerking stop on my floor.

"I think we'll have plenty of leftovers," I said as I struggled to open the metal door. "I picked up Indian."

"Great."

"Listen, so have you thought any more about the fact that Leblanc was at Ethan's hotel?" I asked as I stepped out onto my floor. "We definitely need to talk to him again."

In the couple of hours since we'd discovered this information, I'd decided it was a valuable clue and one we'd really needed. Finally! A clue that moves us in a positive direction!

"Let's discuss it later," Jean-Marc said.

I was all the way down the hall and gearing up to argue the absolute necessity of doing this interview when I realized that my door was open.

I set down the bags of Indian food.

Jean-Marc was still speaking, but I wasn't hearing him anymore.

I wasn't hearing anything because all my senses were absorbed by the fact that there was a body lying in the foyer of my apartment.

A body lying in a pool of dark blood.

43

The body lay on its side, sprawled across my foyer, the puddle of blood surrounding the head and seeping into the cracks of the parquet flooring. An acrid scent of iron and death hung in the air. I felt a tremble of horror creeping up my arms and into my brain.

"Madeleine!" I screamed as I stepped over Jimmy's body into my apartment.

My heartbeat was thrashing in my ears as I ran to the guest room, my heart pounding in my throat, images of Madeleine lying dead across the bed racing through my brain. The bedroom door was closed. I flung it open and nearly whimpered with relief when I saw the room was empty.

I looked at the fire escape out the window and then turned to look again at the body in the foyer. It was impossible for me to tell if Madeleine had been dragged through there.

She's not dead, I told myself. *Focus on that. Kidnapped isn't killed.*

Whoever killed Jimmy had taken Madeleine with them.

I reached for my phone and called the police. Since I'd

gotten disconnected from Jean-Marc, I texted him telling him what had happened.

Then I took in a breath to get my bearings and regain my nerve. I knew I needed to take advantage of the few moments I had with the crime scene before the police arrived. I looked around my living room and tried to imagine why Jimmy was here in the apartment. Probably Madeleine had invited him.

Trying to check for fibers or any other kinds of clues was a little out of my wheelhouse and I was wary of doing anything that might contaminate the crime scene. However, I also knew that my only chance to find any clues about what had happened was *before* the crime scene techs arrived.

I didn't bother examining the body. The medical examiner would do a better job of that than I could. But I looked around my living room to see if anything was missing. Then I walked back to the guest room to see if anything of Madeleine's was not where it should be.

I also looked for a note.

I hate to say that I consciously looked for it because that would mean that a part of me wasn't sure this *was* a kidnapping. When I didn't find anything, I think I breathed a sigh of relief.

I stepped back into the living room with its gruesome evidence of violence and death. I felt sorry for poor Jimmy. There was no explanation that I could imagine that would account for why he would be killed.

None except he'd been trying to protect Madeleine when she was abducted.

I felt a throb in the back of my throat that I couldn't swallow away.

Jimmy had been doing his job. He'd failed at it. But he had given his life trying.

44

A cacophony of noise rang out from the apartment, echoing down the stairwell as the police focused their attention on the foyer in my apartment. And the dead body there.

I stood in the doorway of Geneviève's apartment, listening to the ticking of cameras photographing poor Jimmy from every angle, as well as the murmur of voices. A steady stream of police officers ran by Geneviève's apartment door hurriedly donning latex gloves, while forensic techs gathered evidence for analysis.

Jean-Marc arrived at about the same time his ex-colleagues from homicide did. I assumed, since he didn't approach them, that he believed he'd be relegated to the role of civilian. The two of us sat in Geneviève's apartment while Geneviève kept Robbie distracted, and while my apartment was systematically torn apart, photographed, and dusted.

I'd gone upstairs twice to try to talk to the person in charge —*Inspecteur Principal* Chantal Resnelle—and both times had been rudely instructed to wait downstairs. The last time I'd gone up, Robbie followed me and, to my extreme dismay, had glimpsed the sight of Jimmy's now thankfully draped body in our foyer.

"Why is that man sleeping on our floor?" he whispered at my elbow.

I was able to stop my shriek of horror just in time as I grabbed his hand and took him back downstairs.

"Just somebody who's had too much wine," I said.

"In the morning?"

"Yes, for some people it can be any time and we need to pray for them, right?"

Jean-Marc came running up the stairs panicked and obviously looking for Robbie.

"We're all good," I said to him. "Just going back to *Mamie's* for more cookies."

While Geneviève fed Robbie his cookies and kept him otherwise entertained, Jean-Marc and I stood in her doorway to bar any more escapes.

"I just can't believe this," I whispered to Jean-Marc. "What can it mean? Jimmy was our lead suspect. What does it mean that someone killed him? Was it the same person who killed Ethan?"

Jean-Marc just shook his head. He didn't often put forth theories or speculate. It made us a good partnership since that was practically all I do.

"Who would kidnap her? For what reason?" I asked.

"I don't know, *chérie*."

"I just keep thinking, *what if Robbie had been in the apartment*?"

"I know."

"Remember Ethan's hotel room was searched. And he was tortured before he died. Does Madeleine have information that someone wants?"

"If she does, I don't think she knows she does," Jean-Marc said.

We were quiet for a moment listening to the sounds of the police activity on the floor above us.

"I feel terrible," I said. "I didn't really think anyone was out to get her."

"Nor me, *chérie*."

But knowing that even Jean-Marc hadn't thought Madeleine's fears were justified didn't make me feel any better.

After a few moments, one of the detectives from upstairs came downstairs.

"Do you want me to step outside?" Jean-Marc asked the detective.

"Do you intend to speak while I get her statement?"

"*Non.*"

"Then, you may stay."

The detective introduced himself to me as *Inspecteur* Victor Durand. I immediately asked if we could talk in the hallway since my grandson was in the apartment. Durand agreed and the three of us stepped outside.

I quickly outlined what had happened—how I'd come home and at what time.

"I went upstairs, saw that my door was open and saw the body. Then I called you."

Durand nodded. "Did you touch anything?"

I hesitated. "No," I said.

"Did you enter the apartment?"

I sighed and saw Jean-Marc turn to look at me since I hadn't yet mentioned to him that I'd looked around before I called the police. And since I knew that they might be able to tell I'd done that, I decided to be honest about it.

"Look, I was afraid that Madeleine might be injured somewhere in the apartment," I said.

The detective frowned. "So, you went inside?"

"I told you. I had to."

The detective blew out a frustrated snort. "Did you step—?"

"I was very careful where I stepped. I went nowhere near Jimmy's body."

"You knew the victim?" Durand asked.

"Yes, he was the hired protection for the woman who was staying with me, Madeleine Andrews, who, as I told the dispatcher, is missing. Are you in touch with the American embassy? I can give you a contact number for Stanley Cole. He's the diplomatic coordinator there. Madeleine is an American citizen—"

The detective snapped his notebook shut and gave Jean-Marc an inscrutable look before turning to me.

"You may be called to come downtown to give a more detailed statement," he said.

"You don't want the Embassy contact information?" I asked.

"We have everything we need."

Then he turned and walked back upstairs, leaving me and Jean-Marc standing in the hallway feeling dismissed. Jean-Marc turned to me as soon as Durand was out of earshot.

"You stepped over the body and went into your apartment?"

His eyes widened as he stared at me in disbelief.

"I had to!" I said. "What if Madeleine had been in the bedroom bleeding out?"

"Yes, yes, all right." He ran a hand through his hair, always a sure sign that he was frustrated.

"Now what?" I asked as I stared up the stairs where the detective had gone.

"You probably should call the embassy yourself," Jean-Marc said. "Somehow I don't think the Paris police are going to go in that direction."

45

The hotel Robbie, Geneviève and I moved to was on rue du Grand Prieuré not far from Père Lachaise cemetery. It was fine for our needs, small but quaint, with moonlight lavender walls, white wood faux antique furniture, and several framed posters of Paris landmarks on the walls. It had a kitchenette, small dining area and two adjoining bedrooms.

I called Stanley before we left the apartment, and he was floored when I told him what had happened. He asked me if I thought the cops were doing everything they could. The fact that he even asked made me think Stanley was of the same mind as Jean-Marc and I that they likely wouldn't.

He promised he'd reach out to Madeleine's mother Dilly as soon as he hung up with me. I didn't envy him that call.

"Just tell her you have every confidence in the police finding her," I'd urged him.

"In other words, lie," he responded.

"For heaven's sake, yes."

Once we'd settled into the hotel, Geneviève kept Robbie engaged with a game he liked to play on his electronic tablet, allowing me and Jean-Marc to debrief over the terrible events of the day.

As I'd said to Stanley, my main concern was that I didn't think the police really cared about finding Madeleine. I didn't know if they were complicit or merely out of their depth.

Jean-Marc and I settled onto the little bistro chairs on the small balcony overlooking a courtyard. As soon as we shut the sliding glass door separating us from the hotel room, I wasted no time asking the question on my mind.

"Do you think Resnelle is crooked?"

Jean-Marc rubbed a hand over his face and looked out over the courtyard, his eyes darting everywhere at once as his brain worked.

"I don't know, Claire," he said finally. "I didn't really know her. She came after me."

"Surely you've heard things?"

"I've heard that she's tough and maybe inflexible," he said. "Whether or not she's taking bribes is not something anyone in the department would know about."

"Unless they were crooked too," I said.

He gave me a frustrated look but didn't try to defend anyone.

"What happens next?" I asked, although I was fairly sure I knew.

"They will set up an outpost with the police and the FBI in Atlanta at Madeleine's mother's house for when the ransom request comes in."

I blew out an exasperated breath. "So we just wait?"

"Basically."

I turned away, to look down on the peaceful little courtyard, filled with potted geraniums. My thoughts were churning in overtime.

"It occurs to me that it would've been a lot easier for whoever killed Jimmy to just kill Madeleine too," I said.

"I thought about that," he said. "But remember, her father's room was ransacked, and he himself tortured."

I realized with a sickening feeling that the kidnappers probably hadn't killed Madeleine because they thought she knew something—the same something they thought her father had known.

"Have we gotten this all wrong, Jean-Marc?" I asked. "Was Madeleine the target all along?"

"I don't know, *cherie*."

"It's just that there are so many holes in everything she's told me. Maybe she *does* know something but didn't trust me to tell me."

The golden light of the setting sun reflected off the rooftops around us. I could hear the buzz of city traffic one street over, and the distant laughter of children, up late and playing on the cobblestone streets or perhaps one of the many parks we'd passed on our walk to the hotel. I turned my head at the sound of a faint jangle of bells as a bicycle sailed by on the street beneath us.

Guilt burned in my stomach like acid when I thought of Jimmy. We'd definitely gotten him wrong. I think because he was so rude and thuggish, I just didn't see that, like Roger O'Connell had observed, he was devoted to protecting Madeleine.

"I feel sick about Jimmy," I said.

"Don't be so hard on yourself. Remember he had a sealed juvenile record for sexual assault."

"I know," I said. "But people can change."

He snorted and I gave him a rebuking look.

"Ethan obviously thought so," I said, "or he wouldn't have hired him to protect his daughter."

"If you say so. Me, I think politicians have a singular and self-serving way of viewing the world."

"You think this is about optics?"

"I think it might have looked good for the Senator to be seen as compassionate to at least a certain segment of his constituents."

Jean-Marc was even more cynical than I'd realized. I felt a wave of discouragement. I literally had no idea of how to move forward from here.

And Madeleine was counting on someone doing something to move forward.

"We've got no leads, no clues, and Madeleine is in imminent danger," I said, feeling my chest tighten uncomfortably. "Is there any real chance the police are working to find her?"

"I'm sure they don't want the murder of a prominent American statesman *and* the kidnapping of his daughter to sit on the front page of *Le Figaro* for too long," he said. "They'll try to find her."

"At least they can't fake this," I said. "Nominating a likely suspect for Ethan's murder is one thing. But if they fail to find Madeleine alive, there's no spin they can put on it that isn't disastrous."

"They will try, *chérie*. I'm sure of it."

I heard his words, but they didn't help. And I think they didn't help because deep down I just couldn't believe them.

46

An hour later, Geneviève lay down for a late nap, and Jean-Marc took Robbie and the dogs to one of the parks that we'd seen earlier. Robbie was up much later than he was ever allowed but I could tell he was wired. Short of drugging him, there was no way anyone was going to get any sleep unless he was able to run off a little steam.

While they were gone, I called David Fontaine again. It wasn't that I was necessarily keeping the call from Jean-Marc—even though David and I had dated over Christmas—but I got the feeling that Jean-Marc was feeling less than confident these days. The last thing I wanted to do was goad him into getting beat up again because he was trying to prove his worth and wasn't able or willing to judge the signs of danger.

"Hey, David," I said, when I reached him.

As a public defender, David was run ragged all the time. Forget ever having time for a wife and family. He barely had time for friends.

That tended to be an undesirable trait in a potential boyfriend. But for a solicitor, I think you want an obsessed workaholic on your team. But maybe that's just me.

"What do you need?" he asked.

I could tell when he answered that he was doing three things at once.

"I need to talk to Désirée again," I said. "I just need to ask her one question."

"Can you tell me the question and I'll ask her?"

When I hesitated, he sighed heavily.

"If I apply to have you talk to her," he explained, "there's this whole process I must go through. I must submit your name to the homicide department. It might be easier—"

"You've convinced me," I said. "Ask her if she remembered seeing anyone she recognized in the Sofitel hotel lobby that night."

"There were many well-known people there that night," David reminded me.

"Ask her if there was anyone there who she knew personally."

"You mean, as a client?"

"Yes."

He was silent for a moment, and I got the impression he was jotting down my question.

"When do you think—" I started to ask.

"I'll call you back in an hour," he said and hung up.

Thirty minutes later, Geneviève and Jean-Marc with Robbie and the dogs converged into the dining area of the hotel room, the scent of chicken makhani reaching to every corner of the room. Robbie looked glassy-eyed, and I was pretty sure he wasn't going to make it through dinner before he collapsed.

I envied the easy exhaustion of youth. There have been so many nights when I was so weary, I was literally seeing double. Yet I still couldn't fall asleep.

"Mm-mm!" I said as Jean-Marc set the bag of take-out on the dining room table. "What did you get? Smells amazing."

"We got butter chicken and tandoori chicken!" Robbie said. "And we saw a man with a monkey making music."

"My," I said as I pulled the boxes of Indian food out of the bag. "Such an upscale neighborhood we've moved into."

"Can we move here, Grammy?" Robbie asked excitedly.

"Wash your hands, darling," I said as I caught Jean-Marc's eye over Robbie's head. He grinned at me, but I saw the weariness in his face, too.

An hour later, the food was eaten, the dogs had gone out one last time, and Robbie never made it to the rice pudding before Jean-Marc carried him sound asleep to the bed in the other room.

Geneviève had been quiet all evening, but she insisted she was fine and soon retired to her own room a little after Robbie did.

I hated uprooting her from her apartment like this. In fact, it seemed as if I'd been doing that ever since I dropped into her life—four and a half years ago. I know she claimed the activity and excitement kept her young, but honestly, I was seeing much more disruption and weariness than engagement recently.

As Jean-Marc was throwing out the takeout containers, my phone rang, and I saw it was David. I stepped onto the balcony but kept the door open. Jean-Marc turned to watch me and then, after drying his hands, joined me outside. I put the phone speaker on.

"I've got you on speaker, David," I said. "I'm here with Jean-Marc LaRue."

"Hello, LaRue," David said.

"Fontaine," Jean-Marc said.

"I talked to Désirée," David said. "And I think I got more than you asked for."

I glanced at Jean-Marc and his eyebrows shot up into his hairline.

"What did she say?" I asked.

"She said she was starting to get bits of her memory of that night back. She remembered that one of the docs at the hospital told her she'd been roofied, but the forensic report doesn't support that."

"Okay," I said, frowning. "What else?"

"She did remember seeing someone taking the elevator up to the third floor—"

That was Ethan's floor. I felt a burst of excitement.

"—and she confirmed that he was one of her clients from a few years ago."

"Did she describe him?"

"She did better than that. She identified him. It was Michel Leblanc."

47

The next morning, the sound of the lamp breaking followed by two dogs barking was nearly the final straw for Jean-Marc. He left the kitchen where he'd been preparing breakfast and found Robbie standing beside the broken lamp on the floor.

"It was an accident!" Robbie said, his eyes wide with guilt.

Jean-Marc had been up for hours. He'd been scrolling through his police contacts to see if there was anyone he could call for an update on Jimmy's murder. At one point, he was tempted to call Étienne, but he was fairly certain he'd be lied to, and he wasn't sure he could trust himself not to confront Étienne on the faked surveillance video. Jean-Marc glanced over to see Claire at the dining room table on her laptop, oblivious to all the noise around her.

"Robbie," he said as Geneviève and her little dog came into the room from the second bedroom. "Help me with breakfast?"

"Why can't I go to the park?" Robbie said as Geneviève knelt on the carpet to pick up the bigger pieces of the broken lamp. "Izzy hasn't even been outside yet. She needs to wee!"

Claire stood up and quietly picked up a dog leash that was looped over the back of her chair.

"I'll take her," she said distractedly.

Jean-Marc tossed down a dish towel and went to where Geneviève was kneeling on the carpet.

"Let me do that," he said. "Why don't you and Claire take Robbie and the dogs downstairs?"

"Are we going to the park?" Robbie asked, jumping up and down.

"Perhaps in a bit, *mon vieux*," Jean-Marc said, as Claire hooked up both dogs to their leashes. "Are you all right, *chérie*?"

"Yes, of course," Claire said dully. "Come on, Robbie."

Jean-Marc took the leash from her.

"On second thought, you and Geneviève stay here," he said. "Monsieur Robbie and I will take the dogs out."

"To the park?" Robbie asked, snatching Izzy's leash from him.

Jean-Marc put a hand to Claire's cheek. "We will find her, *chérie*."

"I know," she said as she sat back down at the table in front of her laptop.

"I will go with you, Jean-Marc," Geneviève said, following Robbie and Mignon and Izzy out the door. "I could use some air."

Across from the hotel there was a tidy pocket park, encased in a hip-high wrought-iron fence. Robbie and Izzy instantly ran across the street to the park.

"He is an active child," Geneviève said. "He can't stay cooped up in a hotel room all day."

"It won't be that long."

"Measured in little boy hours," Geneviève said, "it is an eternity."

Jean-Marc crossed the street with her, feeling a sudden urge for a cigarette although he'd given them up years earlier.

The small park was dotted with flowers and lush greenery. Tall trees gave shade to the benches and cobblestone path that led to a small pond. Geneviève and Robbie walked around the gravel path and Jean-Marc sat on a bench. He pulled out his phone and called Claire.

"I'm glad you called," she said breathlessly. "I need to run an errand."

Although Jean-Marc was glad to hear her more animated than when he'd just left her, something in her tone worried him.

"What kind of errand?" he asked.

"Look, Jean-Marc, don't get all nineteen fifties on me, okay? I have to do this, and you can't come."

"I'm listening," Jean-Marc said in a slow, measured voice.

"I need to talk to Michel Leblanc."

"Absolutely not."

"Remember what I said about the nineteen fifties? So just stop it. I'm a professional private investigator—"

"In her mid-sixties."

"How dare you! So are *you* for that matter! And I don't want to argue with you about this. Someone needs to talk to the man and it can't be you. Are we at least agreed on that?"

Jean-Marc growled and turned away as he watched Robbie and Geneviève stroll down the path, stopping now and then to point out a squirrel or some other interesting feature.

"Look, we knew he was at the hotel and now we have an eyewitness who saw him take the elevator up to Ethan's floor," she said. "We know the video was falsified so there's every reason to think he went to Ethan's room."

"He wouldn't do his own dirty work!" Jean-Marc said.

"We don't know that," Claire said. "Why else would he go up there?"

"Perhaps his room was on that floor."

"It still warrants another conversation," she said, her tone reasonable. "I'll be there in broad daylight. Leblanc is a seated member of the French Senate. He won't risk attacking an American national. I've got the US Embassy behind me."

Jean-Marc knew she was at least partially right. They did need to talk to Leblanc again. Especially now that they knew he'd been at the hotel that night. And that he'd seen Désirée. All of which he'd conveniently not mentioned up to now.

"Turn your phone recorder on," he said.

"I will."

"Don't call for an appointment. The surprise element is your best approach."

"Agreed."

"Charm him first."

"Jean-Marc, I know how to question a suspect."

"He's powerful, Claire. He has people in high places to protect him."

"You mean like Chief *Inspecteur* Resnelle?"

Jean-Marc blew out a breath.

"I don't know if it's her specifically that he has in his pocket, but it will be someone inside."

"I'll be fine, Jean-Marc."

"Call me as soon as you're done. If you don't call within the hour—"

"You need to give me time to get there! I'll call you. But if you don't hear from me by…three o'clock, then call me."

Jean-Marc's jaw tensed and he blew out a frustrated breath. He hated every part of this. It occurred to him that he could go to the Palais Bourbon himself and wait across the street. That made him feel better.

Geneviève and Robbie looped back around the path until they stood in front of him.

"All good?" Jean-Marc asked as he stood up.

"Actually," Geneviève said, "I think Monsieur Robbie and I have an idea."

Jean-Marc looked from one to the other before putting his hands on his hips.

"Well, then," he said. "Let's hear it."

Thirty minutes later, Geneviève and Robbie had packed a satchel for the visit to a public swimming pool two blocks from the hotel. Claire had already left for her meeting with Leblanc and Jean-Marc was just waiting for Geneviève and Robbie to leave so he could follow her.

He was confident that the indoor community pool was secure, but he'd walk them to the front door to make sure they got there safely.

"You'll call when you're ready to come back?" he asked Geneviève.

"Yes, Jean-Marc," she said. "But I'm sure we don't need a police escort."

"Nonetheless," he said. "you'll have one. He turned to Robbie. "And you will behave, *oui?*"

Robbie gave him an indignant look. "Of course."

"We'll be fine," Geneviève said as she tousled the top of her little dog, Esmé. "And we won't be long."

After walking the two of them to the indoor pool—a tall modern looking building with streams of children and their handlers going in and out of it—Jean-Marc walked back in the direction of the Latin Quarter. His plan was to take a taxi to the Palais Bourbon to make up for the time he'd lost in order to catch up with Claire. As he hurried down the block, he felt his phone vibrating in his pocket. He pulled it out and saw he was getting a phone call from a number from within the police department.

He felt a stab of suspicion in his gut. Why would anyone call him from there and not use their own number? They wouldn't unless whomever was calling was trying to be covert.

"*Allo?*" he said, answering warily.

"Jean-Marc?" the woman's breathless voice said. "I need to meet with you."

He hesitated.

"May I ask why?" he asked, setting his jaw tensely.

"I don't have time to explain it to you. An hour from now, Square Paul Langevin."

The line disconnected.

Jean-Marc stopped walking and stared at his blank phone screen. There was no doubt in his mind that it was a trap. He touched the bruises on his face and sighed.

But that didn't mean he wasn't going to meet her.

48

Leblanc walked out to the waiting room to greet me. I smiled and stood up as if expecting to follow him back into his office. I'd told his receptionist that I was Michel's girlfriend from Lyons. I thought that was a safe bet since he was such a sleaze and he travels a good bit.

Sure enough, when he came out to the waiting room with a worried look on his face, he saw he'd been fooled. But he was just relieved enough that I wasn't his girlfriend from Lyons, that he gestured for me to follow him.

"Five minutes," he muttered over his shoulder as we walked down the hall.

The room he led me to was quite impressive. One wall was covered with floor to ceiling bookshelves stuffed with leather-bound books. The wall behind his desk was adorned with matted maps of all the countries of Europe. I'm pretty sure Hitler's office looked similar when he was planning to invade Europe.

Leblanc took his place behind his desk and folded his hands on top of it before regarding me almost primly.

"*Four* minutes," he said.

I sat in the single wooden chair facing the desk, making no show of hurrying. I noted there was also a small marble fireplace in the corner of the room with a small fire burning in the grate—*in June*. But of course Leblanc was all about appearances and nothing said *elegance* and style like an office fireplace, regardless of the season.

"I haven't heard from Joelle in a while," I said matter of factly. "How is she?"

My strategy, such as it was, was to remind him that I was at least nominally related to his current girlfriend. It was true that Joelle had warned me off him—three times now—but I couldn't help thinking that Leblanc might at least hesitate to hurt me because of my connection to her.

That was only a gut feeling and nothing I'd bet my life on, especially after what happened to Jean-Marc, but I figured mentioning her couldn't hurt.

Leblanc leaned back in his chair and then reached into his pocket and drew out a packet of cigarettes. He shook one out and placed it languidly between his lips. He paused for a moment and then reached in his desk for a lighter which he flicked open. With the grace of a practiced hand, he lit the cigarette and inhaled deeply, letting the smoke drift lazily out of his mouth where it slowly made its way over to me where I sat.

I smiled, determined that I wouldn't react by waving away the smoke.

"I thought the *Palais Bourbon* was a nonsmoking facility," I said sweetly.

"Three minutes," he said, sending another long puff of smoke my way.

I almost felt sorry for Joelle's involvement with this wretched man.

"I think you killed Ethan Andrews," I said.

I watched his face, but it was impossible to read. Maybe

that's why he started smoking. With all the sucking and blowing involved, it's quite difficult to tell if someone is also attempting to dissemble.

"I know you have a motive for wanting Ethan dead," I said.

"I'm curious to know what you think that might be."

"Because he torched you in the Pardeux Committee. From everything I've read, you were determined to be on that committee. One word in a certain ear, and you were no longer being considered. The press seems to believe it was Ethan who delivered that one word."

A wreathe of blue smoke shimmered between us, but his face hardened at my words.

"That was five years ago," he said.

"Ever hear that revenge is a dish best served cold?"

"Do you have proof of this preposterous accusation?"

I hesitated because all I had was circumstantial evidence and hearsay. But he was watching me closely as if wondering how much I knew. That told me that proof *was* out there. He just wanted to know if I'd found it.

"Show me your proof or I will call the gendarmes and have you removed," he said pleasantly, opening his hands as if he had just made me an amazing offer.

"How about the hotel surveillance footage that shows you outside of the Senator's door the night of the murder?"

This was a bluff since I not only had not seen anything on any video footage to suggest such a thing, but there was no witness to corroborate it either. But my bluffs have paid off in the past more than they haven't.

He snorted in derision.

"Does this footage show me entering his room? Or knocking on his door? If so, I will have my IT experts examine the footage to prove that you didn't tamper with it to falsely indict me. If so, you will go to prison, Madame. Your American Embassy will not be able to help you."

The way he said that made me think he had absolutely no love for Americans. It was a wonder he was able to bring himself to go to the US Club gala at all. His ambition for power and wealth must be off the charts if he could hold his nose to that extent.

Just then, my phone rang, and I saw it was Jean-Marc. Because Jean-Marc knew where I was, I was tempted to let it go to voicemail. But because I also knew he was with Robbie, I couldn't *not* take it. I held up a finger to Leblanc.

"One moment, *s'il vous plaît*," I said to him. His brows furrowed in suppressed indignation at my obvious affront.

"Yes?" I said tersely. "Kind of busy here."

I listened quietly to the information that Jean-Marc gave me —gleaned within the last few minutes from a contact within the Paris police department.

"I trust her, Claire," Jean-Marc said on the line. "I would bet my life that the information is good."

When he finished telling me his Intel, it was clear *why* he'd thought it important enough to interrupt my interview with Leblanc.

"Thank you," I said to him. "I'll be in touch."

I hung up and looked at Leblanc who was now glaring at me from across this desk.

"I can see your point about the video footage," I said. "You're right. It doesn't show you going into the senator's room, as you say."

"You were trying to trick me," he said, squaring his shoulders, his chin held high, his lips curled into a jeer. "Did you really expect me to break down and confess to a crime I did not commit?"

"Like I said, I admit, the video doesn't show you doing that. But I know you were there. I have an eyewitness."

"The prostitute?" he sneered.

"I was going to say Joelle," I said. "Or were you counting on her to give you an alibi? Honestly, I've found that it's very tricky lying to lie to the police to support someone with a false alibi. I personally think Joelle is an amazing woman on many different levels, but I'm not sure even she could pull that off. Were you counting on it?"

"I have a good mind to call your embassy and make a complaint. In fact, I think that's exactly what I'll do." He reached for the phone on his desk.

"Be my guest," I said. "Because you're right that the hotel's video footage does not show you doing anything wrong." I hesitated. "But I wonder how you feel about the kind of story that forensic accounting can tell? Would that be proof enough for you?"

I watched his face drain of blood as he stared at me, and I knew I had him.

49

The sun beat down onto the sidewalk outside the Palais Bourbon, reflecting off the parked chrome-plated cars, and glinting off metal awnings on the sidewalk cafes that lined the road.

It was all I could do not to laugh out loud, I felt so euphoric after my meeting with Leblanc. The information that Jean-Marc had called to give me in the middle of the interview was pure gold. And from the look on Leblanc's face, this time, also absolutely true.

Jean-Marc told me that there existed concrete evidence of a wire transfer for three hundred thousand euros that had been traced from one of Leblanc's bank accounts to an account believed to belong to a high-ranking chief of organized crime. The look on Leblanc's face—devoid of color, his jaw dropping nearly to his desk—told me that Jean-Marc's information was good. That, and the fact that Leblanc then threw me out of his office confirmed it.

Once outside on the street I had half expected to see Jean-Marc waiting for me on the sidewalk. I was disappointed we weren't going to be able to immediately celebrate his information and Leblanc's resulting reaction.

I don't know where Jean-Marc got his information this time, but I couldn't wait to let him know how proud of him I was. While it wasn't quite a lead, or even a clue to help indict Leblanc, it was a step in the right direction. Now I just needed to figure out who he'd paid and why.

As I walked back to the Metro station, trying to be careful to keep my eyes open around me I pulled out my phone. It was broad daylight, but I didn't trust Leblanc not to send his thugs after me no matter the time of day. He was that sure of how untouchable he felt he was.

"Jean-Marc?" I said breathlessly as my line connected. "That was brilliant! You should have seen his face. He totally looked like he'd just gotten some important body parts caught in a pincer."

Jean-Marc laughed. "I thought he might have that reaction."

"Wherever did you get the info? Not from Étienne?"

"No. I got it from Colette Girard."

"I thought they were all shunning you."

"I did, too. It seems Colette wasn't happy about that. She apologized to me."

"Jean-Marc, I'm so glad. I think I remember you talking about her. Are you sure you can trust her?"

"Did Leblanc act like the Intel was good?"

"Good point," I said. "He definitely did. But why now?"

The sunlight seemed to soak into the cobblestones of the walkway that paralleled the Seine as I made my way to the Metro station.

"She said she felt guilty. She knew Resnelle didn't want any of her people talking to me and that never sat right with her."

"As I remember she has had a crush on you, right?"

Jean-Marc laughed. "I prefer to think that her better nature came to the surface on this one."

"Maybe. What are you up to?"

"Geneviève and Robbie are at the community pool on boulevard de Reims. I will collect them when they're done but Geneviève believes it is best to tire the young monsieur out as much as possible before taking him back to the hotel room."

"Sounds sensible. Did Colette have anything to tell you about the status of the crime scene in my apartment?"

"No. At least nothing she felt comfortable sharing."

"But we can't move back yet?"

"Perhaps one more night in the hotel. Or we could all come and stay at my place?"

I'd been to his place. Four people and two dogs in what was basically a studio flat would be a serious crush.

"That's all right," I said. "We'll manage. I'm heading back to the hotel now. Can I pick up anything?"

"*Non*. I thought I would swing by Madame Ferguson's apartment to give her the photos of her husband's extracurricular activities and pick up our check. I will run by my flat afterwards to pick up some clothes. Unless Geneviève calls, and then I will go straight to the pool."

"Don't bother, Jean-Marc. I'm closer than you are. I'll text Geneviève and let her know."

"*Bon*. It was good work today, *chérie*. Not case-busting, perhaps..."

"But the bird builds its nest twig by twig, right?"

Jean-Marc laughed. "So you do listen to me."

After that, I made my way to the subterranean entrance to the Metro station for the ten-minute ride to the eleventh arrondissement. The victory with Leblanc began to fade quickly when compared with the fact that Madeleine was still missing. By the time I emerged from the Metro station at Philippe Auguste, I was feeling antsy and apprehensive again.

She'd been gone for twelve hours. Had a ransom been demanded? I prayed that someone had heard from the kidnappers. I knew from past experience that it was definitely time to worry if they hadn't.

As I walked to the hotel, I stopped at a delicatessen and picked up a chicken and pickle sandwich and a soft drink. I texted Geneviève who responded by saying they were still at the pool, and she was still waiting for Robbie to tire out.

<we are fine chérie. Run your errands. I will call when we're ready to come home>

I nearly got tears in my eyes reading her text and wondering what in the world I would do without her.

As soon as I got back to the hotel, I connected both dogs to their leashes and took them out for a quick rotation around the small park in front of the hotel before going back upstairs to eat my sandwich—most of which I then fed to the dogs. I briefly considered a nap, but I was too restless to do it, so I pulled out my laptop to try to do a little more research.

It was so frustrating not to know what the police were doing as far as Madeleine's abduction was concerned. It occurred to me that they might be forced to keep Dilly informed but before I interfered with what had to be the worst week in that woman's life, I called Stanley first.

"Hey, girl," he said, his weariness evident in his voice. "I just got off the phone with Dilly. Dear Lord, that woman is going through hell."

"I can only imagine," I said. "Do you have any news at all?"

"About the abduction? Nothing. Dilly said she got a single phone call from one of the cops—probably Resnelle—whose English was impossible to understand—why don't they just break down and hire a damn translator?—and Dilly was told to call them immediately if the kidnappers contacted her."

I was flabbergasted. "She's on her own?"

"I think she has a sister with her, but the Georgia Bureau of Investigations said it didn't look like a real kidnapping, but they'd stay in touch. And the Paris police haven't even called."

"And you have no idea what the cops are doing about finding Madeleine?"

"Me?" Stanley snorted. "I can categorically tell you that the group of people the French police disdain more than American tourists is the American Embassy. They are refusing to keep us in the loop."

"I wish I could do something," I said, gnawing a fingernail as I watched Izzy and Esmé begin to playfully wrestle with each other. "But I haven't a clue as to where she might be or who might have taken her."

"I know. It's awful to feel this helpless."

"I was thinking of giving Dilly a call," I said.

"You're an angel. Give her my best if you do."

"I will."

After ringing off with Stanley, I made myself a cup of tea, sorry that it wasn't a little later in the day so I could feel justified in pouring myself a glass of wine. I didn't think I'd be able to help Dilly. I hated knowing that my calling her would probably only get her hopes up until she realized it was only me.

I dialed the number that Stanley had given me.

"Yes?" Dilly's voice was fragile and fearful.

"Dilly, it's me, Claire Baskerville," I said.

"I...yes, how are you, Claire dear?" she said, pulling herself together with the strength of ten Southern women, her accent long and drawn out. "I was so sorry to hear about Bob."

"Thank you, Dilly," I said. "I am heartbroken over the news about Ethan. I saw him that night."

"You did?" her voice rose in hopefulness as if I might drop some morsel of the man back into her life if only for a moment.

"I can't imagine what you're going through with Madeleine," I said. "I wanted you to know that the Paris police are competent. I do believe they'll find her."

"Thank you, dear," Dilly said. "I'm afraid Ethan never had

much confidence in the French police, but I'm glad to hear differently, especially now."

"Are you alone?"

"No, my sister is with me. She and Madeleine were close since Flo is closer to Madeleine's age than mine. Flo was a late-in-life baby for Mother. A boon to us all, but a surprise nonetheless."

I settled in for a good long listen. If Dilly needed to talk, I was happy to provide that for her. It was the very least I could do.

"Flo used to advise Madeleine during her high school boy-crazy phase," Dilly said with a smile in her voice. "My sister wasn't long out of it herself, so she was a good one for Madeleine to talk to. And then, there was that awful time in Riverwood Manor in Eatonton. Did you know about that?"

I was aware that Riverwood Manor was a residential mental health care facility seventy-five miles southeast of Atlanta.

"I don't think so," I said.

"Well, for a while we just thought Madeleine had a wild imagination but there comes a time when that only goes so far. Ethan and I finally had to admit that there might actually be something wrong with the girl. Don't misunderstand me, we love our Maddie to bits. But during this time, let's just say she did some things I can't even imagine wild Yankee girls doing."

"I had no idea," I said.

"Yes, well, she was in Riverwood Manor for nearly two years. Oh, she broke our hearts when we came to visit her, begging us to let her come home. But we couldn't handle her. The lies, the drugs. It was for the best."

"I'm sorry to hear that," I said. "How long ago was this?"

"Oh, I don't know," Dilly said, as if thinking about the current tragedies playing out in her life.

I tried to remind her—hopefully without upsetting her too much—of all the things she and Madeleine had to look forward to. In my mind, when you're going through a bad time, I believe hope is the best way to weather the storm. I know a lot of people don't like this approach because they feel the pain will be all the worst if there is not a good outcome.

But I always say, every day you can keep sorrow at bay, is one day in the positive ledger.

"You both have so much to look forward to," I said. "When she's found."

I was hesitant to mention the baby in case Dilly didn't know about that. The last thing I wanted to do was make things even worse for her by giving her yet another person's life to fear for —especially if she didn't know about it.

"Have you contacted Henry yet?" I asked. "Or did the police advise you against telling too many people?"

"Who?"

"Henry," I said. "I'm sorry. I don't know his last name. Madeleine's fiancé?"

"Dear Claire, I don't know what Madeleine has told you, but my daughter has no fiancé and I have never heard of anybody named Henry."

50

After hanging up with Dilly, I sat in that hotel room and thought back to all the things that Madeleine had told me over the last couple of days. I found myself reflecting on the fact that so many of them had turned out not to be true.

Had she really been attacked? Was the arm in the sling real? Was she even pregnant?

Her mother had basically revealed that Madeleine had been in a mental institution for intense emotional distress and self-destructive behavior. I stood up and began to pace, agitated and angry at myself and confused about what was happening.

Has Madeleine been playing me all along?

Or is she a foolish young woman who pushed the wrong people and gotten in way over her head?

There's nothing so vulnerable as a child—unless it's the mentally impaired. One thing I knew, one way or the other—whether Madeleine was complicit or a victim—she was in danger.

The question now was, *how do I help her?*

For me, when in doubt, I go back to the Internet. As a

private investigator I have a wide range of online tools to help locate people who don't want to be found or to uncover secrets people don't want discovered.

While it was beyond my ability to find out who had taken Madeleine—or where—I could at least see if there wasn't a trail that I'd overlooked that might point in the direction of who was holding her.

It was a long and tedious way to go about things, but I wasn't starting from nothing. I'd already done a fair amount of research on her father and Leblanc. As for Jimmy and his juvenile record, it would probably take someone with more access than I had to find any trail surrounding that. But, I tried anyway.

Usually, especially using the databases that I do, I can get a hint if a record exists—even if I can't actually see it. With sealed juvenile records, that's true too. There would be some sign that *something* exists, even if it was expunged or sealed from prying eyes, like mine.

I worked for an hour before accepting that there was no hint at all that Jimmy had ever been arrested even for a parking violation.

I sat back and stared at my laptop screen.

Was this another example of one of Madeleine's lies? But for what possible purpose?

As I was trying to figure out how a lie about Jimmy's record might fit into Madeleine's predicament today, my phone rang. I picked it up, noting Adele Cote's picture on the screen.

"Hey, Adele," I said.

"Bonjour, Claire," Adele said. "I was having lunch in the morgue lunchroom, and I don't know if I told you, but I couldn't ever get the third page to the post-mortem to send."

I frowned, trying to think if I even knew a page was missing. I think I was so bowled over by the fact that Jimmy's DNA was on the pillow from Ethan's room that I didn't even look for more.

"Anyway, since I was right there in the ME's office and since I have access, I went to the physical filing cabinet and I pulled the forensic report. You are not going to believe this."

"Believe what?" My stomach had already begun to churn with anxiety.

"It's not the same as the one I gave you," Adele said.

I frowned in confusion. "What does that mean?"

"It means the report I gave you was the one accessed from the online portal—and I know for a fact that it's the same report that the homicide team is using. But it is not the same one on file with the ME's office."

"What are the differences?"

"Well, first of all, the victim and the suspect did not have the same drug in them," Adele said. "Andrews was scopolamine or Devil's Breath which is used to incapacitate the victim until death. But Désirée was drugged with Rohypnol."

I felt a chill at her words. Désirée told David that the admitting physician on the night she'd was arrested had said she'd been roofied.

But her taking a date rape drug would not have lined up with the picture of her as Ethan's killer.

The report had been altered to frame her for his murder. The sudden memory of Désirée in the surveillance video—wobbling down the hall until she knocked on Ethan's door—came to me.

Désirée been drugged before she even got to Ethan's room.

The false forensic report kept her a suspect, but the real report did everything but exonerate her.

"Are you still there, Claire?"

"Was there evidence of Senator Andrews' DNA inside Désirée?"

"Glad you mentioned that, because that's the other thing. There wasn't. Not at all."

I felt a wave of elation to the point that I nearly stood up, as if my body couldn't contain the energy coursing through it.

Désirée had been telling the truth. She and Ethan hadn't had sex. Somebody had falsified the report to make it look as if they had.

Who was powerful enough to have done that? I felt another wave of elation at the realization.

Michel Leblanc.

Who else would have the power to have an official police document faked?

Before I could process what all of this meant to the case or even to where Madeleine might be at this moment, there was a knock at the door.

Expecting to hear *"Housekeeping"* called out, I stood up when I didn't hear it. Nobody was supposed to know where we were.

It occurred to me as I walked to the door with Adele still on the line, that we hadn't been doing a very conscious job of keeping a low profile or watching for anyone following us.

I went to the door and looked through the peep hole before telling Adele I would have to call her back and hanging up.

Then I opened the door to face my stepmother standing on the threshold.

51

Joelle pushed past me and stalked into the hotel room, her posture rigid and her jaw clenched. She surveyed the room, her back to me, her gaze sweeping the drab walls and threadbare furniture. I could feel anger radiating from her. She turned to me, her eyes blazing with rage. Her voice lashed out like a whip, every syllable dripping with malice.

"I thought we had a deal," she said.

"Remind me what I got out of this deal," I said. "And how did you know I was here?"

"Why are you doing this?" she said, ignoring my question. "Is it not enough that you have taken everything of mine?"

Joelle lived in a two-million-dollar Haussmann-style apartment on rue Moncey in the most expensive zip code—if Paris had zip codes—in the city.

"As usual," I said, "this is not about you. I am trying to help a young woman."

"A young woman whose father you have accused Michel of killing."

I was impressed that Leblanc had called Joelle and told her

of our little meeting. Perhaps she meant more to him than I thought. Or perhaps he simply saw her as useful to him.

I shut the hotel room door, grateful that the others were out for the moment. I moved to sit on one of the dining room chairs but didn't bother offering her the same. She'd do what she wanted regardless of any invitation from me.

Watching her now, haughty, hateful and full of spite, it was hard to remember that the last time I'd seen her was a year ago —the night Maddie was born. It was the night that so many people had died, nearly me and Joelle too.

If I'd ever thought even for one mad moment that that night might have bonded us—and trust me, I did think it—I was wrong a thousand times over. Whatever we'd shared that night was gone in the time it took Joelle to dust off her Chanel suit and walk out the door.

As I watched her now looking at my hotel room as if she was sure she was about to contract Hep-C from the doorknobs, I felt a powerful compulsion to tell her that her boyfriend hired hookers.

"He didn't kill Ethan Andrews," Joelle said to me. "He was with me all night."

And there it was. The alibi. Ergo the reason for this visit.

"Well, then he has nothing to worry about," I said.

"Trust me, he is not worried."

"Then why are you here?"

She turned to face me, her eyes narrowing.

"I'm here to give you some information I think you need to hear."

She was here to get me to back off and leave her boyfriend alone, but I'd bite.

"Okay," I said. "Hit me."

"You know Michel and I were staying at Sofitel Paris le Faubourg that night."

"I do. Remind me, what floor were you on?"

A cruel, knowing smile formed on her face. "The second floor," she said.

I had no way to check that, short of bribing someone from housekeeping at the Sofitel. Even then, I couldn't be sure they'd remember correctly.

"As I was saying," she said, "on the afternoon of the gala I saw Ethan and his daughter in front of the elevators."

As soon as she said that, I knew she'd given herself away as to what floor she and Leblanc had been on. Ethan and Madeleine's rooms were both on the third floor. How would Joelle have seen them if she and Leblanc weren't also on the third floor? I felt a wave of satisfaction that I'd gotten my answer.

Leblanc on the third floor gave him opportunity. And I already knew he had motive.

"They were arguing," Joelle said. "And then Ethan slapped her."

She raised an eyebrow at me as if challenging me to believe her. At first, I honestly didn't know what to think. If she was telling the truth, it had to mean something important. But was she telling the truth?

"The girl's bodyguard made a move toward the senator," Joelle said.

"Like he was going to attack the senator?" I asked.

She held up a finger as if to correct my assumption. "He made a move like he might," she said. "But the girl stopped him. Then, Ethan said something to her before storming off."

This was very interesting. Again. If true.

"Do you remember what it was that Ethan said?" I asked.

"It was partly garbled," she said. "And as you know, English is not my first language. But I believe it was an American idiom."

"Yes?" I prompted.

She sighed dramatically and smoothed down the peplum of her cotton jacket. "It sounded like he said, *over my dead body.*"

My mind instantly whirled in dread and bewilderment with what possible kind of reason Ethan could have said such a thing to his daughter.

And why hadn't Madeleine mentioned this to me?

Joelle turned and walked to the door. "Michel won't hurt you, you know."

"I appreciate that," I said.

She put a hand on the door handle but didn't turn to face me.

"He thinks he's doing it on my account."

She opened the door and stepped into the hall before turning to look at me.

"But we both know I don't care."

Then she turned and walked down the hall, leaving the door open behind her.

∽

With its mocha-chocolate walls and orange fleurs-de-lis stenciled over the doorways and windows, the chocolate shop provided an instantly warm, inviting atmosphere. Jean-Marc inhaled the scent of cocoa beans and caramelized sugar as he perused the displays of hand-crafted chocolates and truffles lining the walls in glass cases.

A special treat, he'd decided, as he bought a pound bag of assorted chocolates and candied fruit. Robbie would be thrilled. And of course, Claire loved chocolate. He stepped back out onto the street, feeling tall, strong, and confident.

His meeting with Colette could not have gone better. He had hardly expected to be physically assaulted but he'd been prepared to be lied to, as he had been by Étienne. He'd gone to the meeting combative and angry.

And Colette had quickly disarmed him.

"I need to first apologize to you for how I've treated you," she had said, her plain face twisted in shame. "You deserve better than that."

Jean-Marc had softened immediately. He knew this woman. Had known her for a decade. It was the reason why her initial rebuff had hurt so badly. And why he believed her now.

"You were under pressure," he'd said to her. "Forget it."

"Well, I won't forget it. It was cowardly and not the kind of person I like to think I am. I've come today with apologies. And bearing gifts."

At that point, Jean-Marc had looked around the park bench because Colette had only her jacket and not even a purse.

"Not that kind of gift," she'd said with a wan smile.

That's when she told him that she'd heard of his beating at the hands of Leblanc's men. She reached into her jacket and extracted a sheet of paper. It was a copy of the wire transfer from Leblanc's offshore account.

"It's not proof of wrongdoing," she'd said.

"But it's a strong hint of it," he'd replied, looking at the paper. "Thank you, Colette."

"Use it as you like. I didn't want the bastard to get the idea he could treat the Paris police force as he might anyone else. Bad precedent, you know? And regardless of who will or won't have a drink with you right now, LaRue, I want you to know I'm not the only one who thinks that way."

"I appreciate it."

"Still, I'd steer clear of Étienne Benoit."

"Thank you. I've discovered that on my own."

Jean-Marc had interrupted their meeting long enough to call Claire, knowing she was interviewing Leblanc at that moment and could use every advantage.

After leaving the park, Jean-Marc had headed back to the eleventh arrondissement when he spotted the *chocolatier* shop on the way. Emerging with his chocolate purchases, he found his phone vibrating with an incoming text and saw that it was from Colette.

<It was good to see you today, Jean-Marc. I'm sorry about before>

Jean-Marc texted back:

<No problem. It was great seeing you too>

<I've got an answer to your question about the dodgy bodyguard>

Jean-Marc stepped out of the flow of pedestrian traffic. He had asked Colette if she could use the Interpol database to find Jimmy's sealed assault record.

<You found his assault record?> he texted.

<I did. Pretty unbelievable that a US senator would hire a convicted felon for security!>

Jean-Marc texted back.

< I thought Jimmy was never officially charged?>

<I was talking about the senator's bodyguard> Colette texted. <Roger O'Connell served eight years for sexual assault.>

52

After Joelle left, I needed some time to process what I thought I now knew. The fact that Madeleine had lied to me about just about everything didn't erase the fact that she was now in trouble. I don't know why Ethan had felt driven to slap his daughter—or frankly, even if Joelle was telling me the truth about that, but since the story didn't reveal anything one way or the other, I doubted she made it up.

But if Ethan and Madeleine had fought publicly and Ethan really *had* slapped Madeleine—ending, according to Joelle—in Jimmy attempting to come to her aid, what did that tell me?

I went to the window and looked out onto the courtyard below, my mind racing, my thoughts and ideas falling on top of one another in my urge to make sense of all that I'd learned. The courtyard was filled with colorful flowers, with lush green trees lining the edges, and a tidy gravel pathway that snaked through the center.

As I stood there, I felt my thoughts begin to slow until they finally settled into place. I walked around the room, taking in every detail and sensation around me.

For whatever reason, my brain kept going to the idea that

Madeleine was involved in some way—possibly with Jimmy's help—in her father's death. I hated thinking that and even when I did, I got an image in my mind of her tears right after her father's murder when she came to my apartment that first night. But I've been around the block a few times, and I know for a fact that one can kill and still mourn the loss of that person.

Bizarre but true.

Could Madeleine and Jimmy have been lovers? Did they murder Ethan together? It would explain why Jimmy's DNA was on the pillow. And Madeleine would have easily been able to get him inside the room.

But in that case, who killed Jimmy?

From what I'd seen of his body in my foyer, the attack had been vicious. It was true that Madeleine could have gotten close enough to him to do it, and he likely wouldn't have expected it. The lack of visible defense wounds—from what I'd briefly been able to see—was compatible with an attack by a person the victim trusted.

Does this mean Madeleine isn't abducted?

I rubbed the tension out of my neck, trying to massage away my growing frustration. I heard my phone ringing from my purse where I'd put it when Joelle knocked, and I hurried to answer it, thinking it might be Geneviève ready for me to come and walk her and Robbie back to the hotel.

Now that I thought of it, a nice walk to clear my head was exactly what this maddening puzzle needed. I picked up my phone and looked at the screen. My stomach tightened.

The call was coming from Madeleine's phone.

53

Jean-Marc looked at his watch as he hurried toward the Hotel Gabriel. He pulled out his phone, noting the low battery icon, and called Geneviève's phone to see if she was ready for him to come and collect them. There was no answer, so he left a message.

They were probably in the pool. He tried Claire again. She hadn't answered the first time he'd called and what he had to tell her was not something he wanted to deliver in a voice mail or text.

This time, however, when he tried calling, his phone went dead in his hand.

Cursing, he shoved his phone in his pocket and increased his pace. He was only about six blocks away from the hotel, his mind whirling with the information Colette had just given him.

Why did we assume Jimmy was guilty and not even think of a possible police record for Roger O'Connell?

It was the sort of amateur mistake he would've called a rookie on if he'd still been in the department. To assume that the loutish thug had a prior—only because they nearly almost always did—and the affable avuncular chap was decent and upright—was the sort of mistake the old Jean-Marc would've made.

The one prone to stereotypes and typecasting, he thought bitterly.

He didn't even want to think what Claire would say when he told her about O'Connell's record. He shook his head in befuddlement.

What is it with Andrews that he wanted to surround himself with convicted sex offenders?

But right now, that was irrelevant. When they'd interviewed O'Connell yesterday, it had been before Jimmy's murder and before Madeleine's abduction.

Jean-Marc's stomach lurched with realization.

Did O'Connell have her? Even when they were talking to him, was Madeleine bound and gagged in a closet? Or in the trunk of a rental car? Or in a shack on the outskirts of town?

He cursed his stupidity for accepting the man at face value.

Am I losing it? Am I getting too old to make simple, accurate character assessments?

And then it occurred to Jean-Marc that they really only had Madeleine's word that Jimmy had been accused. Jimmy hadn't denied it, but he hadn't actually admitted it either. Was it possible Madeleine's father told her a pasteurized version of what had happened to *Roger* but made it sound like it was Jimmy?

Jean-Marc tried to think if this was information that he should pass on to Resnelle. She had her murder suspect for the Senator. But she hadn't arrested anyone yet for Jimmy—although Colette had said there was talk of naming Madeleine as Jimmy's killer.

Jean-Marc snorted in disgust. It was true he didn't know Resnelle personally and had never worked with her, but if she was truly reaching for Madeleine as the bodyguard's killer, she was only a tad better than a bent cop.

But he needed to let her know what he'd discovered about O'Connell. As an ex-convict O'Connell's prints would be on file to support his assertion. Jean-Marc felt a boost of spirit as he ran up the stairs of the Hotel Gabriel, nodding briefly at the desk clerk who looked up when he came in. He skipped the elevator and took the stairs two at a time, arriving at their room breathless and excited to tell Claire what he'd learned.

He opened the door onto an empty room. Deflated, he dropped the bag of chocolates on the dining room table and then checked both rooms, looking for a note. People didn't leave notes these days, he thought in annoyance. Not with text messaging so handy. He rummaged through his carryall for a charge cord for his phone, but he knew he hadn't packed one. Would they have one at the reception desk? Or should he just calm down?

He could wait to tell Claire this new development when he saw her later this afternoon. He assumed she'd gone to pick up Geneviève and Robbie, but if they weren't back in a few minutes, he'd walk over there himself.

In the meantime, it would be helpful to have an idea of their next step. He went to the kitchenette fridge and pulled out a bottled water and then seated himself at the dining table. Claire had left a small pad of yellow, lined paper and a pen on the desk. She was curiously analog in the way she often preferred to write things down, rather than input them as notes into her phone. He reached for the pen and paper on the desk and wrote:

O'Connell served time; Jimmy didn't. Did Madeleine know? Why did Ethan tell her Jimmy had a record? Or is that a lie too?

He sat back and looked at what he'd written, tapping the pen on his bottom lip as he tried to think what the current situation meant through the lens of this new information of both Ethan and Jimmy dying the way they had. As he thought, his gaze wandered to the wastepaper basket and caught on a crumpled scrap of yellow paper inside it.

Curious, he pulled the scrap out of the trash and straightened it out to read, in Claire's handwriting:

Saint-Denis, 16 Av Lucette Mazalaigue

He stared at the note and frowned. Why had she written this?

Is this where she is?

Suddenly he was on his feet, a hard thump of fear pulsing through him.

Had she heard from the kidnappers?

Saint-Denis was not a safe part of Paris. The only thing Jean-Marc could think of was that Claire had somehow gotten a lead, and she had gone to meet someone here in the worst section of Paris.

He snatched up his dead cellphone and hurried to the door. He would plug it in at the reception desk. If they didn't have a charger, he'd use the downstairs hotel phone to call her to find out what was going on. And then he'd get over to this address as fast as possible.

He jerked open the room door and ran straight into the arms of Victor Durand and Paul Olivier.

"Jean-Marc LaRue," Durand intoned holding out a pair of handcuffs. "You are under arrest for destroying key crime scene evidence and interfering with an active investigation."

54

A line of decrepit, graffiti-covered warehouse fronts, their windows boarded up and barred, faced me from the street which itself was strewn with refuse and trash. Somewhere in the distance I heard the sound of a train.

I hesitated in front of the warehouse matching the address I'd been given, the window in the door to the warehouse was broken out. I swallowed hard. If the door was locked, I could easily snake my arm through the broken pane to unlock it from the inside. I took in a breath.

If it hadn't been Madeleine herself on the phone begging me to come to this address, I would never have come without an armed escort. But she'd been hysterical on the phone and pleaded with me to come alone. She gave me the address and then disconnected. I'd tried calling her back the whole way here in the back of a speeding Uber but only got a recording that told me the line was no longer in service.

As I stared at the warehouse door, my mind was racing with the possibilities of who could be behind this kidnapping and the possible reasons for it. Kidnapping Madeleine made no sense at all. But the terror in her voice on the phone had sounded real.

If she's mentally unbalanced, she will sound real, I reminded myself.

It all seemed too messy to be the work of a high-ranking politician like Leblanc. Maybe I could imagine him killing Ethan out of revenge. But kidnapping Madeleine? For what possible purpose? The man was rich. It was impossible to imagine he'd do it for the ransom.

It didn't fit for him kidnapping her, but did it fit for him as Ethan's murderer?

On the drive over, I'd reached back into my brain to my interview with Roger O'Connell to try to see how *he* could fit here. He was fond of Madeleine. Wasn't he? Maybe too fond?

I groaned with indecision as I stared at the door. Right now, none of the pieces fit together. The picture that was trying to emerge was grotesque and misshapen. But was it the truth?

The warehouse door appeared to be made from reinforced metals, its surface blackened from years of neglect and rust. Its edges were mangled and twisted from time and wear, with a few scraps of paint still clinging to its surface.

I put my hand on the metal handle of the door and tugged, my mind still running obsessively through all the events—much like what I imagine you see when your whole life flashes before you.

What was the purpose of my attack in Switzerland? Was it even connected? Was Madeleine's attack here in Paris while I was gone even real? It hadn't occurred to me to question her about her injuries. All she'd have had to do was take a slap to the face and add a fake sling.

Maybe not even a slap if she was good with contouring makeup.

But what reason would Madeleine have had to fake the attack? Or to send me to Switzerland?

Crazy people like games. That's what this feels like. Games.

As I tugged the heavy door open, a smell of mustiness and oil mingled with the smell of rat droppings hit me. What would I find inside? Madeline not a hostage at all but a ringleader for some demented game with me at the center? Why?

Did she kill her father? Jimmy?

I held my breath and stepped inside. It was eerily silent, and the acrid smell of rust and oil intensified. I moved further inside, regretting that I needed to shut the door behind me, but I couldn't see anything to use to prop it open.

Suddenly I felt my phone vibrate in my pocket. I pulled it out and looked at the screen which showed an unidentified number.

I answered in a low voice, my eyes darting around the dark recesses of the interior.

"Yes?" I whispered.

The walls were stained a dull gray and the floors were littered with debris. Cobwebs hung from the rafters. Broken furniture and crates were everywhere.

"Madame Baskerville?" Désirée said hoarsely. "I remembered something else. My memory is coming back in pieces. David said you should know."

"Can you call me back later?" I asked, hearing how my voice was echoing throughout the warehouse interior.

"I remember about that night," she said excitedly. "I had a drink at the bar with someone. Monsieur Fontaine thinks he must have put the drug in my drink."

"You already told me this. You saw Députée Leblanc," I said impatiently. "But right now really isn't a good—"

"*Oui.* I *saw* him but we didn't speak. This man bought me a drink."

"Call me later and tell me," I said hoarsely. "I don't have time to—"

"It was the Senator's bodyguard," Désirée said.

55

At that moment an impersonal, robotic voice interrupted the phone line with a recording. "*An inmate of the Paris Police Detention Center has reached the maximum phone time allotted,*" it intoned before disconnecting the call.

I stared at my phone and felt dread creeping up my arms like a living thing.

Roger O'Connell drugged Désirée.

O'Connell killed the Senator.

"Claire?"

I whirled around to see Madeleine morphing out of the shadows.

As I'd guessed, she wasn't tied up, she didn't have a gun to her head, she was nobody's prisoner.

But that didn't mean she wasn't in hell. Her eyes were unfocused, her gaze darting from one side of the warehouse to the other, like an animal in search of prey or a way to make sense of her fractured reality.

She wore a sundress I'd seen her in before, its once bright white cotton fabric now badly wrinkled and stained.

"What the hell, Madeleine?" I said when I saw her.

None of this made sense. Not her, not this warehouse meeting, and definitely not the bombshell that I was still reeling from.

Roger O'Connell killed Ethan.

"I'm sorry," Madeleine said, coming closer. "I thought about calling you back and telling you not to come but that would've made things worse."

I approached her, my phone still clutched in my hand, my anger and frustration welling up inside me.

"What are you playing at, Madeleine? The cops are looking for you. Your mother is beside herself with fear."

"Give me your phone, please, Claire. I'm sorry but I can't trust you not to call the people who want me dead."

I reminded myself that I was likely dealing with a person with serious and long-term mental health issues, including delusions and paranoia.

"You know I'm on your side, Madeleine," I said, trying to modulate my voice and strip the tension and anger from it. "What are you doing here? Are you alone?"

"Do you mean, have I been kidnapped? No. But I was there when they killed Jimmy. I couldn't wait around and let them do that to me, too."

Madeleine's mother's words about the stint Madeleine had done in the mental institution came back to me as I stared at her. Half the things she'd told me were lies.

"Maybe you'd better tell me from the beginning," I said.

"I didn't want to involve you. I knew my father wouldn't want me putting you in danger, so I couldn't tell you everything."

"Is your arm really broken? How about the baby? Is that real? Because I already know the fiancé is a lie."

"What?" Her eyes continued to dart wildly around the

warehouse space. "What difference does all that make? No, I'm not pregnant! I did what I had to do!"

"Why? Why did you do it?"

"I told you! Someone is trying to kill me! The same people who killed my father!"

"You mean because of the animal right's bill? Because I know that's a lie, too."

She tightened her mouth in a grimace of distaste or guilt.

"Okay, yes, the animal rights bill isn't true," Madeleine said. "But the rest of it is. I am following in my father's footsteps. Don't you see? I'm doing what I know he'd want me to do. I'm finishing his work. And they want to kill me for it!"

"Who does, exactly?"

"I don't have time for this! Don't you get it? It's happening! Now!"

"What is happening?"

I either needed to call an ambulance or I needed to get Madeleine to come with me. But she was acting so frantic, I didn't think my chances of doing either were great.

"I got a message delivered to my father's killer," Madeleine said. "He's meeting us here."

I frowned. "You called the killer?"

"No, I called my mother. Why are you deliberately misunderstanding me?" she shouted in frustration.

"I just talked to your mother, and in addition to telling me she never heard of anybody named *Henry*, she didn't mention that she'd talked to you. In fact, she sounded beside herself with agony about your so-called kidnapping."

I held up my phone.

"Let me call her," I said. "Let's relieve her mind. Okay?"

Madeline lunged at me and slapped the phone from my hand where I heard it break on the hard floor.

"I'm not lying!" she screamed, her hands clenched them into fists, her body tense and rigid. "I paid a homeless guy ten euros to read a two-line script telling my mother that I'd been kidnapped and where I was being held. I did it knowing my father's killer was listening in!"

She's mad. Whether or not she killed anyone, she's definitely unbalanced.

"Look, Madeleine—" I said gently, placatingly.

"No, *you* look! They're trying to kill me, and you don't even believe I'm in danger!"

"Sure I do," I said, trying to calm her down. "Especially after what happened to Jimmy."

"Somebody has to get his throat cut before you believe I'm in danger!" she cried. "It could've been me! You didn't help! I had to do it all myself."

"Do what yourself, Madeleine? Why did you call me here? Because I do believe you're in trouble. I promise you I do."

Madeleine wiped her eyes and made a visible effort to calm down. She took in a breath and looked around the warehouse space at the shadows that surrounded us.

"You have something they want," she said.

"I have no idea what you're talking about."

"Don't play games, Claire! They killed Jimmy! They killed my father! They want to kill me!"

She seemed to think that more than one person killed her father. Had Roger been working with someone?

"I have nothing they want," I said, furrowing my brow in confusion.

"Yes, you do! The night of the gala, I saw my father pass it to you. And I'm not the only one who saw it."

I frowned in bewilderment.

"What is it you think he gave me?" I asked.

"A jump drive. He gave you a jump drive with all the evidence he'd gathered about the cabal."

"I'm sorry," I said with a helpless shrug. "I don't know what you're talking about."

I watched her grit her teeth in frustration.

"I know he made the jump drive," she said. "He *told* me so. I begged him to give it to me because nobody would suspect me, but he wouldn't."

Tears streamed down her face, and she gulped down her words.

"He was only trying to protect me, but he was so angry. I was there when he got the final message..."

"What message?"

"About the sex cabal! I overheard him talking to them on the phone. He said he'd bring them down and he'd name names. He said he'd go to the media!"

I stared at her and something in the back of my brain gently told me that at some point this had stopped sounding like the ravings of a mental patient and had started to hum with the unmistakable ring of truth.

"A sex cabal?" I repeated, dumbfounded.

"Yes, but I don't know the details," Madeleine said. "When Dad saw I'd overheard, we argued. It was horrible! He didn't want me to know anything about it and I only wanted to help."

"You were seen arguing in front of the elevator," I said, not even sure if I was believing what I was hearing.

She nodded.

"When he wouldn't let me help, I ran out of his room. I was so mad at him, and he followed me. He caught me by the elevator and I...I guess I was hysterical. I said I'd tell Mom if he didn't let me help."

"He slapped you," I said.

She nodded, tears streaming down her cheeks. So Joelle was telling the truth.

"He said people high up in the government were involved." She shook her head. "But I don't know the details. And it's the details that got him killed."

I watched her for a moment, my stomach grinding with acid as she was speaking.

"So, there was never any congressional animal rights bill?" I asked.

Her eyes flashed angrily at me.

"Look, I'm sorry, okay? Yes, I lied to you! I did what I had to do. I needed your help. I needed to know what the Paris police knew about the case. They certainly weren't telling *me*—and I thought you had an inside track with them."

The realization of what she was saying came seconds before I rewound my memory tapes to the point where I saw the trap she'd laid—and had dragged me into the center of it.

People were coming.

Bad people.

"I need that jump drive!" she said urgently. "I need to finish what my father started!"

Did I believe her? I realized it didn't matter at this point.

"You saw what lengths they'll go to," she said. "They'll stop at nothing to get that information. I need to release it to the media before they can get their hands on it."

"I don't have it," I said.

"You're lying!" She took a step toward me in frustration.

"We need to call the police," I said. "They're looking for you. Your mother is losing her mind with worry over—"

"That's not important!" Madeleine screamed. "Only the jump drive matters! Where is it?!"

Her face was contorted with rage, as tears streamed down her cheeks. She threw her head back and screamed in frustration, the noise echoing off the walls all around us.

"Madeleine, get a hold of yourself! Your father only passed me a note asking to get together the next day at his hotel."

She gazed at me in agony.

"You're lying." But the fire had gone out of her voice. She knew it was the truth.

"If people are coming to this warehouse, we need to go," I said. "Did you lure me here so they could torture the information out of me about this jump drive?"

She looked at me, dully as if now that her plan had fallen apart, she was having trouble fully comprehending anything else.

"What? No. I...no."

"How did Jimmy know I was in Switzerland? Was it you that sent me the text?"

"None of that matters!"

"Well, it matters to me if you want me to trust you."

Madeleine shook her head vehemently.

"Look, Jimmy knew about Switzerland because I told him I'd sent the text to you. I said it was a secret so when he accidentally blabbed it out to you, he thought I'd be angry and that's why he refused to say any more. But really, he didn't know any more."

"How did you set up your henchman to attack me on my way to the clinic?"

"That wasn't me, I swear. All I did was try to get you to leave Paris."

I felt a throb of premonition. "Why?"

"I truly thought I was doing you a favor by getting you out of town until I could flush out whoever was behind my father's murder. I felt like I'd involved you and now you were going to get hurt."

"Why did you think that?"

Right then Roger O'Connell stepped out of the shadows.

"Because she received a note from me," he said. "Saying I was going to kill you."

56

"You bastard!" Madeleine said, rushing him and pounding his chest with her fists. "I knew it was you!"

"No, you didn't, Maddie," he said, smiling sadly, holding her away from him.

"Don't call me that. You killed my father!"

As I stared at O'Connell, so much larger and more physically imposing than I remembered in our interview, I cursed the fact that I hadn't done more research on him. Why had I assumed he was the loyal, long-suffering servant who'd dedicated his life in the service of one man and then just wanted to retire quietly?

I saw what I wanted to see.

"He loved you," Madeleine sobbed, wrenching herself out of his grip. "He loved you like a son."

"If you say so," O'Connell said with a shrug. "I hate to tell you, girl, but killing him wasn't personal."

"You're a monster," she said, covering her face with her hands.

"How did you get the hotel surveillance tape?" I asked

coolly, wishing I had my phone. It would only take one button push to have the cops alerted to our location.

"That's an interesting story," he said, turning to me with a grin.

I knew he intended to kill us both. And I knew he felt his confession wouldn't be heard by anyone but us. I prayed he was wrong about that. But at the moment there was no reason to believe he was.

"I timed it exactly right," he said. "Five minutes after the hooker went in, she was passed out and Mr. Andrews was so relieved to see me. I walked in and stabbed him with the hypodermic."

Madeleine gasped and put a hand to her mouth.

"I asked him nicely for the jump drive."

"With a lit cigarette," I said.

O'Connell turned to me and cocked his head as if suddenly finding me interesting.

"He was a stubborn old bastard right to the end. When he finally passed out, I put on gloves, and used the pillow to finish him off. I was thinking about killing the girl too, but I decided she'd be the perfect suspect. I was right, too. The cops went right to her. Badda-bing!"

Madeleine began to weep.

"How did you drug her?" I asked.

"Easy. She was waiting in the hotel bar before going up to the Senator's room. I bought her a drink and prepaid for a visit with her later if you catch my drift."

"And you drugged her drink."

"*Voila.* As they say over here."

"And Jimmy? You killed him, too?"

"That guy was a moron." He turned to Madeleine. "Totally devoted to you, by the way." He shrugged. "I told him to disable the video cameras in the hallway after the hooker went into the senator's room. I said it was to preserve the senator's privacy. I told him if he wanted to make amends with the senator, he'd do it."

"You're a monster!" Madeleine said again.

"Well, I couldn't have him telling people I'd told him to disable the video camera, could I?"

"And his DNA on the pillow?"

"Nice touch huh? Just a comfy backup for yours truly. Not worth the effort, in the end. The police didn't even question him. They had their suspect. I guess all the rest was just information overload." He laughed.

"Now the only question I have," I said, "is why?"

His face hardened, his fun clearly dissipating.

"That's unimportant," he said.

He turned to Madeleine.

"Sorry, girl. It was nothing to do with whatever crap he thought he was doing with his stupid bills."

"Who are you working for?" I asked. "If it wasn't personal, you must have been paid."

He turned again to me, his face clearly showing he was impressed that I was still asking questions at this point.

"It could've been blackmail," he said. "Did that ever occur to you? Or maybe he was holding somebody near and dear to me in a shack outside the city?"

"You have nobody near and dear," I said. "A snake doesn't mate for love."

"Ouch. Touché," he said, but there was no softening in his expression.

"So never mind who or why," he said briskly, as he pulled out a wicked, curved knife from his vest pocket. "I'm going to ask you the same thing Miss Maddie asked you. But unlike little Maddie here, I'm willing to carve big pieces off you until I get what I want. So where is it?"

My eyes went to the knife which I knew this man would not hesitate to use. My heart pounded in my throat.

"I have no idea," I said.

He walked over to Madeleine and jerked her to him by the hair, forcing her head back, and put the knife to her throat. Madeleine gasped.

"How about now?" he said to me.

I dropped to my knees and clasped my hands in prayer.

"I'm begging you," I said, my eyes filling with tears to watch Madeleine struggle in this man's hands.

"No joy, huh?" he said, abruptly releasing Madeleine and digging in his jacket pocket for his phone. "Maybe this'll convince you instead."

I was still on my knees when he shoved the screen of his cellphone in my face. When he did, I saw a shaky video time-stamped fifteen minutes earlier.

It was a video of Robbie—dressed in the same color block sweat suit I'd bought him last weekend at Monoprix. He was walking hand in hand with a strange woman with a harsh face.

I stared in horror and disbelief.

"Tell me where the jump drive is," Roger said, "or I'll tell her to kill the boy."

I barely had time to process the horror of his words before Madeleine launched herself at him, her taloned hands out. When she hit him, I fell over backwards. By the time I scrambled to my feet it was over.

Madeleine was on her knees in front of him, her hands clasped to her stomach where I watched with horror as blood seeped out between her fingers. O'Connell stared at her, his own mouth open in shock as she crumpled to the ground.

"Aw, Maddie," he said sadly.

Without thinking, I grabbed his knife and as he turned to me, and plunged it straight up and into his chest.

He grunted, made a feeble move to clutch at his chest and gave me a brief look of surprise, before collapsing to the cement floor.

I ran to Madeleine. Her face was contorted in pain. I saw the growing red stain spread across the front of her white sundress.

"You're okay, Madeleine," I said frantically. "You're going to be okay."

I pressed directly onto the wound, trying to remember how long to do it for the clots to form. I knew stopping too soon could be deadly—if she was even savable. I saw her eyes close but I continued to press, my mind racing with terror. I could hear O'Connell groaning from where he lay a few feet away from me but I didn't stop to check on him. When it finally looked as if the bleeding had stopped, I ripped the lower hem of her dress and quickly wrapped it around her middle.

"You'll be safe soon, Madeleine," I said, talking close to her ear.

Her eyes fluttered once but I knew she couldn't hear me. I patted her down looking for her phone but there wasn't one. I turned to O'Connell who was now lying still, his eyes open and glassy. I found his phone in his jacket pocket and held it to his face to unlock it.

I called the number to report a terror attack—thinking that was the best way to get the police to come as fast as possible, but the call failed. Twice. Cursing the bad reception inside the warehouse, I jumped up and raced toward the exterior door of the warehouse and slammed right into someone who must have been standing in the shadows all along.

I pulled back to look into the steely, calculating eyes of Stanley Cole.

57

The cloying scent of iron and copper from all the blood mixed with the sickening odors of mildew and stale air in the warehouse. Underneath it there was the omnipresent smell of sweat and fear.

Most of all, fear.

Stanley's hand tightened on my arm from where he'd dragged me back into the interior of the warehouse.

He stood now looking down at O'Connell's body.

"I knew that idiot would screw this up," he said.

I was still too shocked to speak. Even now, I couldn't believe he wasn't calling for an ambulance or putting an arm around me to comfort me.

What a fool I am.

He turned to me and grinned.

"You never guessed, huh, Claire?" he said. "I'm so much smarter than you ever gave me credit for."

"I thought you were my friend."

He snorted. "I'll bet you'll never make that mistake again. Oh, wait. You'll never get a chance to."

I jerked my arm out of his grip but made no motion to run.

He was thirty years younger and fit. I would never make it to the door.

"You might get away with one murder, Stanley," I said. "But now there's Jimmy and O'Connell. And if you don't let me call for an ambulance, Madeleine, too. Do you really think any of these deaths will make things *less* problematic for you?"

"I'm not worried. I know people."

I stared at him until it clicked in my brain what he was saying.

"You have someone inside Paris homicide," I said.

"Aren't you clever?"

I wondered if it was Resnelle.

"How did we get here, Stanley?" I asked. "Can you tell me that?"

He threw back his head and laughed.

"Oh, my God, you should hear yourself," he said. "Here's you being all reasonable like you don't know I'm going to kill you. Do you really think you can talk me out of this?" He shook his head as if regarding a disappointing but bright child. "I mean, I know you're good, but I guess I hadn't seen the arrogance before."

"I don't have whatever it is you're looking for."

"Well, here's the good news, Claire. I believe you. If you didn't cave when O'Connell showed you little Robbie marching off to get his throat cut, I figured it was a pretty safe bet you didn't have it."

I tried not to hear his words. Of all the times Stanley had oohed and ahhed over pictures of Robbie as a toddler, for him to speak of him like this now was almost more than I could bear. I didn't care what happened to me as long as Robbie was somehow safe.

And as long as Stanley died a gruesome, long, drawn-out death.

"So to show you what kind of a guy I am," he said, nudging

O'Connell's lifeless body with his shoe. "I'm going to treat you to the details. I know how you love knowing the ins and outs of all your cases."

"Stanley, Madeleine needs a hospital," I said, my eyes going to her. She moaned once so I knew she was still alive.

"Well, that's unfortunate then," Stanley said, glancing at her. "Do you want to know why, or not?"

I nodded numbly. Keeping him talking meant more seconds or minutes for me to figure out a way out of this, a way to save myself and Madeleine.

"It's very simple," Stanley said. "We have a little club. Let's just say some very high-altitude flyers. Some celebrities, but mostly politicians. A few billionaires. A very exclusive club."

"Madeleine said her father told her it was a sex cabal."

He flushed angrily and looked again at Madeleine on the ground.

"Ethan," he sat out. "He didn't understand so of course he denigrated it."

"So, it's not true? No rapes and snuff movies being made with refugees and undocumented immigrants?"

"Give me a break, Claire. By rights, these people should be at the bottom of the Mediterranean. Our club gave them a few more weeks of life."

A few more weeks of torture and terror and murder, I thought, my stomach turning to imagine it.

"So Ethan found out," I said. "What happened? Did you give him an invitation and he decided to expose you instead?"

He smiled at me.

"Have I ever told you how incredibly impressed with you I have always been?"

"That means so much to me, Stanley."

"You have every right to be angry with me. I get it. But it's still true. Remember when you found out from that stupid hotel doorman that Ethan and I had a huge fight in front of the US Club?"

My heart sank as I realized what he was going to say.

"And I told you it was probably Leblanc because we look so much alike? And you bought it?"

I bought it because Stanley had been a friend who knew about my face blindness. And knowing it, he'd been able to use it against me.

"And then your boyfriend's confidential informant? Étienne? Did you really believe that Étienne *accidentally* bumped into him?"

I mimicked handclapping for him and his face reddened with annoyance.

"You forget that I know you, Claire," he said. "I knew you'd investigate Ethan's death."

"Because Madeleine came to me."

"And she did that because I told her she should ask for your help."

He glanced at Madeleine and shrugged.

"We'll never know if you'd have decided to investigate it on your own, but my guess is that you would, and I needed to know everything that was going on with your investigation."

"Madeleine was your spy?"

"Well, *she* didn't know that," he said with a grin. "Welcome to the world of international politics where even your assets don't know what side they're working for."

"So you thought you were embedding Madeleine in my camp and then you set about feeding me false information about the case. Why bother?"

"It was no bother, my darling. The fact was I wasn't worried about the Paris police—for reasons you've already figured out —but I needed to make sure you weren't going to be a problem for me either. I have the highest regard for your talents, my dear. Over the years you have done nothing but impress me."

"You won't get away with any of this, Stanley. Tell me, is Jenny in on it, too?"

He laughed. "Don't be ridiculous. Anyway, having Jean-Marc come to you with information he was being fed by one of my people was just a little insurance on my part that cost me very little."

"And the false autopsy report?"

"You figured that out, did you?" He smiled approvingly. "Well, I figured as long as you didn't dig too deep, that was well worth the money too."

"I understand the correct one is on file in the ME's office. Anyone could've found it."

"But they didn't, did they? The police had their suspect, and because the false report had been handed to them, nobody in homicide bothered looking at the one on file in the medical examiner's office."

"Or talking to the ME himself?"

"I have to say he was a worry for about five seconds. I always hate taking out police personnel since it makes the police—both bent or not—very crabby. Fortunately for the ME, and his life expectancy, the detective on the case—"

"Your man on the inside. Durand, is it?"

My mind raced as I glanced at Madeleine on the ground. I tried to remember how long someone can survive as they lose blood. She was unconscious which I knew happened at forty percent blood loss. After that death came quickly. But a person might merely black out like Madeleine had with twenty percent blood loss. How much time did that give her? How long had she been out?

"As it happens. Yes, well, Durand certainly wasn't going to talk to the ME about his findings. And luckily, the ME didn't volunteer."

"You'd have had him killed if he had?"

"You make it sound so coldblooded."

"And the hotel surveillance video?"

"As you may have heard tonight from Mr. O'Connell, there was more that happened that night than what was captured on the video camera."

"And the police never questioned the validity of the video?"

"Why would they? They had everything they needed to support the evidence against the suspect they had in custody. You know how cops are. They like things neat and tidy. Unlike you and your constant fascination with loose ends."

"So Resnelle is crooked too?"

He cocked his head at me.

"Not that it'll do you any good but no, she's not crooked. Just inept. Which in many cases is nearly as good. She saw the easy way out and she took it."

"By *easy way*, you mean she opted to trust her detectives who had been bought and paid for by you."

"*C'est ça*, as the French say." *Just so.*

At that point, he pulled out a small caliber pistol and pointed it at me.

"Sorry, my darling," he said. "Places to go, people to meet, money to make."

My throat dried up knowing how close I was to never seeing Robbie or Jean-Marc or Geneviève or Catherine or anyone I loved ever again.

"Now there's an access to an open sewer line about twenty yards from here," Stanley said, indicating with his gun the direction he wanted me to walk. "I'll need to drag O'Connell and Miss Madeleine there, but you can walk and save me a little wear and tear on my back. Let's go."

I turned in the direction he indicated. There were lights on overhead but the illumination they afforded was still dim. My mind raced, looking for a place to dart where I wouldn't be trapped like a rat, trying to imagine where if any of the exits might be. With every step I took, I became more and more panicked.

I heard the sounds of the rushing water first. There was no way out.

The idea of being forced into the filthy vortex of the Paris underground sewer system was nearly the most horrible thought I could imagine. And yet, there was also the barest glimmer of a chance for me nestled there amongst the horror.

"Go to the edge, Claire," Stanley said. "Hurry, please. It's freezing in here and I've got two other bodies to—"

I didn't even choose the spot where I went in, nor did I bother diving. I just turned and leapt into the murky churning water.

The instant I hit the water the current snatched me with a gut-wrenching power and flung me down the open pipeline. The sounds of gunshots rang out overhead—muffled by the roaring water and my own terror.

58

I clawed desperately at the sides of the slimy cement walls as the powerful current dragged me. My hands searched desperately for a crevice to arrest my being carried down the pipe. I fought for breath, my vision blurring with each passing second and I fought to come up for air. As soon as I broke the surface, gasping and coughing, the sound of the rushing, gurgling water filled the air around me, echoing off the walls.

I widened my eyes but all I could see was a world of murky green and darkness. The dark waters churned around me and I felt pieces of debris hitting me. The fetid smell of the filthy water filled my nostrils as I breathed in great gasps of desperate breath.

The water was black, the stench horrible, and the cold was all-consuming as I felt the pressure build up in my ears and behind my eyes.

I had to get out of the water.

My feet couldn't touch the bottom. My hands slipped against the slick sides of the sewer wall. Twice I tried to climb up the side of the pipe, using rough spots in the stone walls of the pipe but the rushing water kept knocking me back into the vortex. I allowed my head to go back under and when I did I felt a powerful exhaustion shudder through me.

Just let go. Let nature happen. Let it be. I was drowning.

Suddenly an image of Robbie blazed into my brain. I focused on his face and pulled harder from some indefinable place deep inside me than I ever have before. I struck out with both hands, my frozen, nearly numb fingers searching for a grip. Just as I felt my strength fading again, my fingers caught onto a small crevice in the wall. I clung to it for dear life.

The force of the current threatened to pull me down again. But I held on with every ounce of energy I had left, my nails digging into the rough surface of the wall.

My clothes were sodden and so heavy I felt as if someone was tugging me downward. I'd lost my shoes but now, even as cold as I was, I needed to get out of my denim jacket. Or I'd never be able to pull myself out.

I waited for what felt like centuries clinging to the side of the slippery pipe wall until I knew would only become weaker if I waited any longer. Keeping a mental picture of Robbie firmly in my brain, I pulled myself inch by inch down the length of the long pipe wall, one crevice and fingerhold at a time, until I found the half-submerged ladder that I knew had to be there.

I grabbed it for the lifeline it was. Then, after a small moment of rest, and with shaking arms I climbed up onto the narrow cement walkway and collapsed.

I lay there for a moment, trembling with relief and exhaustion and cold. I didn't know how far away from Stanley I was. In my mind's eye I saw him drag poor Madeleine to the sewer—injured but alive—and push her in. A sob caught at my throat. I couldn't save her.

Suddenly I felt footsteps. Rumbling and vibrating underneath me as they pounded closer and closer towards me. I looked down into the whirling water. But I couldn't.

In the end, whatever was coming for me, I couldn't do that again.

59

Jean-Marc wasn't the first person through the breached door of the warehouse, but he was close. When Colette had come forward to back his insistence that he knew where Madeleine was being held, Resnelle couldn't resist the possibility she might be a media hero by rescueing the young American. It hadn't taken Jean-Marc long to convince her that bringing him along, in case they failed, would ensure that any failure was not laid at *her* door.

He didn't know for a fact that Claire had gone to the warehouse on a tip about Madeleine, but it was a gamble he felt was worth the risk.

Why else would Claire have come to a place like this? It had to be because of Madeleine's kidnappers.

The police stormed into the warehouse with Jean-Marc leading the way. The first thing he saw was the body of Roger O'Connell—and then Madeleine.

"Call for an ambulance!" he shouted, racing over to Madeleine. He knelt beside her and felt for a pulse. She'd been stabbed in the stomach and the blood had saturated the fabric that someone had tied around her middle. But she was still alive.

Colette knelt at his side.

"The medical responders are right behind us," she said. "Is that O'Connell over there?"

Jean-Marc heard the others in the group shouting "Clear!" as they systematically made their way through the interior of the warehouse. Fear gripped him as his heartbeat raced.

Where is she?

He glanced at O'Connell. A knife protruded from his chest.

"Did the victim kill her own kidnapper?" Colette asked. "Or was that *your* girl's work?"

Jean-Marc sat back on his heels, his mind whirling. If Claire wasn't here...where was she?

Suddenly the EMTs swarmed the area, pushing both Jean-Marc and Colette back to the perimeter of their activities. Resenelle walked over to them.

"Where's the American woman?" she asked.

"She isn't here," Jean-Marc said.

He watched her face tighten. He knew she'd gotten a checkmark in the "win" column with this raid. She'd rescued—*alive*—the kidnapped daughter of a prominent American statesman. Finding an elderly American woman who had never been reported missing in the first place was not on her list of action items. Jean-Marc felt his stomach tighten in dread.

He scanned the room, forcing himself to stay calm. Then he jumped to his feet.

"That's her purse!" he said, running to it and then turning to see Claire's phone lying beside it. "She was here!"

The EMTs were already putting Madeleine on a gurney for transport. Colette came over to him.

"I'm staying to process the scene," she said. "But Resenelle said you're free to go."

Jean-Marc looked around helplessly when his phone

vibrated in his pocket. He pulled it out and looked at an unknown phone number on its screen.

"Yes?" he said answering it.

"It's me, Jean-Marc," Claire said breathlessly.

∽

The very kind, very astonished city waterworks workmen who found me wasted no time in wrapping me up in a canvas drape and half carrying me to their enclosed subterranean office where they made me a coffee and offered me an assortment of pastries.

As I sat shivering on a metal folding chair cupping a ceramic mug of very good coffee with cream and sugar, I pointed to a cellphone I saw on the console.

"M-m-may I?" I stuttered, my body seemingly incapable of getting warm.

"*Chérie*, where are you?" Jean-Marc said, when I put the call through to him, the relief and joy evident in his voice.

"Jean-Marc, go to the warehouse in Saint-Denis," I said, my voice shaking with the cold. "The address is—"

"I am there now, *chérie*," Jean-Marc said. "We found Madeleine and O'Connell."

"Madeleine—?"

"She is on her way to the hospital. She is stable."

I couldn't imagine what he was saying could really be true. But the relief coursed through me.

"Oh, thank God!" I said, my voice thick with emotion. "And Stanley?"

"Who?"

"Stanley Cole. Is he there?"

"No. Just Madeleine and O'Connell."

Stanley must have heard them coming. He must have hidden and then slipped away as the police were dealing with Madeleine and Roger.

"They have Robbie, Jean-Marc," I said, the very sound the words making my throat close up in terror.

"What? Who does?"

I gulped down my emotions and tried to speak clearly.

"O'Connell showed me a video on his phone of Robbie being taken away by some woman. You've got to find him!"

I heard him turn away and speak to someone, likely one of the people processing the crime scene at the warehouse.

"Was O'Connell one of the kidnappers?" he asked.

"There was no kidnapping," I said. "Find his phone, Jean-Marc. Better yet, find Stanley! He's the big boss!"

"Stanley? From the American Embassy?"

I wanted to scream. It was taking forever trying to make Jean-Marc understand what was happening. In the meantime, where was Robbie? Would they kill him when they realized they didn't need him anymore? Had they already killed Geneviève?

"Stanley is the head of some kind of sex cabal," I said, trying to force myself to remain as calm as possible to get the information out. "He thought there was a jump drive floating around with evidence on it to incriminate him. He thought Ethan passed it to me the night of the gala. They showed me a video of Robbie being kidnapped to get me to give them the jump drive."

I could tell that halfway into my description, Jean-Marc had turned on the speaker function of his phone and that his ex-colleagues at the crime scene were now hearing what I had to say.

"But you don't have this jump drive," Jean-Marc said.

"No, of course I don't have it!" I said, feeling myself beginning to border on hysterical. "Don't you think I would have mentioned it to you? All Ethan passed me was the note! You need to tell the police to arrest Stanley Cole at the US Embassy! *He* was the one who ordered O'Connell to kill Ethan and Jimmy—and me and Madeleine too!"

"Who killed O'Connell?" one of the detectives asked.

"Not important!" I nearly screamed. "You need to arrest Stanley Cole! He knows where Robbie is! He's the one who tried to shoot me! He's why I jumped in the damned sewer!"

There was a pause on the line. I looked at the two men who had rescued me and who were now staring at me, their eyes wide with disbelief at the wild story they were hearing. They must have thought they'd just fished a mad woman out of the sewer.

I could only imagine what the police thought.

"Jean-Marc?" I said weakly.

"I'm on my way," he said. "Hold tight. I'll be there soon."

"And...and the police?"

"On their way to the American Embassy."

60

When Jean-Marc appeared in the doorway of the subterranean outpost of the Saint-Denis sanitation department, he took two strides to reach me and gathered me into his arms. At that moment, I finally felt warm after what felt like a lifetime of shivering.

The workmen had given me a pair of canvas overalls so I was at least dry. But all I could think of was my darling Robbie walking away with that strange woman. I had no idea if she'd killed him or sold him into human trafficking or left him at the first public toilet she came to.

And not knowing was very nearly killing me.

As Jean-Marc shepherded me down the long hall and up the iron ladder to the interior of yet another warehouse, I worked hard to force my mind not to think. My body was moving but no good could come of letting my mind have free rein.

Whatever would happen next would happen regardless of what I did or thought.

A police car was waiting for us on the street when we emerged. Jean-Marc quickly bundled me into the back of it.

His friend Colette Girard was in the front seat next to the driver.

"Hello, Madame Baskerville," she said. "We have Stanley Cole in custody."

I felt a spasm of relief at her words.

"Is he...has he told you where Robbie is?" I asked.

"Not yet," Colette said, her eyes darted to Jean-Marc in apology. "But everyone is out looking for him. We will find him."

I nodded my thanks, but I wanted to break down and cry. All I could think was: *what is the good of solving any of these terrible crimes if I lose Robbie?*

"*Courage, chérie*," Jean-Marc said as he rubbed my shoulder. "We will find him."

I tried to nod for his sake. But if I lost Robbie, I would leave Paris. I don't know where I'd go but I would never come back here. I would never...

I dug my fingernails into the palms of my hands to force myself to stop the downward spiral of my thoughts. The game wasn't over yet. I needed to play it to the end. There would be plenty of time for grief and tears later. Not yet.

I stared out at Paris as it flew by my window. It was an overcast day, unusual for Paris in June, but I don't think I could've borne a sunny day. The streets that sped by were filled with colors from the awnings and umbrellas of the cafés and shops we passed to the many window boxes of geraniums and petunias. I stared at it all now, numb and detached. I'd forgotten how much color there was everywhere in Paris.

The car pulled up in front of the Hotel Gabriel. It occurred to me that I hadn't even asked about Geneviève. I grabbed Jean-Marc's hand.

"Geneviève?" I asked him.

He shook his head and gave my hand a squeeze.

"They are looking for her, too," he said.

I knew that Geneviève would give her life for Robbie. If

someone tried to take him, she would fight back. She would have flung her body in front of a moving train to protect him.

"Have you tried calling her?" I asked.

"It goes to voicemail," he said.

We walked across the hotel lobby to the bank of elevators. I knew we must look a sight. The hotel staff glanced up when they saw us, me barefoot, in my floppy men's work overalls and Jean-Marc beside me. By the time we reached our floor, I wasn't sure I had the strength to put one foot in front of the other.

Deep down I was a coward because I wished at this moment for nothing more than a drug that would make me sleep for the next two weeks.

Anything to avoid the terrible news I feared was coming.

As we walked down the hall, I saw two uniformed policemen standing by our door and heard the crackle of their radios. One of them spoke into his and said, "We have visual on them now."

We were halfway down the hallway when I heard Izzy bark and my heart lurched at the sound.

And then Robbie popped his head out from the open door.

"Hurry, Grammy! We're having ice cream!"

∼

I'm not sure I will ever want to fully unlatch from this child. When I gasped at the sight of him, he romped down the hall and threw himself into my arms, knocking me over. I covered his face with kisses until he fought to free himself and Jean-Marc helped me to my feet.

I staggered into the hotel room to see Geneviève sitting there with Esmé on her lap and a bowl of ice cream in front of her.

"Hello, *chérie!*" she said cheerfully. "What on earth are you wearing?"

"Phew! Grammy, you stink," Robbie said, wrinkling his nose.

Tears streamed down my face as I regarded the scene, stupefied, as Jean-Marc talked to the police at the door. Then he came into the room, shaking his head.

"They only just found out that they were here," he said to me. "They reported that they were here but the line of communication..." He gave a shrug as if to suggest that perhaps he hadn't been first on the list to be informed.

It didn't matter. None of it mattered.

"But how?" I asked as I sat down, too numb to even know what question to ask.

"Shower first, *chérie*," Jean-Marc said, pulling me to my feet. "Answers and a stiff drink *anon*."

It was hard to leave the sight of Robbie eating ice cream and teasing the dogs, but Jean-Marc was right. I needed to scrub away the experience of seeing that terrible video. I gave his hand a squeeze and found my way into the bathroom for a good long and very hot shower.

Later, I sat in the living room with Izzy at one hip and Robbie next to the other as he played one of his video games. Geneviève had been apprised of all that had happened by then. She was alternately worried and outraged.

"I can't imagine," she said, shaking her head. "When we found Robbie's clothes had been stolen, we didn't think anything of it because I'd just discovered that my phone had fallen into the pool!"

"Accidentally?" I said.

"Well, I *thought* it was an accident until Jean-Marc told me what happened. Now I think it was kicked in."

Of course, disabling Geneviève's phone would have been

the first step after stealing Robbie's clothes and dressing up another boy in them to make the video. In the video I'd only seen the child from the back. I'd jumped to the conclusion that Roger O'Connell had intended for me to jump.

"It makes sense," Jean-Marc said. "It is much easier to steal clothes from a locker at a public swimming center than to take a screaming child out the front door. Not to mention his very protective *grandmère*."

My heart swelled with joy at the sight of Robbie. Now that I knew that Madeleine would likely survive her injuries and that Robbie and Geneviève were safe, I allowed myself to feel the full extent of the relief I craved.

As I snuggled with Robbie and Izzy, Jean-Marc got a phone call and stepped out onto the balcony to take it. When he returned, Robbie was fast asleep on my shoulder, but I didn't have the heart for Jean-Marc to move him into the bedroom just yet.

Geneviève kissed me goodnight.

"It has been a big day for everyone," she said, putting her hand on Robbie's head. "And we have all ended up together and safe at the end of it."

"I know," I said, reaching out to take her hand. "Thank you, Geneviève. For keeping him safe and for reminding me of what matters."

She patted my hand and left the room. Jean-Marc did pick up Robbie then and put him to bed. I was glad he did. The child had had an exhausting day swimming and then watching the police come and go for most of the evening. Tomorrow we would return to our apartment. And to some semblance of a normal life.

Jean-Marc sat down with me on the couch.

"That was Resnelle," he said.

My eyebrows rose. "She's calling you, now?"

"I do not think she will ever want to involve me in the business of the department," he said. "But perhaps she got some clarity as to how she was being seen."

"You mean like showing herself to everyone as insecure and unsure?"

He smiled. "Something like that."

"So what did she say?"

"She said the woman in the video with the boy was apprehended. She was someone who Cole knew—"

"An expat?"

"Yes. I'm sorry, *chérie*."

"He probably had some dirt on her," I said.

"It seems she was a part of the cabal herself."

"Oh, dear. What about the child?"

"It was her own son. His father is flying over from the US to take custody."

I was quiet for a moment, digesting that. To think that the innocent child whose video I'd seen and who'd so terrified me, was a young boy about to lose his mother and have his whole life rearranged—well, it made me sad in spite of all the things I had to be grateful for today.

"Cole is still refusing to admit to anything, but Resnelle is confident that will not last. In the few hours that he has been in custody and his house searched, there is more and more evidence to show what he was doing. Plus, they have already pulled texts off his phone from him to O'Connell. Other arrests will soon follow."

"Resnelle must be feeling pretty good about herself about now."

"It will make her career, these arrests," Jean-Marc said with a shrug.

I watched him for a moment, wondering if he was thinking how, if he'd just stayed in the job a little longer—after thirty year's service—it would be *his* career these arrests would be making. I couldn't see anything like that in his face, but then he's French and his face rarely lets me know what he's thinking.

"The embassy has put Cole on administrative leave until the allegations of sexual misconduct can be resolved."

"Not to mention, murder," I said. "But basically it means his support is gone."

"*Oui.* He is alone now. No one will dare come to his aid lest the world think they were involved in this sex cabal."

"I wonder if his wife knew what was going on."

"There is no evidence of that," Jean-Marc said. "She is making plans to return to Texas."

"I'd call her, but I don't imagine she would want to hear from me."

"I don't imagine so, *chérie.*"

He got up and poured us both a glass of wine before reseating himself.

"Oh, and Resenelle got word that Madeleine's mother is flying in tonight."

"I'm glad," I said.

I sipped my wine, feeling a warmth settle over me, comforting and peaceful. Everything outside of this moment felt distant, like a dream.

Jean-Marc pulled me close, and I let myself relax into his arms. The weight of the world seemed to be lifting off my shoulders. We sat in comfortable silence for a few moments, just enjoying being together. I closed my eyes as he kissed away the last of my worries and fears.

We stayed there, motionless, as if we were carved from stone—his strong arms providing protection and security while I breathed in his familiar scent of lemons and, somehow, leather. And for just that moment, I have never been happier in my life.

61

Many people know Parc Monceau as the famously unusual tableau of English gardening in the heart of the French capital. It is also known for its incredible statuary—a rotunda built in the late seventeen hundreds, a colonnade half submerged in a duck pond, and an Egyptian pyramid, of all things. But I know it as the park nearest my apartment where Robbie is allowed to run and climb and make noise and be a rambunctious little boy.

Today, he was doing all that as I sat on a bench with Adele Coté and Jean-Marc. Robbie had connected with a few of his pals in order to run through the lush green grasses of the park which were today dotted with tulips, daisies, and daffodils. All around us, families picnicked on the grass, while couples took romantic strolls hand in hand down the winding pathways leading to the ponds and past the playgrounds.

It had been three weeks since that terrible showdown in the warehouse in the Saint-Denis section of Paris. It was one week since Madeleine had been discharged from the hospital, and two weeks since the murder cases against Stanley Cole had become inviolate.

Jean-Marc got up to rummage in the picnic basket on the bench. We'd already eaten lunch, but he always packed extra since Robbie inevitably became hungry thirty minutes after eating.

"Anyone want a plum?" he asked, holding the fruit up in his hand.

"I wouldn't mind," Adele said, reaching for it.

I watched Robbie laugh with his friends, the happy sound of it seeming to drift on the breeze along with snatches of conversations from parents and child minders around the park. When I closed my eyes, I heard his laughter laid over the sound of footsteps crunching the gravel paths and the rustle of the trees in the summer breeze. Not too far from where we sat was a fountain making a soft bubbling sound as its water cascaded over its ancient and worn tiers.

I felt more at peace today than I had in weeks. Two weeks ago, we discovered that Ethan had mailed the infamous jump drive to Dilly in Atlanta. She brought it with her when she came to sit by Madeleine's bedside at the hospital and had a copy of it couriered to the US Embassy, as well as to the Paris police department, and the *France 24* news station. I think Madeleine stopped her from sending it to *Le Monde*, or publishing it on Instagram, but it probably wouldn't have mattered. The jump drive filled in all the gaps of what we knew about the sex cabal—and from the prosecution's point of view, it hammered the final nail into Stanley Cole's coffin.

Jean-Marc had heard from someone within the department who'd seen the contents of the jump drive who said that it revealed all about the cabal—including naming names.

"I can't stay long," Adele said. "I've got a date."

"Oh?" I said turning to her.

"Don't do that," she said, still munching her plum. "It's early days."

I smiled at her and shrugged. Adele wasn't determined to get settled down and I admired that about her. I didn't understand it, but I admired it.

Anyway, because of the incriminating jump drive making the rounds, Stanley Cole finally confessed to all his crimes and then promptly tried to kill himself. The effort wasn't successful and was universally seen as a blatant confirmation of his guilt. Jenny, who was now living in Texas, had begun divorce proceedings. It was a sad end for her tenure in Paris, but it was hard for me to feel too sorry for her. She was rich and she'd lived with a monster that she had somehow never recognized.

"What exactly was this cabal?" I asked abruptly. "Did anyone ever find out?"

"Yes, well," Adele said, wrinkling her nose, "it was a private club of a small subset of men who paid a large premium to have certain things—mostly illegal things—done to them by women who were usually abducted from foreign countries or in other ways simply unwilling."

"How was Stanley involved?"

"He orchestrated the influx of women," Jean-Marc said, still rooting in the picnic basket. "At times finding specific women to perform specific tasks as requested by the members."

"How did he hide his wealth?"

I'd seen Stanley and Jenny's apartment. It was nice but not what I'd call on the level of a Sexual Crimes Czar.

"The usual places. Offshore accounts," Adele said.

Adele's mention of offshore bank accounts reminded me of Leblanc and how I was so sure he was involved in Ethan's murder. The fact was, the sex cabal itself sounded like it was right up his alley. But Jean-Marc said that of the twenty or so members who had been rounded up so far, Leblanc was not among them.

I'm not sure what I had been expecting. But to have to

admit that Leblanc had had absolutely nothing to do with Ethan's death was hard for me. I know he's a crook. We have evidence of that. Just not this.

I waved to Robbie as he turned to look at us and waved back.

Whenever I think of Leblanc, I tend to think of Joelle and these days, since the smoke had, for the most part cleared, I found myself wondering whether or not she and Ethan had really had an affair. I guess I'll never know. Joelle hasn't reached out to me since all of this came down and anyway, she would have no reason to change her story. And of course, Ethan isn't talking. I guess that little mystery will have to go to its grave with the man.

"But why did Ethan have to die?" I asked, although I basically knew the answer.

"Stanley invited him to join the club," Adele said with a shrug as she gathered up her purse and small gym bag.

I snorted. "Talk about not reading the room."

"Yes," Jean-Marc said. "What I heard is that the Senator was so appalled he swore to Cole that he would bring down the cabal, including Cole. As I understand it, Cole attempted to backpedal his involvement in the club, but Ethan wasn't buying it. When that happened, I'm afraid the Senator essentially marked himself for death."

My phone rang and I saw I was getting a call from Madeleine.

"I need to take this," I said to Adele. "Don't leave until I get back."

"Is that Madeleine?" Adele said. "I've been meaning to ask you why in the world did she lie about having a fiancé? Surely that could have nothing to do with her father's murder."

"I think she figured that since I was from the South, same as her, that I'd trust her more if I thought she was normal not crazy."

"She didn't think making up a pregnancy and a fiancé wouldn't make her look crazy?"

I walked away toward the front gates, a glimpse of the Arc de Triomphe just visible from where I stood.

"Hey, Madeleine," I said. "How are you feeling?"

"Better," she said. "My mother and I have been going out a little bit each day. She wanted to take me right home, but I convinced her to stay."

"I wish I'd met your mother," I said. "She sounds like the real deal."

Madeleine laughed softly.

"Yeah, why do you think she's called Dilly?" There was a moment of silence on the line before she spoke again. "Listen, Claire, I want to apologize again for everything."

"Don't worry about it," I said. "You were going through a lot."

"I know, but Dad would not have been happy with how I involved you."

"On the contrary," I said. "I think he would've been proud that you reached out for help."

"Well, in any case, it's over. Did you hear about the jump drive?"

"I did. Stanley was right to fear it. Jean-Marc says it's the end for him and about twenty very famous people."

"I'm glad. But more than that, I wanted to apologize for nearly getting you killed. That was the opposite of what I was trying to do."

I'd already been told by Colette that when Madeleine paid the homeless guy to call her mother, Stanley, who had in fact tapped Dilly's phone, was then able to trace the call to Madeleine's cellphone and pinpoint it at the warehouse where he then sent O'Connell to dispatch her, and then, not trusting O'Connell to do it, went himself.

"After I had the homeless guy call Mom, I guess I started to lose my nerve. I could hear her on the line as he was talking, and she was just sobbing. It took everything I had not to jump on the phone and tell her what was going on, but I was convinced her line was bugged. That's when I called you, Claire. I'm so sorry about that. I put you right in the middle of everything and nearly got you killed. I'm so sorry."

"It all worked out. I have to thank you for attacking Roger when you did. If you hadn't, I think we both would've died."

"I just couldn't bear hearing the things he was saying about Robbie," she said, her voice thick with tears. "And along those lines, I need to apologize for getting your hopes up about the baby. I know that was cruel and I hope you can understand why I felt like I had to do it."

"Roger said he sent you a note threatening to kill me?"

"I guess I panicked. I felt like I needed to get you out of town fast. And since we'd just had that conversation about your missing grandson, I used that."

"I understand why you did it."

"But I also know it caused you serious mental anguish."

We talked for a few more minutes before promising to stay in touch. She and Dilly would be going back to Atlanta at the end of the week, but I rarely went back to the US unless it was to see Catherine in Florida. And these days those invitations had pretty much dried up.

After I hung up with her, I said goodbye to Adele so she could go on her date, and I sat back on the bench to watch Robbie toss an American football with Jean-Marc who seemed to know how to handle it. It occurred to me as I watched them, that I still didn't know who it was who had sent the man to attack me in Switzerland. Madeleine swore she didn't do that part.

So if not her, then who? And why?

My mind went back to thoughts of my father since something like this was so his style. But that couldn't be, since my father was dead.

Right?

62

As usual when we spend a lot of time at the park, Robbie conked out that night much earlier than usual which, I have to say, I appreciated. I adore him, but at my age, I can only hear so many Knock-Knock jokes before I want to go screaming out of the building.

Jean-Marc had made *coq au vin* for dinner, a favorite of Robbie's. After Robbie had his bath—in which he'd nearly fallen asleep—and gone right to bed, Jean-Marc and I retired to the living room with two glasses of a very heady red Jean-Marc had found in a small wine shop in the Latin Quarter.

We'd had a lot to process since everything had happened, ending with my icy plunge into the underground sewers of Paris. But I honestly think we'd talked it all nearly half to death. I was ready to focus on philandering spouses and people trying to skip out on their credit card debt for a change.

"I think I want to have a boring life," I said.

Jean-Marc laughed softly.

"I will believe that when I see it."

"Oh! One last question and then we can put this whole thing to bed."

He raised an eyebrow at me.

"Étienne," I said.

Jean-Marc sighed.

I knew he had confronted Étienne but he'd yet to tell me the outcome of that encounter.

"He said he'd been approached by someone who knew he'd done coke on duty—and had the pictures to prove it. In order to save his career, he agreed to give me the video, although he swore he didn't know it had been faked."

"I see." I remembered that Étienne had a baby on the way. "So you let him off the hook?"

Jean-Marc snorted. "Absolutely not. He did drugs on the job and made himself vulnerable to blackmail. And he lied to me."

"You're a hard man, LaRue," I said fondly as I leaned over to kiss him. He pulled me closer to him and I let out a contented sigh as his arms enfolded.

"But we did get good Intel from Colette," I pointed out.

"For all the good it did us coming as late as it did."

"Maybe the information about O'Connell's rape conviction," I said. "But I'm talking about Leblanc's suspicious money dealings."

"Yes, except, that was, at best, a red herring since he ultimately wasn't involved in the Senator's death."

"Agreed, but it wasn't a total loss."

Jean-Marc turned and looked at me questioningly.

"I'm just saying, you never know how it might come in handy in the future," I said. "We know he's up to dirty dealings, moving money around from his offsite account. And now he knows we know."

He said nothing, seeming to think about that for a moment.

"Did you ever find out *why* O'Connell killed for Stanley?" I asked. "At some point in the warehouse, I thought he hinted that Stanley had him over a barrel."

Jean-Marc snorted in derision.

"Stanley paid him," he said. "That was the barrel O'Connell was over—not wanting to leave money on the table when it could be in his pocket."

"I'm sure you're right," I said. "You know, I didn't want to say it in front of Adele, but Stanley admitted to me that Victor Durand was in his pocket," I said.

"You mentioned that," Jean-Marc said.

"What do you think that will mean going forward?" I asked.

"I doubt it will seriously impair his job function at the Paris police department—especially now that Stanley Cole won't be able to pull any strings from prison."

"Should you tell Resnelle?"

He snorted.

"If I tell her, she won't believe me. And if I tell her and it gets revealed that I was right, she'll hate me even more than she does right now."

"Does that matter so much?"

"That depends on how much hope we have that I might be able to use the department for inside information going forward."

"Seems like a long shot."

"Right now, it does. Did you ever ask the Senator's wife about his predilection for helping felons?"

"I did," I said. "It seems it was a second-chance sort of compulsion he had. His brother killed himself in prison."

Jean-Marc shook his head.

"How did *that* information not end up on his public dossier?"

"You know politicians," I said with a sad smile. "They're masters at having you know only what they want you to know."

Later after arranging to meet the next morning at a new café that Jean-Marc had discovered to discuss our new roster of cases, we parted for the evening, lovingly and affectionately.

After he was gone, I went into the kitchen to see he'd cleaned the kitchen so there wasn't much to do but rinse out our wine glasses and take Izzy downstairs for her last call of the night.

I stopped at Geneviève's apartment and tapped on the door. Sometimes, if she was still up, I'd take Esmé down with me to save her the trouble. Tonight, she came to the door with Esmé already on her leash.

"You had a nice night with Jean-Marc?" she asked.

She'd been invited for dinner, but I was not surprised that she'd been ready to have some time on her own.

"Very nice," I said.

"I am sorry Robbie and I caused you so much anxiety."

"Don't be silly," I said.

"It is the price of love, *n'est-ce pas*?" she said.

I paused when she said that. Because that's what people say at funerals. There was no doubt in my mind that Geneviève was talking about Baby John.

"Someone went to a lot of trouble to create him," she said. "Wherever he is, he is loved, *chérie*."

I nodded but I couldn't speak. I guess I never thought of Baby John being abused. I knew that likely wasn't the case. He probably wore princely robes and sat on a velvet cushion all day.

"I know," I finally managed. "I know he's okay."

"He *is* okay." She reached out and gave my cheek a pat. "And so will you be, *chérie*. In time."

I knew that everyone had accepted that we'd never find him. His mother, Catherine, certainly had. And if *she* had, then it was probably time for me to accept it too. Just thinking that that part of my life—the search for Maddie and then for John—was to end hit me as hard as the current in the sewer when it threatened to drown me.

People don't talk about closure as being anything but a good thing, a healing thing. But closure is also a heartbreaking thing. It's a giving up and failing thing that sweeps away hope and important moments in its path until all you're left with are memories and debris.

There were times when I felt I had been so close to finding him. But the wall I faced now was insurmountable. There was no toe hold, no crevice to reach for. And no babe in arms at the end of the hard climb. Only emptiness.

As I turned to walk both dogs down to the courtyard, I found myself trying to imagine a different way to stop what I was doing. Instead of endlessly, hopelessly looking for Baby John, I might look for closure for that loss through Catherine. I hadn't talked to her in weeks and then not in any depth. I could talk to her about my feelings—and hers—and perhaps ask her if she would be willing to do something symbolic for John; maybe a memorial service or planting a tree in his honor.

I just needed to do something that would tell the universe —and possibly, somehow John—that no matter where he was or how he grew up—his grandmother wouldn't forget him.

I just needed him to know that.

For my sake if not for his.

∼

To follow more of Claire's sleuthing and adventures, order *Murder Carte Blanche, Book 12 of The Claire Baskerville Mysteries!*

ABOUT THE AUTHOR

USA TODAY Bestselling Author Susan Kiernan-Lewis is the author of *The Maggie Newberry Mysteries,* the post-apocalyptic thriller series *The Irish End Games, The Mia Kazmaroff Mysteries, The Stranded in Provence Mysteries, The Claire Baskerville Mysteries,* and *The Savannah Time Travel Mysteries.*

Visit www.susankiernanlewis.com or follow Author Susan Kiernan-Lewis on Facebook.

Printed in Great Britain
by Amazon